THICKER THAN WATER

THE BORROWED DESTINY

By Daniel Arthur

ISBN: 9798686104334

Contents

Prologue

Dear Reader,

There are some things you need to know about this story. Over the course of the book and particularly the first chapter, certain actions take place that are probably going to divide some opinions.

While Lady Lilah of the Thurston dynasty is the first character you will meet in this story, you need to know that this tale isn't hers, though it could have been. You see, in another realm or parallel universe, some alternate reality or even a diverged timeline, this story would be hers and she would indeed be the protagonist of this tale; she should have been the strong female lead that we need to see more of.

Had Lilah felt that she had the support of someone who could have helped her, or someone to reach out to, this story may well have been an entirely different one. Instead, she makes a choice – the only choice she deems fit – and it subsequently influences and changes the lives of those around her.

I ask that you aren't harsh on her. Despite her extraordinary gifts and talents, Lilah is only human and like most of us, she's perfectly imperfect and certainly not immune to the effects of guilt, heartbreak, isolation and misplacing her trust in a loved one.

Good people can do bad things, but that doesn't mean that they are innately evil and beyond reproach. It also means that they should not be judged based on a single choice they made. We can all stand to show a little more forgiveness in our lives, not only to those around us but especially when it comes to accepting our own actions.

Before leaving you to get on with the story, read this tale knowing that although Lilah Thurston's part is small, she is at peace and is forgiven by the one who can grant it. Show compassion, but don't be sad. You don't have to understand everything but you should try and accept the big things.

Because sometimes, dear Reader, we make decisions that mean our destinies aren't what they're supposed to be and other people might have to borrow them on our behalf.

Thankfully and sensitively yours,
Your omniscient and equally flawed Narrator

Part One

1. Lilah Thurston

"Today is the day I kill myself."
"I am going to kill myself today."
"*Today* is the day I end my life."
"I'm committing suicide shortly."

Lilah mulled over today's to-do list with nothing less than mild indifference as she lay restlessly in the confines of her cold bed.

The season had crept in unusually early for the time of year and during the night a fur of powdery frost had spread over the autumnal landscape outside her dorm room. Morning's arrival was slow and gradual, whilst the evenings rolled in earlier and earlier with each passing day.

The restless girl shivered in the cold draught of her bedroom as she stared from her pillow to the ice-dusted landscape that lay beyond her window. The golden-brown carpet of discarded leaves smothered the ground outside and was peppered with a layer of precious frost. Her tired eyes surveyed the picturesque landscape, noticing the morning silence and that the birds no longer sang as she had remembered them.

"Today *is* the day I give it all up" she affirmed.

6:45 am

An old-fashioned brass clock perched eagerly on her bedside table and like a hysterical creature made of cogs and screws, it jittered loudly from behind her. She turned her head to confirm the time, clicked off the alarm with a lazy hand and continued staring idly out of the tiny curtain crevice to the bleak morning outside. Just a few moments longer.

Over the last few months, she had grown to appreciate the simplicity of ordinary and mundane pastimes, like laying in bed and looking out the window.

She sighed, rolled on her back for a change of scenery and stared at the ceiling instead. The night had been spent charting the shadow of the lampshade as it rolled across the whitewashed plaster under the sway of rolling moonlight through the gap in the curtains.

Lilah lifted her head decidedly and swung her feet out of the bed. The freshly disturbed air kicked a spiteful chill up her legs that rolled across the rest of her body, causing her to shudder softly under a wave of goosebumps that shimmered up her skin. The solid wooden floor was painfully cold as she stepped onto it. Her bare feet felt tacky against the hard surface. With weary steps, Lilah solemnly padded across the room and made her way to open the bedroom door, which creaked with a mournful and guttural groan.

With the laborious approach of dawn, the hallway of her dormitory was dimly lit due to the blanket of clouds that smothered the sky outside. Knowing the harsh halogen bulbs would be torture to her eyes, Lilah refrained from flicking the lights. Instead, she pulled her gown close to her body, and with the silence of an icy apparition, glided down the hallway to the dingy bathroom.

Glossy white Victorian tiles glimmered like freshly laid snow blown against the walls of the communal bathroom. The glass doors of the shower cubicles complemented the wintry scene, like a perfect sheet of concealing frost. She reached in and wrestled the stubborn tap with one hand. After a little effort, the faucet gave way and the head of the shower hissed to attention.

The ancient plumbing groaned as the metal veins from the heater struggled to warm the dormitory bathroom. Pulses of ghostly steam meandered through the cold air and in the moments waiting for the water to heat up, Lilah stood in a state of catatonia contemplating the crucial task she must complete today.

She caught sight of her sallow frame in the mirror. Unlike Dorian Gray, Lilah's body was indeed her soul's canvas where the anxieties of what she had endured had manifested in her physical appearance. She barely recognised herself; her eyes had become sunken and dark, her skin papery thin and her hair fell lank and dull at her shoulders.

"Get with it, Lilah," she told herself, "don't chicken out now. You know what has to be done."

The girl stripped swiftly and stepped into the envelope of steam, taking solace from being out of the chilly air. The jet of hot water should have been invigorating against her milky skin, but the rejuvenation was superficial and did little more than warm her outside.

Lilah was not in the habit of talking to herself and otherwise remained silent this morning. Aside from the occasional reminder that she would be taking her own life shortly, as though it were as casual as remembering to get milk or check you turned the oven off, she said nothing else. There were too many voices crowding her mind and much guilt in her soul. To engage them in conversation or address them would be the cause of her emotional undoing.

He doesn't know it yet, but I'm doing this all for him. He's relying on me to do what I have to – it's the only way.

Stepping out of the warmth of the shower cubicle was a shock to the system. She fastened a towel around her chest and threw her gown over her body, hastily gathered her belongings and made her way back down the hallway to her bedroom. Walking along the tired corridor, Lilah was not at all unnerved by how the dormitory was dead-still. She passed the door that she would soon knock on one last time. Like the occupant, no one would stir for hours, which was good in order for her to set about accomplishing the final touches to her fatal task.

The sun had illuminated the bedroom only slightly through the slash of the partly prised curtains with what can only have been described as overexposed grey. The dense layer of murky clouds sealed the world below in a dull vacuum.

Lilah removed a comb from her vanity table, and lazily combed her yellow hair. Ceremoniously, she caressed each lock attentively as if each limp strand of soft gold were a lethal viper. Having taken the time to untangle any knots, she then made the extra effort to dry and style it properly.

Once done with her yellow mane, she idly took a brief moment to find suitable underwear; something to mark the occasion since it's not every day you're going to kill yourself. She dropped her towel, threw it in the laundry bin and put the black lace on. She recognised how little things such as these seemed so trivial in the grand scheme of what she needed to do today, but she relished them nonetheless, realising that she had taken so much in her life for granted.

Moving away, she made her bed with military precision. Each corner was tucked neatly under the mattress and the plumped pillows were sitting erect and proud at the head of the bed like duck-down tombstones.

7:15 am

"I'm late," she muttered to herself, so quietly that it was barely even a whisper.

Lilah turned to the beautiful vanity table that sat opposite her bed and took a seat on the blushing cushion of the white stool to apply her makeup. As she sat in front of the vintage mirror she admired the French antique that her father had once given her mother. When Lady Thurston had died, Lilah's father had offered it to her, knowing how much she had admired the unit.

Lilah thought back to fond memories of sitting at her mother's feet, watching in admiration as she painted her face and accentuated her beautiful features. Lilah remembered gazing with such eagerness, wanting to be so much like her when she grew up. Like the stool she was perched upon, the white varnish of the wooden frame had seen better days. It was so old, yet no less beautiful. Despite being worn and fragile, it still had a purpose. Cracked, mottled and slightly yellowed, Lilah couldn't help but admire its charm. She affectionately brushed the carved roses, all the while imagining the faces that had once gazed into the glass; her mother's being one of them.

With that thought, she took an eyeliner pencil and accentuated her warm chocolate eyes, layering a small amount of mascara to frame them just so. A light dust of coral-coloured blusher emphasised her ever more prominent cheekbones, whilst she slowly traced the curve of her once plump and shapely lips with an application of a warm shell-pink lipstick. As before, she brushed her silky hair once more and admired the soft strands between her fingers, whilst inhaling the fresh scent of clean hair and continuing to try and appreciate the small things.

Finally, she made one last examination of the beautiful, yet pathetic face staring back at her in the romantic mirror only to snigger gently to herself. Then, with a long, sad breath she wiped a single tear from the corner of her atoning eye. She felt ridiculous but knew that this had to be done.

Over to the wardrobe, a black dress hung at the end of the rail. She stroked the coal-coloured satin and idly admired the subtle lace pattern between her fingers. Earnest, modest and tasteful, it was perfect for a funeral. Dressing quickly, she zipped the back single-handedly; she was used to taking care of herself. Finally, with a flick of her golden hair, she stepped into her shoes and was almost ready for her task.

Today was definitely an occasion for the silver locket that once belonged to her grandmother. The antique silver locket no longer shimmered as it once had. The polished sheen had tarnished over the decades giving it a creamy hue the colour of champagne, though the engraved pattern was still as intricately defined as the day the smith finished it.

She fastened the delicate silver chain around her neck and once again caught her own reflection out of the corner of her eye. It was as though it were trying to get her attention and tell her something of grave importance; she ignored it.

Lilah longingly fingered the thumb-sized locket with one hand, before dropping it to her chest and dusted away any last imperfections on the dress. She decidedly passed her own inspection and nodded to herself reassuringly.

7

"Right, that will do. Almost ready."

The sombre girl then turned and left the peripheral of her reflection, making her way to the chest of drawers that stood stoutly under the elegantly curtained window of her private school dormitory. Opening the top draw, she pawed through the sentimental clutter, which consisted of a few of her favourite books, tiny knick-knacks and a series of old photos. She caressed each item gently and smiled to herself, admiring the photo of her mother and father in the manicured garden of their stately ancestral home, Thurston Manor. A magpie, which she had never noticed before, sat atop a nearby branch, staring down at the subjects of the photo. Her father, Lord Jude Thurston, stood proud and stern, boasting a tamed mass of thick black hair that had since withered to a steely shock of grey in later years. Lilah was unnerved by his piercing, almost hypnotic eyes, knowing that their intensity was not a trick of the camera. His arm enveloped her mother, Evelyn, in a strong embrace that looked fierce, like he planned to never let her go. Her mother's admiring face was in profile, looking up to her brooding husband eagerly. The hand on his wide chest was tender yet powerful. From under her pale blouse, the apparent swelling that would eventually sprout Lilah and Lars was faint but noticeable.

Lilah put the photo to one side, wiping another dewy tear from the corner of her eye. She sifted through pictures of loyal old pets, forgotten family members and dear friends; all of whom she had loved and lost over the years.

At the bottom of the small pile of paper memories, lay a tatty old photo, dog-eared and slightly torn. It was well-loved. The picture was of herself and her twin brother, Lars. Putting them both at about thirteen years old, she noted how they both shared an identical large, carefree smile. Lars had no doubt said something funny or done something childishly boyish and probably slightly outrageous at this point when the picture was taken.

This particular photo wasn't staged or professionally shot in any way, just a nameless occasion such as a summer holiday when they would have been reunited after another year at different boarding schools. The picture may have been the christening of a new camera, or just two siblings messing about when it was taken. Lilah realised that she didn't even know who had been behind the lens.

Lars was never a naughty child, just defiant. She remembered how he was quiet and kept himself to himself, yet would always have an answer for everything; a trait that he expected others to share.

Growing up, why had incessantly been his favourite word. The simple question was also a wonderful way to get a rise out of somebody with minimum effort. 'Why?' becomes insanely irritating when you persistently test the knowledge of someone senior to the point where you don't even care about the answer. It's probably why he and their father never saw eye-to-eye growing up. She silently wondered if this was a trait that her brother had grown out of in later years.

Lilah snapped out of her memory. The very thought of her brother made her throat tighten and her eyes sting. Had it not already been broken, her heart would have shattered at the thought of how close they should have been and how much she missed him.

As one expects of twinned siblings, Lilah and her brother had been inseparable when they were younger and had looked very much alike. As puberty set in and she developed her womanly features, he had shot up and grown out of his boyish visage, and their resemblance was less alike. His hair was still their natural golden brown, whereas she had enhanced hers with highlights over the years.

They still shared the same shaped, warm brown eyes but that was where their shared aesthetic stopped. It was only now that she really noticed how different they looked compared to when they were younger. Catching a glimpse of her own reflection in the grey window, she truly saw how her eyes had lost that warmth from the photo and she hoped that her brother had still managed to retain it.

Their father had always been strict on them both, especially Lilah. It sickened her to think how much she resented Lars and his ignorance of not knowing the true cost of being their father's favourite, and in turn, how much it had truly cost her.

With desperate hands, she clutched the photo tightly. It was the remainder of a distant memory; a glimmer back to an era that still sparkled with the youth and innocence she had once shared with her brother. Laying it to one side, Lilah's eye caught sight of something in the drawer and instinctively made to retrieve it from amongst the tortured trove of other treasures.

A small, highly varnished wooden trinket box hid at the back of the drawer buried amongst the other personable knick-knacks. The polished wood was old and musty, but rich and deep like the fragrant pages of a book.

Resting the base of the box in one hand, she brought it closer and prised open the lid with the other. Opening with a springy-snap it revealed a quilted inlay of royal blue velvet. The lid sighed from Lilah's fingers to expose the balmy breath from within, where the scent of the box was richer and far more intense. It exhaled an intoxicating aroma of history and magic that flooded all of Lilah's senses. Nestled within the centre of the cavity, like the sleeping character of a fabled fairy tale, lay the antique fountain pen.

The pen was incredibly old and had belonged to their father, having been a gift from their mother. The pen had been an heirloom of their mother's and it was tradition for a father to give the pen to their daughter so that she can bestow it to her husband upon their wedding day and he too can bestow it to his daughter.

At the time of receiving it, Lilah had been obnoxious, thinking that it was a ridiculous tradition. She thought back to how disenchanted she had been with her father's gift knowing what a vile little brat she had been about the situation. Their mother was ill at this point and not getting any better.

It was after their mother's death that Lilah and her father similarly withdrew from domestic matters, both opting to be in their own company. Lars had never been privy to their self-pity. Their mother, Evelyn, would not have wanted them to behave in such a way.

Having forgotten that she owned the precious artefact, Lilah took time to admire her once spurned gift. The pen itself was particularly unusual as it was carved from real ivory, that much was fact. However, common conjecture was that the fountain pen probably originated from the East, before the Crusades. It was also presumably carved from an elephant tusk, but this was admittedly just the twins' own speculation. After all, fountain pens were a relatively modern instrument.

Ornate engravings had been embossed into the pen, but there was nothing legible scribed into the pale bone but merely elaborate swirls and patterns. Lilah and Lars used to pretend that these carvings were ancient glyphs of a forgotten civilisation, holding all of life's secrets or the whereabouts of some forgotten treasure. As she held it in her hand, it seemed to hum with life, speaking with silent words that she could not understand.

The nib of the pen was made of real gold, and bleeding blue ink that had dried and stained the very tip. The vicious point was razor sharp and Lilah remembered the scratching sound orchestrated as her father signed various documents, cheques and branded his signature with it.

Flipping the photo to test the pen and in turn re-enact the glorious scraping sound, she scribbled something on the back. Though she was neither signing a legal document or cheque, she wrote simple words that bore the weight of a lifetime. Returning the picture the right way up she placed it back in the box, followed by the pen. Not able to fight back tears, two lonely teardrops escaped from her eyes, plummeting and landing on the ivory fountain pen. She did not notice and closed the lid of the wooden box regardless, sealing not only the artefact, but in time, someone else's fate as well.

She knew that time was running out. She got up, took the box and made her way out of her bedroom. Once again Lilah was in the same corridor as earlier, which despite the elapse of time was still not any brighter, nor was it any warmer.

On the tip-toes of her shoes she dashed along the dormitories, looking for that very specific one from earlier, hoping that the person in it would have remembered their part in this solemn task.

Arriving at the door, she clutched the box and gently knocked upon the solid wood. There was controlled movement from the other side. A bolt clicked and a chain slid slowly before the handle relieved and the door opened with a long creak.

Lilah instinctively placed a desperate finger upon her lips to silence her helper, who naturally obliged and stepped out of the way to permit Lilah's entry to the room.

Before the host could speak, Lilah thrust the box eagerly into their apprehensive hands and told them with desperate firmness: "You know what to do. Get this to Lars... and tell him... Tell him that I'm sorry." Lilah's brown eyes stared with intensity as she pondered her next demand.

"I'm trusting you to do this for me. Every bone in my body, everything I know about you and what is to become of me and my brother, goes against this whole situation. But the Fold is onto me and I need to help my brother; only he can do what I can't. I'm desperate and you're all I have in this world. Please."

Lilah's host went to open their mouth, offering advice or solace, but could not. They did not agree with Lilah's choice but knew that it was unavoidable and they too, had their own part to play in this, even if Lilah was not aware of how big a part they would play.

The air was rapidly growing more awkward so Lilah shifted the silence and got straight down to business with her muted ally. "Have you got what I need?"

Lilah's host diligently went to the large wooden chest that sat at the foot of their bed. They crouched down, retrieved a small key from their pocket and unbolted the once steadfast lock. In a brief moment, Lilah thought she saw her host hesitate, before going about their business as they were supposed to.

With a lazy creak, the lid leaned open and the host retrieved a slender silver object, which had been buried beneath an array of exotic treasures. Its exposure to the light cast a glimmer of shimmering radiance that slid along the smooth, metallic edge of a dangerous object. The host had found what they were looking for and gave it to Lilah in silence.

"Thank you," said Lilah, as she accepted with sober hands, cradling her friend's gifted knife. The atmosphere between the two was tense and Lilah did not want a drawn-out conversation. Her host looked away, so Lilah planted a delicate kiss upon their exposed cheek, causing them to look further beyond their own shoulder. With no exchange of words, Lilah took the knife and made her way back to her room for the final part of her grave task.

***

Sitting upon her bed, Lilah explored the exotic blade. This strange-looking knife was not something found in your everyday kitchen. The blade had not tarnished with age, and the edge could still split even the finest of hairs. It was very old; older than her French dresser and her grandmother's locket put together, but probably not as old as the ivory of the pen.

The hilt was polished, pale and exquisitely ornate, embossed with flourishes of black and gold painted patterns. The handle bled into the quillon, which smoothed out into a fine and wicked blade. The delicate, but powerfully lethal weapon shimmered strangely in the soft reflection of dancing light that leaked through the curtains.

Lilah expected to feel grief or guilt over what she was about to set into motion. The path she was about to forge for her oblivious and innocent brother was going to be harrowing, but instead, she felt relief. She reminded herself that it had to be this way.

Repeating her actions from earlier, she brushed away the last few imperfections on her dress, adjusted the duvet with her free hand and composed herself. She paused. It was so quiet in her room that she could hear her own heartbeat drumming in her chest. The atmosphere of the room was strangely absent, almost vacuous in that moment. There were no wandering echoes or any background noise, not even the muffled conversations of a nearby neighbour. Even the room refrained from creaking as it appeared to hold its breath, anticipating Lilah's tragic action. She was alone with only her pounding heartbeat and the whistling of blood in her ears.

After a deep breath, she released a loud sigh and wiped her eyes a final time. Then, with both hands, she took the knife firmly and looked straight ahead.

"I'm sorry," she whispered, plunging the knife deep into her chest.

Lilah fell off the bed onto her knees and lunged forward, causing the blade to crack through her sternum, graze her ribs and puncture her heart. She toppled sideways, pulling various items off her dresser and stared up at the ceiling. In those moments that were ultimately her last, she wondered why it didn't hurt. In her final moments, her mind went to the only place it could.

Lars.

After that, not a single emotion stirred until her final breath. Each and every speck of anxiety and guilt seeped from her body with every drop of her now faintly pumping blood.

As she lay there quiet and peaceful, a single magpie squawked from outside on the window ledge, peering through the glass to survey the scene. With a frantic flap of her wings, she squawked and returned to her master.

2. The Grey Goose

The birds had been chirruping in a tree outside the window for well over an hour. Lars imagined with a hazy head that they were gossiping away to one another like little harmonic busybodies. Their urgent melodies had driven him mad, right from the moment he had first heard them some few hours ago.

The sun squeezed through the crack of the curtains and bled murky light through the slats of the blinds that guarded the window. Both the half-arsed sunshine and frantic twittering from the birds' nest outside were not helping his hangover. Lars lay on his back trying to make the room stop spinning. To no avail, he delicately pinched the bridge of his nose in a vain attempt to try and alleviate the cranial pressure that had evidently been caused by an excess of designer vodka.

He recalled not going home – a conclusion that was made apparent by the fact that he was all but dead in a strange bed that was certainly not his own. On top of it all and to add to his growing list of ailments this morning, Lars had also woken up with a severe pain in his chest. It was after a few deep but sharp breaths, he concluded that he had simply smoked too much, or that he had inevitably decided to give the vodka shots an encore of vomit; either way, the sharp stabbing pain was unbearable.

Movement from beside him disturbed his train of thought and stole his attention, which in turn, reminded him of that throbbing headache he was also suffering from. Lars turned his head slowly to admire the pert nipple of the body laying to the right of him. It had popped out from the sheet and upon being exposed to the coolness of the bedroom had become alert to fresh air. At this point, immaturity got the better of Lars and he grinned to himself, like the schoolboy he barely was; being in the sixth form definitely doesn't warrant the schoolboy label, especially when you are no longer permitted to wear the uniform. Distracted nonetheless, he adjusted the sheet to protect her modesty and his desire to giggle.

From what he could remember, she was older than he was. Her mass of thickly tangled hair hung over the side of her face to conceal her full visage. What was visible of her puffy face was smudged with last night's makeup and Lars admired how pretty she was in her vulnerable, sleepy state.

Just as Lars was about to roll over and creep out of the bed, another person stirred to his left and he felt his stomach lurch with the realisation of what else he had done. The muscular back and broad shoulders of the second body flexed and relaxed as it adjusted its weight before nuzzling his face back into the pillow.

This girl's boyfriend.

Lars was swamped with a flood of instantaneous regret, searing panic and beaming pride, as remnants of his busy evening stitched themselves back together and played out on the cinema screen of his mind's eye. He absentmindedly punched his forehead with the flat of his palm, which made a definitively dull slap that regrettably reminded him of both his headache and the predicament in which he now found himself.

Oh, fuck. How the hell am I going to get out of this one?

Taking a deep breath, he squirmed under the cover of ruffled sheets with extra caution so as not to alert either one of them.

Lars had not really considered the repercussions of pursuing the attractive girl in the red dress last night. Neither had he paid any mind to the idea that she may have a boyfriend. Lars also neglected to consider what would happen if said couple would be up for a laugh with an attractive young man. He realised quickly that it would pay to have a bit more foresight in future.

Upon approaching the girl in the red dress and being told she indeed had a boyfriend, a decent person might have backed off immediately on the account of not being a dick, knowing full well that they had overstepped their boundaries. Some might have needed a black eye to persuade them to back off further, but Lars was arrogantly confident. He oozed charm and even the most draconian individual could not help but become ensnared by his wit and humour.

At the potential sign of confrontation, Lars successfully worked his charm on the boyfriend by complementing this large man for his taste in women and winning him over almost instantly. At the memory, Lars felt sick as the taste of his chauvinism repeated on him. The threatened guy whose name might have been Steve, or Stewart, was wary at first, but Lars retrieved a gold credit card from his silver clip and offered to buy him and his female companion a drink like the gentleman he thought he was being. Within five minutes, both guys had laughed it off and were discussing the generic crap that one often speaks when drunk with strangers; the football, London's housing crisis and the gentrification of typically working class areas, Trump and Gal Gadot.

This unlikely, yet enthralling whirlwind bromance continued for some time and both guys unintentionally ignored their pretty brunette companion.

The fact that Lars was on the cusp of his eighteenth birthday had not made its way into the conversation, neither had the fact that he was a student at the nearby boarding school, Kingswould Academy for Boys, for that matter.

He was confident and charismatic, which made him appealing to both his new friend and his new friend's partner. Lars noticed that they had left her in the booth where she sat with her arms crossed and scowling in their direction as she played the third wheel on a night out with her own boyfriend. Quite rightly, he recognised that she was bored and probably angry at having been dismissed. Phase two of damage control would need to commence promptly. Lars felt nauseous again.

Lars ordered another bottle of expensive vodka and led his new friend back to their waiting lady, where they perched down on either side of her. Her legs were crossed away from her boyfriend. Her arm was stretched out in front as she rhythmically tapped her fingers on the table in agitation. Lars assumed that she was not used to vying for the attention of anyone, let alone her own boyfriend.

Whilst the boys joked and laughed over ever-flowing glasses of Grey Goose, she decided to take matters into her own hands and made enticing eyes towards the direction of Lars. He was hypnotised but fully aware of what she was trying to do and he was ensnared nonetheless.

Lightly, she teased the veins that embossed Lars' muscular forearm with her fingers, tracing them down to the glass in his hand and leaving a carpet of golden goosebumps where her fingers brushed. The girl gently prized the tumbler out of his willing fingers, where up until this point, he had been absentmindedly teasing the beads of moisture on the cool surface. Quickly, she snapped the alcohol up to her mouth and necked the clear contents in a swift motion.

Licking her lips, she caught the glint in Lars' eye. He was clearly impressed by her and she smiled coyly before placing a suggestive hand on his knee. He maintained eye contact and his heart raced with anticipation. He felt the churn of his stomach drop, which served as a preliminary reminder that his blood was about to race elsewhere in his body.

She leaned over slowly to manoeuvre herself between the line of sight of both men, edging her face closer to Lars as she did so. He drank the scent of her freshly washed hair and lightly fragranced neck before feeling the caress of her cool breath on his face. She leaned ever closer, only to swerve at the last minute and lean the opposite direction to plant a passionate kiss on her boyfriend's mouth. Lars didn't realise at first, but this was a message to them both.

The confident woman remained there for what felt like ages. Her hand still clamped around Lars' knee, whilst her boyfriend grinned through her reciprocated advances. Eventually coming up for air, she necked another vodka and the boys followed suit.

The roles had switched and Lars enjoyed the thrill of going from predator to prey. What had started out as a simple flirtation had now unfolded into something more complex, challenging and dangerous.

Alex is not going to approve of this.

From what he could recall, the rest of the night had been a blur from that point onwards. Lars remembered the evening drawing to a close very late. The couple had ordered a taxi, offering him a lift home, though they did not stipulate whose home, which was great because Lars could not explain rolling up to the school gates to anyone. While all three sat crammed in the back, she continued to kiss her boyfriend passionately and then turned and planted her soft lips upon Lars' own. After that, everything was lost in a Grey Goose haze.

Now it was the morning and Lars was overcome with panic at the prospect of an awkward confrontation.

Crawling out from the bottom of the bed, Lars foraged for his clothes in the half-light of the bedroom. He pawed at silky material that whispered under the touch of his fingers, which must have been the red dress that the girl had slipped off within minutes of bringing Lars and her boyfriend into the bedroom.

"Shit. It's all in the living room," he hushed to himself, remembering where and how he had undressed.

Naked, Lars crawled along the floor and out of the crack of the bedroom door which had been left ajar. When he had fallen through the door last night with the liberal couple, they had gone to the lounge for more drinks. Neither the nameless girl or her boyfriend seemed to have a problem when she continued to kiss him. The boyfriend remained on the sofa and watched eagerly.

Shuffling along the corridor, Lars remembered how the girl had run her hungry fingers through the waves of his shaggy light brown hair, kissing him passionately. She pulled off his top, admired his tanned coloured skin and hard body, and eagerly pulled off his trousers. At that point, the boyfriend didn't want to miss out on the action and commanded her with a powerful and sensual hand that led her willingly to the bedroom. She, in turn, gestured a bewildered, but eager and very naked Lars to follow through to the bedroom as well.

At the time this had seemed like a great idea, Lars pondered, but as with all plans thought with the downstairs brain, there were always consequences. And as if the hangover from hell and a sharp chest pain wasn't enough, Lars was now without clothes in a strange flat or house with an older couple who, if Lars were a judgmental guy, probably had issues within their relationship. The icing on the cake, however, was the fact that he should not be judging anyone. Afterall, he was going to be nursing the scuff burns on his knees after literally commando'ing through their swanky apartment to avoid an awkward confrontation.

From this far down, the furniture of the lounge prudishly leered over the sneaking nude body that now edged upright and tiptoed through the room. Every picture and ornament cast judgmental looks at the stealth streaker as he urgently rummaged for his clothes.

Lars frantically gathered up his strewn garments in his arms. The first item was a sock that had been flung on the lampshade. Both shoes were conveniently placed by the couch and his royal blue cashmere sweater was wrinkled on the floor, where she had removed it from his body and dropped it at his feet. Lars was nearly onto landing a full house, but his underwear was nowhere to be seen.

The silence was broken when the smash of glass came from the other room. Like a startled meerkat, Lars abandoned the search for his Calvin's and hoisted his skinny jeans up over his bare backside. Grabbing the other sock and wrestling to put the jumper on, he frantically clambered the remainder of his belongings in his arms and wedged his feet awkwardly into his black leather boots.

His heart stopped dead in his chest as a pair of footsteps slowly padded down the hallway and he comprehended the awkwardness of being caught leaving.

Lars was petrified. His heart punched away at the inside of his sternum with a persistent thud that brought a wave of cold sweat down his neck. The nervous beads teased and rolled down his spine. Instinctively clenching his fists in panic, he somehow managed to clumsily drop his recently foraged belongings in an awkward mess at his feet.

With the padded slap of heavy steps on the wooden floor, Lars' stomach dropped and felt as though it plummeted to his kneecaps. The sound of two pairs of heavy feet laboriously trudged down the corridor, where the boards creaked from the other side of the door as they neared the living room.

The couple's struggled breathing rasped heavily in their unnaturally wheezy chests.

Are they asthmatic or did they also smoke far too many cigarettes last night?

Lars was reminded of his chest pain and tasted the Marlboro Reds.

"Crap." he cursed, looking desperately for an emergency exit, to which there was none. He was cornered, and the footsteps drew nearer and louder. The promise of a painfully awkward confrontation drew ever closer with each struggling slog. The last thing Lars wanted the morning after the night before was awkward small talk. Yes, the vodka had been liberal, but so had Lars' morals and he did not want to face the consequences of his drunken antics. Lars had once heard that hangovers are your body's way of saying that you had been a dick, and today was evident to that hypothesis.

Had Lars done this sort of thing all the time, he probably would have been a bit better at handling a situation like this. For all his charm, Lars could be pretty naive and a little hot-headed. Plus he had a habit of jumping headfirst into situations and not always seeing the bigger picture.

This particular liaison had seemed like a fantastic idea at the time. But for all his passion and exuberance, he was indeed young and very, very immature. As such, he was not accustomed to trysts such as these and certainly did not know how to behave respectfully. It was now quite apparent that he had bitten off more than he could chew. That and Lars always thinks he knows better. Had he been a little wiser, Lars should have been out of the building twenty minutes ago.

The creak of the expensive wooden floor from the other side of the living room door brought Lars back to his senses. He could distinctly hear that there were two panting breaths and both were extremely laboured and heavy. If he was not mistaken, Lars was concerned that they might have been struggling for air.

The glossy wooden door whined as it lurched open. Whether it was last night's vodka or the anxiousness of the situation, Lars felt sick with anticipation. Though, the awkwardness and the embarrassment of his behaviour was nothing compared to what Lars was about to face.

The couple plodded monstrously through the threshold to reveal their sickening and fiendish state. This went beyond the hangover from hell; something was hideously wrong with them.

Both were stark-naked as they had been in bed. Dishevelled and unkempt, they looked insanely pale and drained, like the stars of a zombie film. The once fake-tanned pair were now rigid and withdrawn with skin that looked paper-thin and as light as linen. The greying skin on their lips was dry and cracked, while their faces took on a transparent quality that exposed the dark blue lines of their veins underneath.

The most striking quality was that both their eyes had been drained of all colour, looking ghostly pale and milky. Neither were entirely white, but their irises were hollow and deathly.

The girl staggered forward, entering the main room slightly ahead of her lover. Lars coughed, gagging on the sudden smell that they brought with them. Science wasn't Lars' strongest subject in school, but he had done enough chemistry experiments to recognise the distinct smell of sulphur. He had also read John Milton's Paradise Lost and that brimstone had a distinctive smell – evil smelled like eggs.

"What have you two eaten?" Lars tried to force another laugh, not entirely sure about the situation. "Is this some kind of a joke? Where are the hidden cameras?"

The once exotic-looking girl was now waif and stunk to high hell, and her boyfriend was in no better state. She reached her scraggly grey arms out. Lars panicked, stepped awkwardly and lost his balance. He fell forwards, right into her deadly embrace. It was the opportunity she needed to clasp her rotten fingers tightly around his neck.

Whether it was because she was icy cold to the touch or because Lars was panicking, her fingers felt like an intense static shock that gripped vice-tight around his throat. Her piercing gaze was haunting and intense, luring him with a visual grip that seized his very soul. The girl did not blink as she stared into his fearful face.

"Let- go- you crazy bitch!"

The larger guy stepped out from behind his girlfriend and let out an unearthly howl. The now-visible veins of his body looked toxic yellow and were raised against the grey canvas of his papery skin. He fell to his knees, retching from the very pit of his stomach, heaving and then doubled over in an agonising contortion.

Is he reacting to something or fighting something?

The girl gripped Lars' neck tighter and tighter while bringing her face nearer to his own. Her breath was acrid as if something was rotting in her diabolical throat.

At that moment, her pale eyes began to bleed like wax dribbling down a candle. The thick streams of fluid leaking from her eyes weren't the glossy red of healthy blood, but thick and snotty, and a brownish yellow like rotten egg yolks, seeping from her lower eyelids.

From his painful position, Lars saw from the corner of his eye that the guy's eyes were also seeping the same discharge. Streams of congealed mustard-treacle rolled slowly down both their faces.

The screaming naked guy threw his head right back to an unnatural angle and howled with an intensity that seemed to vibrate the entire contents of the room. Lars' chest hummed with panic and fear. The pain in his chest was unbearable and his heart could have exploded with the inhumane pitch of the howler's bawl.

Desperately trying to break free of the girl's grip, Lars pulled at her now wild and matted hair only to find clumps of it in his fingers. "Gah," was all he managed to choke, both in disgust and disappointment as she was unfazed by what should have been very painful. Lars increasingly lacked control of his heavy and clumsy limbs and grew light-headed. His hair-pulling only urged her to hold even tighter to his neck and he choked for breath.

Etiquette flies out the window when faced with certain death; Lars really needed to punch this crazy lady in the face or offer her a shot to the stomach with his knee, but his vision began to blur and his peripherals were getting darker. He wanted to cough, but every desperate gasp for air allowed for the vicious woman to inch tighter around his windpipe like a python.

In the hazy oxygen-deprived blur of vision, Lars was aware of, though could not see properly, the man's violent silhouette vibrating in full-on bodily spasms. Standing mid-howl, the naked man began to convulse and vibrate violently. His girlfriend continued to strangle Lars, taking no notice of the seizure her now demonic lover was undergoing.

In the blink of an eye, the man erupted in an explosion of putrid human entrails. Like a water balloon in slow-motion, the outburst of yellowed tar and brown mush flung across the room with sickening splats and squelches as the rancid missiles made contact with the various furnishings of the living room.

Had Lars not been preoccupied with the crazy possessed lady who smelled of rotten eggs, he would have been equally disgusted by the warm mess that had just splurged across his face and body.

The girl growled and clung tighter to Lars' neck. In hazy desperation he grabbed for anything at his disposal; fingers rummaging awkwardly for anything on the knee-level surface next to him. Papers ruffled as he grazed the polished surface of the wooden table with his fingertips. Then, a large, cold and solid heavy object that was round to the touch made its way into his grasp; a paperweight.

Score.

With one awkward blow, Lars brought the heavy glass object down on the side of her shoulder. Without a moment's hesitation, Lars choreographed a second, more accurate swing that landed right on her temple.

This did nothing but seemingly spur her on with a fiery ferocity that had Lars failing to see a way out.

With a final squeeze around his neck and a shove that caused him to fall back against the wall, he dropped his weapon. It crashed to the floor and exploded into glittering splinters of glass. Enveloped by her vicious gaze, Lars took both hands, reached deep within for a hidden strength and heaved his entire weight forward for an almighty shove in her chest.

She staggered, toppled and landed back on the floor. But it was not over – in that split second, Lars knew that something was still not quite right with his sudden liberation.

Lars looked down to find the rapidly rotting spindly digits of the girl's fingers still wrapped around his neck only the grip had subsided. The fingers were attached to her freakishly strong hands which in turn were still at the ends of her arms. However, tracing his eyes up the pair of wrists, along past the elbows right to the top where they should have met her shoulders, Lars was horrified that there were, in fact, no shoulders, or rest of the body. The shove had forced her torso to come apart, leaving her arms still in place.

Where the shoulder blades should've been, were two oozing wounds. On the floor lay the remains of the now mortified girl. She was dead.

Lars threw the arms that were still clasping his neck to the floor and jumped back in horror.

"What the f—"

He peered down to the body for closer inspection and it began to hum and wobble hideously. Lars was not sure why he wanted to but reluctantly peered his head nearer to the cadaver. Without warning, the corpse exploded into a harrowing mass of rotten puss. Moments later, the arms followed suit at his feet with definitive thuds.

Some brief moments passed. Exactly how long, Lars did not count, but he could not believe what he had just witnessed.

All was still in the living room. He surveyed the rancid splats that adorned the walls and furniture. The air moved and an eggy yellow haze of sulphur wafted up to his nose. Lars looked down at his clothes and then cast a gaze across to the sofa for his Italian leather jacket; it was about the only thing in the room that had avoided being pelted.

Lars' instinct to fight had long gone. All he wanted to do now, was run.

Grabbing the jacket, he dashed out the front door, through the apartment block and flew through the corridor. He darted down the two flights of stairs he had only staggered up a few hours prior and bolted out the main entrance into the fresh air of the chilly autumn morning.

He fell over himself and landed flat on the pavement. The wet concrete slabs were ice cold and numbing to his face. The light was invasive to his eyes and the rays tingled on his exposed flesh. The fresh air hit harder than running into a brick wall. Or falling flat on the pavement, as it were.

With no time to stop, Lars picked up his feet and ran down the street, not really knowing this part of town. Dashing past a milkman, several children and then a postman, all going about their early morning business. He zipped across the road without even looking, causing several cars to screech to a halt. They honked their horns in retaliation. One vehicle clipped his backside with their bonnet causing Lars to tumble, landing on the other side of the road relatively unscathed. He had not noticed the injury at that point but pelted as fast as his strong, yet tired legs would permit.

He was oblivious to where he was going. His head was pounding, his chest ached and his eyes stung as he fought back the tears.

The muscles in his legs burned with a sickening pang. His throat was bitterly dry. Lars' surroundings were significantly quieter than they had been ten minutes ago. He looked around. No longer in the busy suburban area, he now found himself at the edge of a woodland or park.

Stopping to catch his breath, his throat rasped with a continued burning sensation and his stomach was in knots. His eyes were still stinging and his breathing mimicked that of a dog's pants as he tried to regulate. Doubling over and placing his hands on his knees, Lars threw up and took some odd gratitude in his vomit. At least it was not yellow.

He coughed, spat and collapsed to the floor in a swift fluid motion. Lars rolled on his backside, wincing feebly, and muttered a definitive "shit" to himself. He was oblivious to the oversized magpie perched on the branch above his head. She squawked urgently and streamed back to her master on urgent wings.

3. The Headmistress and the Dead Girl

Ms Barty, the school's headmistress careened her way up the glossy corridor. It had not been long since getting wind of her charge's death and immediately went about orchestrating the most extreme damage control. It was gone 11am and Lilah, whom she had been something of a personal pedagogue to, had been duly absent from morning registration and failed to attend a group study period.

Ms Barty's day had started like every other. She awoke on time and performed her daily ritual; half an hour of Pilates before getting washed and dressed. She then savoured a cup of Earl Grey with half a grapefruit for breakfast while going through some paperwork before addressing the school at 8:50 am for assembly. Her day was running its usual course until she was interrupted by a larger than usual magpie convulsing at the window as she chaired a faculty meeting.

The other staff members were perplexed and horrified by such an aggressive show, fearing that the bird was deranged and in danger of hurting itself or breaking the glass. Barty, however, recognised it immediately and knew at once that this was a bad omen. Her instincts screamed from the pit of her stomach while she could only pray that they were erroneous.

She leapt from her seat and adjourned the meeting without needing to say a single word.

"Where's Jennifer?" She barked as her faculty poured through the room. Several of them kept going, whereas one or two stragglers at the back of the bottlenecked door turned around to respond to their headmistress. The history teacher, Miss Harvey, was the only one to answer the command.

"I'm not sure ma'am. She was in the dorms a little while ago." Barty nodded with a sharp abruptness that dismissed her.

The room was sufficiently empty and Barty shot her eyes to the window. The magpie had gone, but she knew that danger was afoot. The bird's presence could only mean one thing. Lilah.

Ms Barty left her quarters and headed to her office to call Jennifer. Marching down the corridor, the headmistress was met by a stout little woman waddling furiously with clapping shoes on the varnished floor. Despite the apparent exertion, her face was drained of colour. Barty knew what was coming before the woman opened her mouth.

"Headmistress!" she sputtered, not able to finish her sentence, "Oh Headmistress, it's terrible! The Thurston girl! She's– she's–"

Barty cleared her throat and snapped, "Good heavens, Glynis. Take a breath and tell me what happened." Rather than await the response, she started in the direction of the dormitory, which in turn was a command for the little fat woman to walk and talk. Barty's intuition meant that she already had a clear idea of what the woman was about to tell her, but no less had to multitask.

– "Er... well, it would seem, Headmistress, that one of the girls found Lady Lilah... this morning..." She paused, which Barty took to mean 'dead'. "The poor girl that found her –

such a little thing she is – and terribly shaken up, oh she was in such a state. Mind you, she was lucky Jennifer was there to console her and keep everything under control until I could find you. I need to tell you that Jennifer brought her to your office and told me to find you immediately."

"And where is Jennifer now?" she commanded.

"At the dorm."

"And the girl?"

"Still in your office, ma'am."

"Very well, console her and get her a cup of sweet tea. This next bit is imperative; call WPC Laura Shilling immediately; she will know what to do. Also, get me Professor Lenton's telephone number immediately as someone will need to tell the boy.

I'm on my way to Lilah's room and will deal with Jennifer. Do not let that girl leave my office until I return. She is not to phone, speak or see anyone but you. This is not to get out to anyone. Am I understood."

The last point was not a question, to which the lady responded with a silent nod.

Barty knew that navigating this tragedy was going to take a monumental amount of skill, even with the aid of her own natural ability. Fate was already changed and Lilah's act could prove catastrophic for all involved, but it was up to her to take the reins and fix this mess.

She marched on sensible heels through the school corridors towards the dormitory, parting masses of schoolgirls as she bound through them like a shark spearing through a school of mackerel. It was not unusual for the girls to be terrified of their headmistress. It was also common lore that one should never look her in her lavender eyes – bad things happened when you made eye contact with the headmistress.

Believe it or not, when it came to infamy and disrepute, Barty had dealt with worse scandals in her four decades of service to Oxney than a dead school girl. No less tragic, this was, however, beyond the school; Lilah's fate was tied to that of their coven and ultimately, the Fold.

Since before her birth, Lady Lilah Thurston had been predetermined to study witchcraft at Oxney under the tutelage of Ms Barty, despite the tragic headstart to their relationship. It should be said that Ms Barty was certainly not running a *magic school* and that being a witch was not a prerequisite to assure a girl's acceptance and attendance. That being said, however, fledgeling witches did indeed flock to Oxney in order to study under the infamous headmistress.

The death of Lilah's mother, before coming into her power, left Lilah without a suitable mentor. It is a mother's sacred duty among witches to guide and mentor her daughter through the coming of her gift. In cases such as Lilah's, which – historically – was tragically common, a surrogate was appointed. A sort of mystical wet nurse as it were.

Since the headmistress and Lilah's father, Jude, had been friends for many years, it seemed only natural that Barty would be entrusted with the care of Lilah's legacy. A responsibility she relished zealously.

Aside from having no children of her own, she was incredibly honoured to have a direct hand in this girl's destiny. Barty was an incredibly proud creature and the Thurstons brought prestige and prominence, which only served to inflate her sense of self-worth.

She certainly loved the child, but it was more complicated than that. Barty loved Lilah like a couturier loves their collection; her blood and soul poured into her life's work for praise and adoration en masse.

Barty had revelled in the fact that Lady Lilah had been predestined true greatness among the coven and was to oversee the girl herald tremendous things for the Fold.

Not anymore.

A gaggle of giggling girls loitered the top of the corridor, whispering and gossiping like a spiteful mob of little meerkats in blazers and tartan skirts. Unlike meerkats, however, this gang had neglected their lookout duty and failed to spot the severe predator viciously strutting up the hallway towards them.

The corridor was out of bounds and the meerkat girls were infringing the perimeter. Barty was itching to let off some steam and these girls were in her crosshair. Barty did not have time for insolence. If she and the covens hoped for any salvation, she needed to get to Lilah's body quickly, otherwise, all might be lost for the Fold.

The gaggle of girls had been fed up with waiting to get back to their rooms and decided to sneak in. The ring leader, Emily Fitzgibbons, had initially needed her laptop charger and managed to convince her posse to creep in and help her collect it. The retrieval had been an in-and-out job and overall success, but being naive and insensitive, the girls' sense of morbid fascination got the better of them and they decided that it would be a good idea to check out Lilah's bedroom.

"Apparently, they found her body this morning. That Susie girl said she never turned up to their study group," piped one of the girls.

"Lilah doesn't do study groups," chided Emily matter-of-factly, "Unless it's to find new ways to torment us."

The girls giggled guiltily. Lilah was not popular among the lower tiers of the school caste and these girls had not been particular fans of their deceased peer. Humans have a difficult time warming to those who are smart, beautiful, traditionally popular, rich and athletic. However, Lilah was generally considered a bitch and had also made every girl's life hell at least once throughout her academic career. This is not to say that the girls thought Lilah's death was deserved, but behind the shock and sadness, many of the girls dared not admit to themselves that some measure of divine justice had been served.

"You're being mean, Emily – especially if she is actually dead," defended another girl, to which Emily acknowledged reluctantly.

"I know. It's just that she's such a bitch. Was a bitch? Is a bitch? Whatever she may be, dead or otherwise. I hated her and her stuck-up attitude – she made my bloody life hell for years – not to mention all of yours." She accused, and the girls ashamedly agreed.

In the case of Emily, Lilah christened her with the nickname Pleb, and like a bad reputation, it had stuck with poor Emily for as long as she could remember. A few years ago, the class had been learning about the ancient Roman feudal system. It was no secret that Emily had earned her tuition thanks to a generous scholarship and as such, was deemed a lesser student; a Plebian among the Oxney Patricians. When Lilah found out Emily's uniform was secondhand, she hounded her mercilessly.

As far as slurs went, Emily had to praise the intelligence behind her moniker and was sort of grateful that it was not any worse. Afterall, according to Lilah, she kept company with sluts, dykes and fat-lesbo-whores.

As the girls squabbled ignorantly amongst each other in the corridor, daring Emily to go to Lilah's room to see if there was still blood everywhere, the impending figure of authority drew closer.

They were still unaware of her presence. And it was too late. The menacing woman swept towards the crowd like a cunning shark in a murky reef. One girl clocked the headmistress, but they had already been spotted and there was no escape. They tried to disperse and leave the vicinity of the forbidden corridor, but they were already done for.

"1, 2, 3 and 4," barked the distinguished yet definite voice counting off her prey as she marched to their approach, "Where do you think you're going? This floor is strictly out of bounds. Get yourselves to my office immediately. Wait for me and we'll discuss your suspensions when I get there."

Each girl dropped her head without argument and made their way down to Ms Barty's office to await their fate. Despite their punishment being wildly unfair, they knew that there was no use in arguing since their headmistress' word was both severe and final.

Emily stewed over the prospect of her parents' disappointment, muttering under her breath, "She's dead and that stupid bitch is still making my life hell."

Ms Barty showed no remorse towards the insolent girls and now stood at the door of Lilah's dormitory. The glossed dark wood reflected her own austere reflection, which revealed her immaculate silver hair and harsh face.

Barty reluctantly placed her hand upon the doorknob. The brass was cold against her uneasy hand. She took a moment to prepare herself. The headmistress was about to come face-to-face with the most brutal tragedy and summoned all the composure she could muster. Without warning, she yanked the handle and thrust the door open into the bedroom and was met with the shocked face of a distinct-looking ginger woman.

"Jennifer?" addressed Ms Barty.

"Headmistress!" Jennifer was startled, hastily collected herself and prattled off an immediate explanation. "Y-you weren't in your o-office and I knew you were making your way here to... I mean, that poor girl... she was in such a shock when she found... A-and then poor Lilah –". She stopped, fighting the instinct to turn around.

Barty was uncomfortable with how uneasy Jennifer looked, especially considering her stature. From her fiery mass of red hair to her strong, athletic posture, nothing about this woman said she was timid or awkward. Needless to say, Barty certainly was not impressed with Jennifer's presence. Fortunately, she stood in the way, shielding Lilah's body and Barty was spared the immediate horror of seeing her beloved Lilah in such an undignified position. Barty still tried to inspect the scene for the weapon.

"Did you touch anything?" she shot.

"No, Ms Barty. I literally sent the girl to your office, left the room, cleared the corridor and guarded the door. It's only because her, I mean, Lilah's alarm went off that I went in the room to turn it off. I... I...

I mean, it's such a – a –" she tried to add, failing to find the words. Barty was uneasy and growing impatient with the woman's stutterings. Jennifer started to sniff and shock began to set in.

"Let's step outside," Barty urged, trying to get out of the room but Jennifer continued to panic-talk.

"What was she bloody thinking?

Barty glared, silently.

"I can't even imagine what the hell was going through her head," she paused, only to utter mindlessly an idle comment through a sob, "S-Selfish."

Whilst the comment had been made idly, Barty pondered her assistant's opinion as she stepped further into the room. In an almost bored manner, the headmistress considered whether or not the careless words needed a response.

Lilah's sodden body leered from the bed in Barty's peripheral. Looking down to her peep toes, the severe woman paused for a moment longer than comfortable. She gently closed her eyelids and sighed. Without warning, something ignited within the headmistress and she struck. Within an instant, Barty flung open her eyelids in cool passion and lurched her head with the sharp control of a serpent's pounce to Jennifer's young face.

The school's headmistress was ordinarily a refined being; one from a generation where leering into the face of anyone was deemed crass and vulgar. However, despite the socially unacceptable distance, the younger of the two ladies could not help but feel the heat of her bosses piercing gaze which in turn manifested prickly beads of sweat that transpired about her collar.

The words that left the older woman's mouth in that next moment were both perfectly pronounced and clear, yet they were also lethal; as if each syllable were a deadly sting.

"If I want your opinion, Jennifer, then I will most assuredly ask for it. However, at this point, neither do I want to know, or even care what you think on the matter." She paused but wasn't finished.

"And may I remind you kindly," she said, almost with something of a snigger, "that you are not under my employment to provide me with your futile notions, and would, therefore, do well to keep your lips shut when involved in matters of little or no concern to you. Do I make myself clear?"

Put out by her employer's comeback, Jennifer sheepishly adjusted her mottled cardigan and wiped her face with the back of her hand. A lump formed in her throat, and she felt as though she were a naked child, ashamed and dirty under the scrutiny of a spiteful adult. "Sorry. Ms Barty, I had no right–" she said through gritted teeth.

For a moment, she thought she saw a twinge of anger or fire, which disappeared from her assistant's aura as quickly as it had possibly begun to surface. The headmistress quickly interjected: "Do. I. Make. Myself. Clear?" It was not a question by any stretch of the imagination.

In the blink of Ms Barty's unforgiving lavender eye, the atmosphere yielded to an instantaneous switch of mood from the viciously angry woman. The clouds seemed to part, Jennifer let out an almost euphoric sigh and Ms Barty's hackles gently subsided.

"Now, what's happened – what do we know?"

Jennifer recapped what she could, just as she had done when Barty arrived at the room. She explained that she was walking through the dorms, noting that one of the girls was knocking on one of the doors. Jennifer had reminded the girl that she should be in class, only to be duly informed that she was sent to retrieve Lilah who had not turned up for a study group.

Jennifer trusted the girl's story and thought nothing more as she continued on her way. She recalled hearing the door go and the girl entering the room before a piercing scream reverberated through the entire corridor. Jennifer then recited how she consoled the girl and sent her to Barty's office immediately, while she guarded the scene until the headmistress arrived. Jennifer explained that she waited outside for some five minutes or so, before hearing Lilah's mobile alarm, to which she went in and rather stupidly turned off.

– "I'm sorry Headmistress, I didn't think. It seemed like the thing to do – an alarm goes off and you respond to it. It didn't occur to me that it could be evidence or that I tampered with the scene. Here –" she handed the phone to Barty. "And that's it. You arrived just as I was about to leave and wait outside again."

"No Jennifer, you did the right thing. It might have drawn unnecessary attention." Barty placed the mobile phone in her pocket. "I'll take it from here. If you would, Jennifer, go back to my office and wait for me. See to it that you and the girl – who was it that found her, by the way?"

Jennifer paused, awkwardly, before offering: "I, er, I... I'm not sure, Headmistress... I can't rem–"

In a terrifying instant, and without warning, Beatrice Barty planted a burning slap across Jennifer's cheek. Instinctively, the victim raised her own hand to her face where the cool of her own palm soothed the already swollen cheek, as she meekly offered: "-Remember."

Fighting back the tears, the fragile girl cupped her burning cheek. Jennifer dared to speak. The words were there, but they were too scared to leave the safety of her mouth. Her throat seized and she could neither speak or move. How pathetic she thought she must have looked.

"Get out of my sight." Ms Barty hissed.

And without needing any more excuses, this was exactly what she did.

Jennifer had elsewhere to be and Lilah's death truly had more of an impact than Barty would know for now.

The headmistress was alone. Coolly, as if nothing had just happened, Beatrice Barty composed herself, tucked her silver hair behind her ear and prepared to examine the room. She thought nothing more of her assistant and respectfully her thoughts turned to Lilah.

To conserve her charge's dignity, Barty would not stare at Lilah's body longer than necessary. She took a breath, placed her left hand to her mouth and looked to the body. The crimson sheets of the bed were sodden. Barty knew how the ritual would have taken place and correctly peered to Lilah's chest to confirm the suspected puncture wound to her sternum.

"Very well, Lilah, but where's the athame?" Barty darted her eyes around the body to see where the blade had gone. It was nowhere to be seen. She dropped to her knees to inspect under the bed and found nothing. Her stomach dropped in realisation.

"Jennifer!"

Without delay, she left the room and raced back to her office, where the four trespassing girls awaited their sentence in the waiting area with the girl who discovered Lilah's body. And just as Barty feared, there was no sign of Jennifer.

"Where is she?" She barked at the girls, each of whom looked more confused and panicked than the next. "Where is Jennifer?"

The assistant came through, bringing the distraught girl a cup of sugary tea. "Headmistress, she never came through."

"Everyone out," she commanded. "Not you, my child," as she isolated the girl that had initially found Lilah, and ushered her through to her room and into the chair opposite her desk.

"Have a seat, little one. You poor thing." The girl remained timidly silent and perched on the leather chair with great trepidation. "My gosh, what a morning you've had, you poor, poor thing. Go on, have a sip of your tea, it will make everything better my angel."

Barty urged with such sweetness that the girl tasted the sugar in every sentence. She made her way around her desk and perched on her own chair, placing her elbows on the desk and her chin on her clasped knuckles.

Barty glared intently at the girl who continued to sip her sweet tea, looking up over the rim of the china to catch the headmistress' eye.

The girl was drawn into the lavender and suddenly found herself aware that she could not move. Barty leered closer and whispered through pronounced lips:

"Forget. It. All." Barty whispered.

The girl nodded her head abruptly, put the tea down and blinked. She looked around the room, unsure of where she was, before realising she was face to face with the headmistress and let out a mild gasp. She had no idea why she was there or why there was such a sweet taste in her mouth.

The headmistress smiled, got up from her seat and encouraged the girl to leave, "Come along now, little one. Thank you for your time and well done on achieving such a tremendous grade. Girls like you are the future of this academy, so keep up the good work."

She undoubtedly had no idea what was going on but was grateful for the headmistress' favourable mood and left abruptly, not quite sure what was happening.

Barty was losing herself. She rambled her thoughts to herself. "It's all going wrong. It's not supposed to play out like this. Where's Jennifer? Lady Lilah must have performed the ritual, so where is the athame? Oh heavens," she realised, "What will Jude say? And what about the boy? Yes, the boy..." she pondered.

With desperate trepidation, Ms Barty dialled the number for Lars' boarding school. As the tone rang, butterflies dashed about her stomach and her heart reprised an encore of drums upon her ribcage. She composed herself and lightly fingered the pearls on her chest.

"Hello?" answered the other end.

"This is Ms Beatrice Barty, headmistress of The Oxney Academy for Girls. I must speak with the headmaster about the welfare of one of his pupils... I'm afraid I have some rather devastating news for him." Her refined voice was pleasant and polite but her tone, severe.

"I'm sorry, but the headmaster-" the voice was cut off by the persistent and forceful headmistress on the end of the line.

"I will speak with him immediately." She noted as the person on the other end of the line had dropped the sing-song tone and sounded a little peeved now.

"As I was about to say, *Ms Barty*, the headmaster is unavailable at the moment but I can take a message for you."

Ms Barty paused, to the point where the assistant or receptionist momentarily doubted that Beatrice Barty was still on the line. Carefully but precisely, she stated in that clear-cut, yet passively forceful tone: "*Excuse me*, but it is imperative that I speak with Professor Lenton *immediately*." She paused to emphasise the severity. "It concerns Lord Thurston."

Again, the girl's tone changed once more, but this time with an urgent realisation of how foolishly difficult she had been. "Right away ma'am. Apologies, I didn't understand the severity."

The phone clicked and a stern voice came to the line. "Barty, old girl, I understand we have a problem."

"I know Headmaster... We've been compromised. I'm on my way to you and the boy."

4. Back to Life

Several hours passed. Not a soul had wandered by to stumble upon the exhausted and confused boy taking shelter among the bushes.

The area was quiet and were it not for the catatonic state of confusion he was suffering from after his traumatic ordeal, every snap of a twig and every scurry of flickering leaves might have had Lars jump out of his skin.

The air was thick with a silence that somehow drowned out the creaking branches as they bent to the force of the wind overhead. The air's density muffled the whispers of the wild vegetation as it gossiped away about the frightened young man, while light rain popped against the dying leaves overhead like atmospheric white noise.

There were occasions when Lars thought he could sense the presence of something pulling him out of his catatonic state, like a lurking tiger about to pounce from the trees. It was a familiar sensation, which made itself known by the materialisation of a dull hum that was both alarming and oddly soothing. At this stage, Lars merely had an awareness of the distant sound, which was accompanied by pulses of faint vibrations, neither knowing or indeed caring, what it was right now.

The hazy state of panic was beginning to clear and Lars could feel the realisation of what had happened creep slowly into his conscience. He had taken obnoxious comfort in his adrenaline-fuelled state of panic. The goal had been to get away to safety and now that he was out of the danger zone, reality was a punch in the gut.

Somewhere after vomiting in the midst of panic, Lars had the idea to hide – not that anybody was about. The area was desolate and his instinct was to bury himself away until he could gather himself and face the ordeal with a clearer head.

He had managed to stagger and enshrine himself under the protection of a sympathetic yew tree so that he was out of sight. Should anyone else come after him in the immediate future, he would at least see them in the distance and be prepared enough to run and hide.

As he took in his surroundings, he noted the mass of woodland that lay behind him. Tree after tree was crammed tightly next to the other, causing a sepia canopy of browns and yellows to smother all the light out of the undergrowth.

The barren meadow he dashed across after the bloody confrontation earlier in the morning stretched out ahead of him. The hypnotic dance of the grey grass ebbed and flowed in the breeze, causing it to wave a lethargic taunt at the outskirts of the town in the distance. Lars could have been entirely alone and possibly the only human for miles.

What the hell happened to them?
What have I done?
People don't just do that.
They melted.
They exploded.
They tried to kill me.

He ran his restless hands from his aching temples to finger the shaggy mat of sandy curls. Lars ducked his neck and wondered in disbelief about the ordeal that had just happened. His eyes stung and his throat tightened. He sniffed his nose as he let out a wretched and uncontrolled sob.

Her eyes.

They were so...

Empty.

Remembering the immense grip she had on his neck, he fingered the tender flesh under his weary jaw.

That smell; I've never known anything like it; beyond decay and past death.

Lars fought the urge to gag violently at another thought of the putrid stench. His stomach was empty, but the involuntary memory revived a bitter tang in his mouth and throat that he had no desire to sample again this morning.

He replayed the hedonistic night and subsequent morning of horror over and over. Lars tried to recall the lead up to last night's events, and half laughed in a delirious fit of disbelief at how it panned out.

He had arranged to meet the boys at 8pm. Always one to see a deadline and surpass it, Lars had strolled into the appropriately-named establishment, The Bar, somewhere after 9pm and his friends were nowhere to be seen.

Scanning the Thursday night crowd of the town's only decent place to grab a drink, he scoured the area in an attempt to recognise a familiar face. He continued to survey the venue as he made his way through the mass of dancing bodies to the bar, and ordered a bottle of beer. He then sat and waited.

The Bar was renowned for serving the underage boys of the local private school. These kids were extremely wealthy and spent a lot of money, more so when they had enjoyed a drink or seven. The boys knew how to have a good time and the owner of the bar lived to indulge their extravagant lifestyles, which in turn, paid for his.

Lars took out his phone from his jacket pocket.

His screen revealed that he had received several missed calls from his friends. He proceeded to return their respective calls but only got their voicemails. The guys had moved on, but not left a message to tell Lars where.

He cast his thoughts to Alex back in the dorms. This was not his scene and a *good ol' piss up* was definitely not Alex's idea of fun. Lars had jibed him for being a nerd, because his friend had opted to stay in and study rather than go out with the other sixth form boys.

Now on his own, Lars could only think of what his friend was up to.

Right before he was about to throw the towel in on the night's shenanigans, a striking female walked by; the then-pretty brunette from last night clocked his attention from across the bar.

She sashayed across the room with a roll of her hips. Her hair fell down her shoulders in brown curls with the glossy sheen of tempered chocolate, parting over and curving around the outside of her breasts.

Abandoning any ideas about giving up for the night and going home, he decided that he had to pursue this girl; in hindsight, a move that would turn out to be very dangerous.

Under a sharp breeze that brought a severe chill over him, Lars huddled his legs to his chest in a tight embrace and rested his nose in between his knee caps. He feared that by letting go of his legs and looking up, he would unravel like a loose thread.

What happened to them?
What did I do...?
I need to call the police.
I smell horrendous.

Breaking the silence, and also his ever-meandering train of thought, Lars once again felt the familiar rumble of that persistent hum from earlier. Unlike before, the noise and accompanying motion successfully drew his consciousness back to reality like a lifeline.

Patting his front, he retrieved the phone that had vibrated in his pocket.

This could have been the hum or rumble from earlier, but this felt different.

The identity of the mystery caller was concealed with the terminally frustrating caption: Withheld Number. Despite having sat on the sodden earth under a tree for some hours, it was still quite early and Lars wondered who the hell would be calling at this hour.

Is it the police?

Does someone know what happened?

Without thinking, he simply clicked the button and cancelled the call, putting his phone back in his pocket until he could see clearer. Lars needed time to think. After all, that couple had just tried to kill him. And he felt that time to collect his thoughts was due to him.

Another breeze kicked up a whiff of the yellow gunk that was spread across his cashmere sweater. A flashback of the lurid gaze of the powdery-white irises of the once attractive woman was all too much. The acrid stench teased his nostrils and Lars wretched another empty offering.

If I'm sick anymore, I swear I will bring up my insides.

With that, Lars clambered to his feet with strong but tired muscles and dusted himself down.

Wiping his eyes, he took a deep breath and navigated his way home.

5. Kingswould Academy for Boys

The walk back to Lars' prestigious boarding school had taken well over an hour, and by the time he got back to the dorms most of the school were ending their second period.

It was now somewhere near eleven o'clock, and going through the main entrance in this state would be suicide; they would literally get a whiff of him before they saw him. Smelling like this makes for a terrible attempt at being inconspicuous and Lars thought it safest to duck through a not-so-secret wooded area that last year's older boys used to skip lessons and smoke in.

The hangover was subsiding and he was feeling more alert as he wove through a series of vines. He hopped over a dilapidated wall and slipped through a broken railing belonging to a longer chain that circumvented the entire academy. Somewhere in the process of infiltrating the school grounds he had snagged a thorn on the front of his already soiled sweater and grazed his skin beneath.

This sweater is definitely going in the bin.

The scratch was merely a scrape to his skin, but stung like a bitch. The injury itself was well-received by Lars because it was the first thing besides fear, sickness and confusion that he had felt in a few hours. Pain was definitive; something either hurt, or it did not. It also meant that the bruise on his backside was coming to life, reminding Lars of the car that had nicked him earlier whilst escaping from the *House of Horror.*

Stepping out of the browning shrubbery that enveloped the autumnal school grounds, Lars combed the scene. From the wooded border, the lavish school building leered with an ageing regality at the centre of a series of manicured lawns. The pale clock face of the North Tower grimaced in the shadow of the tired sun, peering down judgingly at a desperate Lars, on his final leg of the home stretch.

If Lars were to make a dash, he would be exposed and out in the open for several metres. Running across the wide stretch of dewy grass in broad daylight, for the entire student body and staff to see, was out of the question.

Lars always thought of Kingswould Academy as more of a prison. He knew it was cliché but he dreamed with desperation of escaping the pomp and bombastic nature of the privileged establishment. Never, in his wildest dreams, had he ever considered escaping back *into* school.

In a swift dash, Lars beelined along the old brick wall as quick as a fox in pursuit of safety. It was a longer journey, and one that would involve crouching in an awkward waddle as he circumvented the grounds. The crumbling lion figurines that adorned the ageing pillars, sneered with a detrimental gaze as Lars darted to the back door of the sixth form dormitories in a leap that immersed him in the safety of indoor shelter.

Just as Lars reached the back door, it swung open and out dashed a couple of boys from the year below. Fortunately in their hurry, they didn't see Lars as he braced the wall. The younger-looking ginger boy turned up his nose and looked to his friend: "Have you just farted? You stink." Lars felt a little embarrassed that the eggy smell of sulphuric guts and gunk still tainted his clothes.

Flying up the ancient stairway and along the corridor, both of which never seemed to end, Lars made it safely to the sanctuary of his room, where he all but fell across the threshold of his dorm.

Fortunately, upper sixth boys like Lars were privy to their own rooms and were no longer required to share as they had done in the earlier years. He would not have to explain his absence, the cuts and bruises and the god awful pong just yet.

Being Lars Thurston however, came with certain privileges. Throughout the many years he had attended this school, Lars' father had seen to it that his son had the best of everything; an attitude that had not made Lars popular in his early years. For example, having a private room as a first year was unheard of and had meant that two upper sixth boys had to share. To say that the name Thurston came with certain status was something that both Lars and the sharing sixth formers had understood far too well.

Lars thought to how his sister had inherited that sense of entitlement, that was only instilled further by their father. Like him, Lilah took great pride in wearing the Thurston name as a badge of honour, or more aptly, a crown in some instances. Dropping their name got them into specific circles with exclusive benefits. To put it politely, the Thurstons had a lot of money, and for everything that currency couldn't obtain, their surname got them the rest.

Lars, however, had always been uncomfortable with his family and the stuffy old traditions and expectations that often came with it. Despite the privileged lifestyle, Lars had wanted nothing more than to go to a regular school, with regular children (especially girls), and go about relatively anonymously. Instead he and his twin sister were shipped away separately to the country's finest boarding schools and treated like minor celebrities, where pupils and teachers alike would pander and vie for their respective attentions.

Of course, the older he got, the more important material things became and his ethics slipped occasionally.

Lars caught his breath and stripped completely. He bagged up his jeans, sweater and leather jacket and lobbed them out of the window into the bush below before the stench tarnished the room entirely. Later he would burn or discard them properly. Lars completely missed the mysterious rosewood box that had appeared on his desk, dashing straight into his en suite shower instead and scrubbing until his skin practically bled.

Whilst in the shower, Lars' phone buzzed once more from the same withheld number that had called earlier.

Pulses of ice-cold water spat from the shower's slightly lime-scaled head. Lars stepped back with a violent shudder, nearly slipping over on the slimy tiles. He prepared for a second attempt. Bracing himself, he plunged his rigid body, head first, under the spitting stream of water. Lars' skin contracted with goosebumps under the frigid cascade.

The water yielded to the ever-warming current and began to melt the tension and tightness of his aching muscles, where the cleansing water teased and tickled his bumps and scratches. The heat eased the fatigue and frustration, although the hollow feeling in his gut meant that Lars could not fully submit to the releasing qualities of the usually invigorating shower.

Thick matted lumps of rotting yellow mass were woven loosely in the curls of his thick sandy hair. There were in fact a whole host of unwanted entrails and debris about his hair and body. Braving a look to the floor, Lars noted the scraps of twigs and leaves from his cross-country getaway as they fell to his feet amidst the clumps of jaundiced flesh and matted hair from the exploding couple.

He lathered up quickly and watched as mustard swirls bled into the clean water on the canvas of his bronzed skin, greying into an oblivion of clarity. The smelly lumps, of what Lars dreaded to imagine, dissolved and fizzled down the abyss of the plug hole.

All in all it took Lars several attempts with shampoo and soap to feel completely clean, not to mention, to finally get the smell out from under his nose. Lars took a long time to decontaminate and feel relatively human again without the use of industrial strength cleaning agents.

After all the violence and tragedy of this morning, Lars' hangover was long forgotten. When it had stopped exactly, he wasn't sure.

All that remained was a hollow feeling of guilt and remorse gnawing away at his insides. Lars knew he hadn't done anything wrong, but he felt for the couple. He also felt sick with shame about leaving the scene of the crime.

He lathered and rinsed one last time before turning off the shower and grabbing a nearby towel from the heated rail next to the glass cubicle. Once out of the shower, he knew he would have to deal with the next priority; something that he would undeniably have to face sooner or later.

One step at a time Lars.

From his room, Lars could hear the migration of bodies in both the corridor and the school grounds outside his window. From the gay screams, giggles and laddish jeers he knew that this was the mass exodus to third period and the final stretch before lunch.

Lars cleaned his teeth. On autopilot, he ran his towel through his sodden mop of golden brown hair and left it at that. It did not seem appropriate to go all out with a full-on bouffant after his morning. He paused to wonder if they would have hairdryers in prison.

The thought of getting dressed was both laborious and traumatic. He opted for comfortable pants, which he slipped on over his backside quickly and covered the rest of his body in an old pair of jeans and a plain black sweater. Socks were too much effort, so he didn't bother.

Adequately clothed he perched on the corner of his unmade bed and rested his chin on praying fingers, letting out a remorseful sigh.

I'm never having sex again.

The atmosphere was calm, and for the first time in hours he felt safer and more at ease than he could seem to remember. A breeze encroached the cracked windowpane and Lars was able to forget himself in the moment of quiet serenity before he would open the floodgates and get to the bottom of this morning.

At that moment, Lars' mobile phone interjected with a buzz as it vibrated across his desk.

He looked over to it with a startled panic. His stomach plummeted to his naked toes and through the floor as he remembered himself and the current situation he now found himself.

It stopped as soon as Lars plucked up the courage to answer.

The screen revealed that he had already received five missed calls from the same number.

Despite his fear and the anxiety of dealing with whoever was on the other end, Lars couldn't help but feel a little miffed that the caller was using a withheld number and had left no message. Lars would normally assume it was an annoying sales call or something about PPI. On this occasion, he felt that it was something a little more close to home and wondered if this might have had some connection to the dead couple he had sex with last night. The phone buzzed in his unnerved hand. He swiped his finger across the screen and answered cautiously, trying to sound calm and not like he was the major witness to a gruesome accident. "Hello?"

He was shocked by the instant crackle of static on the other end as it scratched at his ear and the morse code of a breaking voice pressed urgently.

"Lars?"

The line snapped and hissed violently, making the caller sound staggered and robotic. Lars couldn't even decipher whether it was a man or woman on the other end.

"Hello?" he asked again, laced with a slightly obnoxious tone at the possibility of someone wasting his time. "Can you hear me? You're breaking up."

"Lars?"

The line continued to muffle and hiss as the incoherent android tried to converse.

"L... Lars... hide." The tone was frantic and panicked. Lars' patience was about to get the better of him and hang up, when the dormitory door wrapped with an urgent pound from the other side.

"Lars are you in there, son? It's Professor Lenton."

At that moment, Lars swore that he felt his heart stop. A wave of paralysis swept across his body with a current of mild trauma. He executed the instinctive desire to hang up, awkwardly ending the call and fondling the phone into his pocket whilst he considered his next move.

Shit. Does he know about this morning?

Lars felt that jumping out of the window would have been a viable option at this stage, had the professor not called through the door in his old schoolmaster tenor.

"Thurston old chap, we know you're in there. One of the first years saw you enter the building."

Crap. So much for my stealthy entrance...

Professor Lenton's voice had the waffly grunt of some Victorian aristocrat from the days of the British Empire.

"Lars, I heard you talking to someone in there," he accused.

He checked the room, looking for any incriminating evidence. Everything had been thrown out of the window and nothing suspicious remained. His desk was scattered with various rubbish and the wooden box sat on top of a few papers like an organic paperweight.

The door banged again, but Lars was captivated by the mysterious box. It was not his and he had no idea how it had appeared on his desk. He picked up some of the papers and threw them over the top to cover it. He could not decide why it was a secret, but felt that the headmaster should not see it.

Lars opened the door to be met with a waft of pipe tobacco and stale brandy, whiskey or possibly methylated spirits. In the doorway stood the robust figure of Professor Lenton. A vision of earthy colours; the headmaster lived for tweed.

He fashioned a curly moustache and was just a monocle away from being a bonafide pompous Victorian gentleman. Professor Lenton had the rosy complexion that became of most men at a certain age, especially those accustomed to a tipple or four throughout the day. His strawberry hair was receding, but oiled back in an unflattering combover.

"Sorry Sir, I was on the phone."

Standing next to the headmaster was an uptight and frigid-looking older woman, whom Lars could not quite place. Her hair was a sheet of silver, curled into a regimented cloud of grey curls. She was immaculately dressed in a simple black dress, with a pastel blue cardigan draped formally over her shoulders.

Her gaze was filled with sadness but steely, and almost spiteful. She had one arm crossed over her waif chest, whilst the hand of her other arm fingered the string of pearls around her leathery soft neck. The woman was composed enough to control her anxiety to a degree, instead channeling that energy into a mysterious determination that terrified Lars.

The professor's tone was stern but sympathetic. "Course you were. No need to apologise..." He paused, as if trying to calculate what he was going to say next. "Err... Lars, may we come in? We need to talk to you."

That hollow feeling in Lars' stomach was expanding with a rapid tenacity. Lars paused awkwardly in the doorway. His palms were sweaty and his heart pounded against the inside of his ribcage. He self-consciously stepped aside from the door and gestured for his guests to come in. Not knowing what to say, he blurted: "Sorry about the mess."

"Rough night?" the distressed silver vixen accused, with the crack of a knowing grin.

"I can explain—" Lars added hastily.

"Argh, *boys will be boys, eh*?" interrupted Professor Lenton.

"Something like that," Lars settled.

As the older couple walked into the room, he caught the look on both of their ageing faces as though a bad smell lingered. Lars leaned to crack open the window further with lightning speed. Turning back around to close the door, sensing the privacy of the meeting, a uniformed police woman entered the room with a brazen stride.

The pearl-necklaced lady gestured to the new arrival, with a severe and uncompromising tone: "Lars, this is WPC Laura Shilling."

Lars knew if he had caught sight of his own reflection he would have seen the colour drain from his face. He sensed the authority of the older lady as she placed her angular hands on his shoulder, ushering him to the corner of his bed for a seat. He knew from the police officer's badge that she was from home.

Lenton ignored the WPC as he pulled up the chair from the desk, sat down heavily, and reached out to touch Lars' knee. "This is Ms. Beatrice Barty." With that minor introduction, the staunch-faced Ms. Barty also ignored the policewoman and sat down on the bed, slightly put out that Professor Lenton had not offered her the chair. Once comfortable, she reached over and put her hand on Lars' other knee and gave him a difficult smile through pursed lips.

I wish people would stop touching my knee; last time didn't end too well.

"Master Thurston, do you remember me?" She glared through her peculiar coloured eyes. They were bloodshot; she had been crying.

His silence spoke volumes.

"Lars, I am a dear friend of your father and have been for many years. Do you know what my job is?" She leaned in with an unconvincing attempt to be sincere that came across as condescending. "I am the headmistress of your sister's school," she said in that school-teacher voice, wiping her tearful eye with a tissue that seemingly appeared from nowhere.

It clicked.

That's where I've seen you from.

Lenton took the pause to try and shoulder in his own authoritative interjection. "Lars, the headmistress is here with WPC Shilling..."

He paused, though only shortly for fear of being spoken over by Ms. Barty, as he tried to find the right words.

"...They are both here, unfortunately, as they have some rather terrible news."

Is this when they arrest me for this morning?

A wave of beads dotted Lars' forehead and sideburns just as the hairs on his neck stood to attention. He was all but about to confess for fleeing the scene of a crime, when something in the air changed.

Perhaps it was telepathy or the fact that Lars was innately in-tune to the psychology of strangers, but he instinctively knew that this news was a little closer to home; as to how or why, Lars did not yet know, though he was moments from finding out.

These people were ignorant to his deadly tryst, but from the way they shifted in their seats, avoided eye contact and spoke with patronising tones, they certainly knew something and it wasn't good.

"Where's Lilah?" He offered anxiously, fighting the urge to panic. Lars could feel his throat contract and his breath shorten. "What's wrong? Tell me why you're here."

The adults all looked to one another with dubious glares, not knowing who should step forward and enlighten the desperate boy. Ms. Barty brought her scrunched tissue up to her mouth and looked away with desperate eyes.

"Where's my father?"

Ms. Barty cleared her throat and adjusted her half moon glasses on the bridge of her nose. Taking a deep death, she straightened the material of her dress that lay across her knees and attempted to come forward with a response. She was as composed as she could be.

"Lars, my darling, I'm sorry to have to be one the one to tell you this, but..."

Had she not spoken with such poise and had such a graceful stature, Lars would have called her out on her pause for dramatic effect. Her loss for words was sincere, though it did manage to irritate Lars, especially when she closed her eyes for what seemed like a lifetime.

Enough with the melodrama. Spit it out, woman.

"... I'm afraid to tell you that dear Lilah is dead."

Shit.

She had just come out with it, so quick and direct. The news diluted his senses and bludgeoned any hold of reality in that moment.

"How?" he whimpered.

But the truth was, Lars did not hear anything beyond the question. The whole room was bursting with a tension that would implode at any moment. The air grew stale and his chest felt tighter. The walls of his dormitory leered tall, lurching over its contents while the people within shrunk and blurred to specks in his peripheral vision.

Lars was overcome with a sudden sense of claustrophobia and needed to move. There was a metallic coat lining his tongue; he had bitten the inside of his cheek to a point where it was bleeding. He hadn't noticed.

Lars leapt from the corner of his bed where he had been perched and inclined towards his chaotic desk under the window. He clocked the war zone of stationery and papers and started to tidy. Maniacally, he flipped his laptop shut and continued to adjust the contents of his desk in futile frenzy, starting with the pen pot, then straightening the picture of his forgiving mother, and ruffling a confusion of papers. Forgetting the adults were present, he looked up and out of the window at the first years running around wildly without a care in the world.

The headmistress was still talking but he did not register a single iota of what she said.

Professor Lenton trudged across the room and placed a chubby hand on Lars' tired shoulder, saying nothing. The older gentleman was clearly uncomfortable and the puffy limp hand on his shoulder was nothing more than awkward. He knew that his headmaster meant well but his gesture of compassion was not helping. If anything his hackles were well and truly raised at this point.

Lars fought every urge not to lash out and shrug the professor's hand off. Instead he let it settle there, knowing that in some way he was doing the teacher a favour.

This whole day had just been a string of bloody and tragic events, each more horrifying than the last. Had someone predicted all of this yesterday, how his world would be turned upside down, Lars would have thought that they were spinning a cruel and elaborate work of fiction.

In a daze of numbness, Lars surveyed the stocky little police officer. Shilling was odd and, for some reason, looked very much out of place. She was uptight and exuded a stuffy aura, much like Ms. Barty, only messy. It were as though the officer's uniform was too tight or she was wearing far too many layers on a hot, sunny day. The uniform should have given an air of authority but it just made her look unprepared.

Lars was struck at the thought that her plump little body would not make her very good at catching criminals. And besides the look of not really knowing what to do or say, he could tell that WPC Shilling similarly thought her own presence was unnecessary.

Her look was that of both bored and uncomfortable. It was quite obvious that Shilling did not know what to do in this situation. The officer just looked about the room, as though Lars' ordeal were going on elsewhere and she had no idea about any of it.

"Just go," he said, "leave me."

His tired and flagging voice interrupted Ms. Barty mid-sentence, who had been wittering away. His request was neither stern or harsh in its tone, but spoken with a voice that had been dealt a lifetime of agony within the space of a traumatic few hours.

Lars was undeniably in shock and had never felt the desire to be left with his own company more than he did right now. "You need to go. Now," he asserted.

The adults were dumbfounded and caught off guard by this simple, yet powerful command. Ms. Barty struggled to fight the look of personal insult, as if Lars had made a slur upon a religious ritual or cultural custom of hers. They looked to one another, knowing that they had to obey his command but equally put out since they had more business, which needed Lars' attention.

"But Lars, old chap..." pleaded the boy's Headmaster with an already defeated spirit.

"Please," Lars commanded. "I want to be left alone."

With a sigh, Lenton rose and ushered his female companions to leave. "As you wish, son." Both women looked affronted by this request, but conceded to the boy's wishes with mild hesitation nonetheless.

Despite looking offended, WPC Shilling left the quickest.

Though obviously put out, Ms. Barty still managed to stride to the door in one graceful swoop. As soon as she met the threshold she turned to bark a sharp statement that could not have sounded more insincere, "I'm terribly sorry for your loss," before quickly realising herself and softening. "You have no idea just how sorry I–" she started, offering a glimmer of genuine humanity, before remembering herself and her composure and quickly changed direction, "You have no idea how devastated we are."

In those few seconds her eyes darted about the room to and from Lars's own gaze, as though looking for something and equally trying to get his attention.

Lars hardly acknowledged the refined, yet sharp, old lady and when he finally looked up he was caught in her crosshair; she had locked his gaze onto her own as she backed out of the room. Her hypnotic eyes seemed to whisper something as she left, but he shook his head and immediately looked away to the open window where two magpies danced from a series of branches, squawking and flapping about amongst the growing leaves of the watching oak tree.

And she left.

Finally, the professor adjusted his enormous weight from one bulbous foot to the other, as he struggled to effectively make an appropriate exit. If he could have just walked out and said nothing he would have been very content to do so. However, that would not be proper or gentlemanly, so he stuttered, "Take your time, Lars. When you're ready, you know where my office is. We'll be waiting for you." Lenton was the last to leave and pulled the door behind him. Lars listened as his heavy footsteps receded away from his room down the corridor.

Lars was alone.

Lilah's gone.

Why didn't I ask them how she–? He couldn't even say the d-word in his thoughts.

Lars continued watching the pair of black and white birds dancing in the tree.

My sister, my twin sister, is dead.

He wondered if he should have felt something. Obviously he felt something, but was there a pang or twinge the moment she died?

Was she in pain? Was she sick? Where's Father? Does he know what's going on?

At this point it was all too much. After last night's ordeal, the grizzly deaths of the couple this morning and now the weight of the headmistress' tragic revelation, Lars had been completely sapped of all energy and feeling. He had gone through the entire spectrum of human emotion in less than twenty-four hours and had nothing left to feel anymore, besides exhaustion.

He collapsed onto his bed and stared up at the ceiling, wanting to process what had just happened.

Why?

Instead, he just closed his eyes to the world.

6. A Voice in Purgatory

A voice whispered to Lars from a stifling darkness through his dream. It was too faint to hear and too distant to decipher its origin and, for all he knew, the voice could have been in front, behind, above or below him.

It was calling eagerly. It was calling specifically to him.

Slithers of air slipped through and around his astral body, ethereally slicing through his skin and eroding his bones.

His ambient vacuum was both suffocatingly dense and vastly empty, and Lars was suspended somewhere in the centre. From this dark and oppressive dream realm, Lars was enthralled with panic and oblivious to where safety lay.

Waves of gentle vibrations rumbled through the atmosphere irritating Lars' senses. In the void, his sight was limited and his hearing was muffled. The only senses he could rely on was the raw metallic tang in his mouth and the chilled temperature that teased his skin from the inside-out.

Neither flying, floating or falling, Lars ebbed with a strange motion akin to treading water against an ocean current. He tried desperately to gather momentum from his state of sensory and gravitational suspension and, while each fruitless stride was fast yet powerless, his arms were heavy and slow in the desperation of trying to get somewhere.

Despite a vague, subliminal sense of heated urgency, Lars was awash with panic and wildly hostile towards his current situation. This dreamy delirium was a superficial state where time seemed to have no consistency. He and his thoughts were apparitions in Purgatory, neither one thing or another.

The voice continued to indistinctly smother the serenely stifled atmosphere. Lars knew it was there and that it was meant for him. He also knew there would be severe repercussions if he did not locate the heavenly voice's menacing source and decipher its monumental message.

Floating closer in a lazy, yet laboured manner, Lars moved what he perceived as forward.

He released a gentle sigh, expelling the contents of his lungs. The air evacuated like a tiny pebble rolling down a snow-capped mountain, gathering in ferocious momentum, growing larger and faster with each passing second. The world shook to its core and every fibre of the realm hummed to the disturbance of the air.

The breath continued to evacuate his mouth, getting faster and longer with every delirious second. The almighty exhalation extended further and longer than any human would be capable.

Like a demonic python, Lars' mouth grew wider as more air erupted from his dislocating cavity, causing everything to vibrate on the spot as the air hummed to the chanting chorus of his swooshing breath.

Then, without warning, the breath took on a life of its own and Lars realised that he was no longer making the infernal noise. In a brief moment of self-awareness, Lars wondered if he had ever made the noise at all.

Cracks began to suppurate across the insipid landscape, breaking down and decomposing the great dark dimension. Lars remained unaffected by the deterioration that now shook the place apart as he remained suspended at the centre of this absurd universe. The world of nothingness melted and crumbled, dissolved and bled away, breaking itself down and devolving into a whole different nothing.

A huge crack of noise came from overhead, a cloud of light and a massive roar of wind heralded an all-consuming white aura that flooded the atmosphere, which made it explicitly painful for Lars to see anything around him.

The world seemed to change direction with the returning snap of an elastic band. Matter shed it's weightless quality and the floor came crashing upwards as if it were the ground that met the suspended particles.

Lars' feet made contact to the floor and the enraged roar stopped to welcome dead silence.

Liquid drip-drip-dripped so close to Lars' ear that it could have been the blood from his own bleeding hand falling to the floor beside him. He turned with the swift swing of a compass and was greeted by the most grotesque vision; a horrific sight that would likely haunt his waking memory for the rest of his life.

A figure just a few steps away.

Matted dirty hair fell in tangled curls about her dirty face, concealing her identity. Mud lined the tips of her fingers and the black lace of her dress looked wet as it gleamed in the blinding light. She looked like she had just crawled through a swamp. Or her own grave.

The girl's dirty appearance was in stark contrast to the harsh white surroundings in which she stood. A shimmer of tarnished silver lie limp around her neck and briefly caught Lars' attention. His grandmother had one very similar, and had given it to–

He knew the figure at once.

The grotesque figure lifted her head with a monstrous snap and Lars glared into the identical brown eyes of his once-beautiful sister.

"Lilah."

Another barrage of horror flooded his senses as he realised that the substance on the tattered dress was not the shimmer of the material but blood from the pulsing wound of her chest. Red liquid dribbled down her front and streaked her pale and dirty legs. Thick red globules matted and clumped to the hem of her dress, plummeting to the floor at her feet. The dripping noise had been identified.

She leapt a superhuman distance so that their faces were practically touching. He could smell her metallic breath as it brushed his cheeks and offended his nostrils. Her clothes and hair smelt damp and musty, a mix of soil and wet concrete. The rancid tang of putrid eggs laced her entire aura.

Lilah hissed at his face. Her message was carried on a hoarse voice, so gravely desperate, yet obscure and imperative, and Lars couldn't understand a word she said. She moved her mouth urgently, but no noise left the once pink lips of her broken face. Lilah's breath was fetid. It pained him to see his sister, once so beautiful and exuding vitality, now so ugly and offensive.

"I can't understand you Lilah — talk to me," he urged.

Her face looked panicked, scared and hopeless.

Then she changed.

In one swift moment, she shook her head to the side as if someone were talking in her ear.

Her face softened under the blood and dirt that had masked it and her beautiful eyes eased to a look of sorrow and pity. She wore his eyes, just as he wore hers.

As swiftly as it had shifted, the white around them began to darken once again, as did her once pretty face. Just as soon as she had appeared to recognise him, she quickly clouded over to reveal the menacing scowl from before.

Without warning, her words were a clap of thunder in the vacuum and in a deafening moment of clarity, she spoke rhythmically with a dry and raspy cadence:

"One for sorrow, two for joy,
three for a girl and four for a boy.
Five for silver, six for gold.
And seven welcomes you to the Fold!"

She repeated the song over and over again until the words lost all meaning.

Lars was awash with her haunting rhyme and was swept away in a terrific tide of terror, forever careening into an abyss until he would wake up.

***

Back in this realm, several magpies watched a sleeping Lars from outside the window as a near-invisible creature made off with his bag of discarded clothes.

7. Alex

Lars had been AWOL since yesterday evening and Alex was rightly concerned. Initially, he had left his own dormitory door ajar in the hopes of catching his friend strolling in from last night. Since his room was on the opposite side and just a few doors down from Lars', Alex would have been alerted to his friend's arrival.

At the moment, this vantage point meant that Alex could stand inconspicuously from the safety of his dormitory and see what was going on in the hallway, which he had already been monitoring for the best part of the morning. He wanted to catch his friend and make sure that he was ok and then extract a step-by-step account of whatever scandal Lars had managed to entangle himself.

Right now, he was watching the headmaster, Professor Lenton, urgently wrap his knuckles on Lars' door. He was accompanied by two women whom Alex did not recognise and one of which had been a police officer, which quickly set about a wave of anxiety for Alex.

Alex had a slight reputation for being a little uptight, and the boys in his year would rib him for it. He had opted to stay in last night and not join his peers in town for a few drinks.

For one thing, Alex didn't drink. This particular life choice meant that he was often the put-out sober friend making excuses for his inebriated mates – or worse, the designated driver. The other thing, he didn't really like 'drunk Lars' because he often had a tendency to show off and generally be a bit of a prick. He was vain, arrogant and obnoxious at the best of times, and booze just made it worse. Also, even if Alex chose to drink alcohol, he would not because he was not eighteen yet.

Prior to the distraction at his friend's dormitory door, Alex had been plonked at his desk trying desperately to plough through some extraordinarily tedious reading. He was in the middle of a free period with no lessons scheduled for the entire morning and was battling a bout of severe boredom.

At Kingswould, it was school policy that *free periods* were called anything but, since it implied that the time could be used for sitting in the common room watching trashy morning TV, or playing pool and napping.

Despite his uptight reputation, Alex was occasionally partial to savouring these deliciously forbidden delights and wanted nothing more than to veg out in the common room this morning. However, there were rumours of Mrs Smith wanting to spice up her history lessons with a surprise mock exam, which meant that it was best for him to stay in his room and swot up on one of the wars. Alex assured himself that he would double-check which particular war that was, right after the makeover segment on the television.

Professor Lenton's arrival was undoubtedly a welcome excuse for an abstracted Alex to do anything other than what he was supposed to be doing. He slid away from his desk, abandoned the dry and stale old textbooks, lifted himself out of his chair with a mild creak and tiptoed to his door.

Peering through the crack of the door with ardent vigilance, he clocked the large, piggish man who was the headmaster. Alex brough his face closer to the door to get a better look of his two mystery guests.

The first was a stout little policewoman, who besides her uniform, was for the most part a very unassuming figure. From this angle she was particularly plain faced, with her dull hair scuffed back from her blotchy features in a crusty bun, having used far too much product to oppress her mane which perched like some fossilised bug in amber resin. This awkward woman was a little on the short side and slightly overweight giving her a dumpy, barrel-like figure.

Alex tried, but could not imagine her successfully in pursuit of some limbered up and light-footed chav who had just mugged the Post Office or robbed some poor little old lady. A group of boys scurried past and she inelegantly adjusted her underwear, which apparently had ridden up somewhere that Alex dared not think about.

He shuddered.

The second woman, much older, stood prudently beside the unpolished WPC. In contrast, she was tall and exuded an air of that old-school grace that one assumes of a certain generation. Alex didn't know her but could tell she was probably the sort to eat a sandwich with a knife and fork. She was immaculately presented in her moderate, yet expensive, black dress with an expensive-looking pastel blue cardigan strewn neatly across her shoulders. Her white-jewel-encrusted brooch shimmered from her collar bone with a sinister sheen from the half-hearted glare of the lights overhead.

This taller lady had a pristine mass of thick silver hair that was neatly constrained into stern silver curls. It was styled so precisely and perfectly that a single hair dared not fall out of place for fear of facing her meticulous wrath. Her face was determined with a penetrating gaze of such severity that it would burst the door open itself, were it not an ill-mannered and unladylike thing to do. Her posture was intense and steely as she, the headmaster and the police officer, stood in the wooden corridor outside the door of Lars' room.

Professor Lenton had been calling through the door between knocks when the elegantly viperous lady turned with sudden mantis severity, making an ensnaring eye towards Alex that consequently sent a chilled surge right through him to the pit of his stomach.

The intensity and severity of her glacial lavender glare startled Alex so much that it left him with an uneasy and queasy feeling. He fought the urge to be intimidated, causing her gaze to intensify so much that Alex was overcome with a sudden urge to retreat further into the safety of his room, stepping back out of her lethal line of site.

He waited silently and held his breath, before peering through the crack to the hallway. In horror films, this is the part when the psychopath disappears, and reappears with lightning speed at the window to be face to face with her next victim. Lars' visitors were gone from the hallway and Alex tried to ignore slasher flick paradigms, before caving and checking behind him, just in case.

Alex paced the floor of his dormitory, anxious to speak with his friend. That gaze left him feeling uneasy and slightly relieved that he himself was not the one having to entertain the stuffy old professor, the chubby little police officer and that terrifyingly austere woman with hypnotic eyes.

He considered what to do. Lars was obviously home now. Whether he was home safe and in one piece, was still to be determined. Something was off.

Alex wasn't in the habit of mothering his friend. However, Lars was a terrible drunk and would knock at ungodly hours to share his cheesy chips before going back to his own dorm, or leave an obscene phone call or message to say he was locked out of the building and needed letting back in. The know-it-all part of Alex knew that something was wrong with his best mate's situation, long before the three adults turned up.

Alex turned to thoughts of whether his friend was in trouble, which then led to thoughts of Lars in general. The friends were different as they were similar. For one thing, they were united in their dislike of school. Alex knuckled down because he was good at it and it was better than being at home. Lars, a little more rebellious, didn't have time for rules and restrictions, and had the opinion that school stifled his spirit and creativity. It came as no surprise that the two boys would sneak out of school whenever possible, just not during lesson times as Alex would refuse to miss a class. In which case, bunking school often came at night time, after dinner and study hour.

The prefects would patrol the corridors making sure that the younger boys were not out of bed. Technically, the same applied to the sixth formers, but Lars would stroll past and tell them what he thought of their system, often with a gesture from his finger. If he were feeling generous, he would give them two.

Some nights in their younger days saw them escape to the local village and loiter in the bus stop or sit in the park where the swings were too small and the slide was sticky. They were older now and both venues had vastly lost their appeal. Other nights would be spent closer to home, where Lars and Alex would duck over the dilapidated wall behind the upper sixth boy's dorms and lose themselves in the wooded area that encased the south of the school. When the weather was especially kind, they would trek through the surrounding forest while the school slept and retreat to an isolated clearing. Lars would be armed with a pack of Marlboros and a hip flask, while Alex had a flashlight and fully charged mobile phone.

Surrounded by a wall of trees, Alex's favourite pastime was to stay silently in his friend's company, looking up to the starless sky, comforted by the simple fact that each was there for one another. This secluded hideaway was a sanctuary for when school was tiresome and boring, or when something was going on at home. Being exposed to the elements in each other's company was always a million times better than being confined to the customs and traditions of their school and respective home lives.

Alex and Lars were drawn to each other for a number of reasons. Both were from incredibly prominent families and despite their wealth and status, the pair were equally uneasy about the preconceived reputations that came before them. Lars came from an old family, where his father, Jude Thurston, ruled his empire with a strict hand that applied most of its pressure within the four walls of the Thurston Estate. After the death of Lars and Lilah's mother, Jude tightened the reins on his children, driving both a wedge between him and his son, and friction between the twins.

As a result of his lineage, Lars was known, and even to a degree feared, by both his peers and teachers. People knew that Lars was untouchable. Whether he had been bullied by a fellow pupil or an ill-advised teacher marked an exam paper all too harshly, it was the unforgiving wrath of Jude Thurston that they would have to deal with. A deterrent that ultimately left Lars ostracised.

There came a point when Lars told Alex that he had long given up caring what others thought. People had a perception of him regardless of how well they knew him and therefore he saw fit to play up to it and give his public what they wanted. Anyone lucky enough to be familiar with Lars Thurston knew that despite coming across as an entitled, cocky and arrogant little shit, deep down he was actually a gentle and shy boy that vehemently detested the thought of being feared by anyone. The sad thing is that no one did know Lars *that* well, except for Alex. Probably.

Alex on the other hand, was from a different kind of prominence and status. Alex's father was none other than Roger Wood, the frontman of 60s glam rock band, Silk Sword. Kingswould, being the prestigious boarding school it was, had been the learning ground for many celebrity offspring, but Alex was the only son of Roger-Fucking-Wood; revered rock god, pop icon, living legend, and current guest of Her Majesty the Queen in a maximum security prison.

Roger had gained notoriety for his string of high profile relationships throughout his career. What had been more famous had been the even more high profile divorces; all five of them. The media had mocked that he was the Henry Tudor of Music, a framed tabloid headline that Roger had in his studio with his many platinum discs.

Alex's mother, a very successful supermodel during the 80s and 90s known mononymously as Saffron, had been Roger's significantly younger sixth wife.

It was from his mother that Alex was bestowed with his supermodel powers of perfect coal-black hair, chiseled features and fragile, yet haunting cobalt blue eyes. Such features were coveted by hungry scouts and shameless agents who promised him wealth and status, which would rival that of both his parents. Fortunately, Alex had a wise head and would rightfully decline each and every time. He knew that Fame was a mistress not to be fooled around with. Afterall, look what it had done to his parents.

In the case of Roger Wood, fame and excess were obtained too readily at much too early a stage in his life. Consequently, Alex's father was always seeking the next big thrill and that ultimately drove him to his most atomic and prolific relationship; the insatiable lust for women, drink and drugs. Roger teetered on and off the proverbial wagon over the years, until he met Saffron. The two had started an illustrious affair, fallen pregnant and married within weeks of their tempestuous romance. Their relationship, which the tabloids shamelessly catalogued and documented, had been fuelled by a concoction of narcotics, stimulants and booze.

News of their biggest spat was unleashed seventeen years ago on the morning of Boxing Day when Alex was just a few months old. Saffron had managed to stay sober and clean throughout her pregnancy, after falling in love with her life coach. On the night of Christmas Day the two spent the evening together on the promise that Roger was AWOL.

Indeed Alex's father enjoyed a festive bender of womanising, drinking and abusing pretty much anything he could sniff, gum or inject. Only when Roger returned, he erupted in a blind fit of anger and humiliation after finding his wife in bed with another man. In his inebriated rage, he struck his wife's lover over the head with a marble pineapple ornament. Too late, Saffron leapt in between her lover and enraged husband, only to receive the second blow. Blindly, Roger left his wife and her lover in the bedroom where he first discovered them and trundled to the en suite bathroom where he passed out in the bath.

An infant Alex had been in the room next door and sources claimed that his screams were heard all night long. The chef had arrived early the next day to prepare the family feast for Boxing Day and discovered the tragedy, where he had hurriedly called the press and then the police.

The ageing rocker had been serving a double life sentence ever since, and yet it was Alex's legacy to be treated like the criminal. For years the press hounded the young boy, expecting him to fall off the rails. He was subject to phone hacking, regular hounding as he made his way to and from school, and informants even stole and published his school reports. Of course, there was never any scandal, especially where the latter source material was concerned since Alex was unanimously a "pleasure to teach".

Unfortunately for the red tops and glossy magazines, Alex grew up to be an intelligent and well-adjusted kid, which meant that they soon left him alone because they didn't make for a good tripe to feed the masses.

Back in his dorm and after several minutes of aimless marching on his carpet trying to think of an excuse to go over, Alex clocked the library books on his desk remembering that Lars had wanted to borrow one. They were overdue and Alex would knock on the door, offering to return them. It was tenuous but all he had at this point.

He scooped up the pile of battered literature, closed the door with a respectful hush, and cautiously crept over to Lars' room.

Raising his free hand in a gesture about to knock, he paused and listened. He could decipher the one-sided tones of the adults, two of which spoke gently but severely. Alex could not make out what they were saying but from the weight of their voice decided that it was probably best not interrupting his friend.

Alex would instead need to kill some time and come back in a little while. Besides, if he looked at another textbook he was pretty sure that he would go mad. For sanity's sake, he decided to run a quick errand and return those books to the library.

Hopefully by the time he got back, the headmaster and his anxious female duo might have finished with Lars.

8. Whispers in the Library

The school library was located on the other side of the campus and rather than take the tiled network of corridors that meandered through the school, Alex opted for a shortcut by running straight across the vast cobbled courtyard. By his own admission, he had time to spare as he was appropriately waiting to disturb his friend. However, like the average teenager, he still wanted to be reasonable and not overexert himself.

From this side of the school, the building forked across in a distinct U-shape with Alex on the east, the library to the west and the large paved courtyard, like a channel of grey, separating the two.

Today was a typical autumn day and much of the school's grounds were shrouded in a silken fog that restricted any typical views of the surrounding landscape. Alex could hear the distinct jeers and clattering of sticks synonymous to a hockey match that was in session somewhere on the field to the south; on a clear day he would be able to see the boys clashing about in their claret and gold jerseys.

The red brick facade bled through the mist as Alex approached the west side of the building and thanks to the camouflage of mist, he had overshot the whereabouts of the entrance by several windows. Following the borders of flowers and shrubs, he etched his way along the path until he reached the elaborate stone porch and proceeded to climb the few ancient steps in order to reach the large oak door. It growled with age as he pushed his way over the threshold and into the corridor.

Alex's shoes clapped and squeaked as he strode across the chequerboard floor in the direction of the library, where a waft of leathery paper permeated the atmosphere that grew heavier with each approaching footstep. Alex breathed deep and savoured the intoxicating smell.

Growing up, Alex had retreated into his books. He knew it was cliché, but to him, they really were gateways to other realms. They whisked him away from his old boarding school and displaced it with one that taught pupils magic or trained the students to be spies. Books were portals from this world to mountains where dragons guarded vast troves of coveted treasure or where men turned to monsters at the sip of a potion or phase of the moon. The characters in his own story had been far more terrible than the ones drawn in black and white words, so when his books whispered promises that a pragmatic Alex knew could not be kept, he loved them even more for their sweet lies of heroes and happy-ever-afters.

He neared the end of the corridor and approached the library doors, admiring the entrance and how it differed from the other rooms in the school. Two giant doors permitting entry to the wealth of knowledge it safeguarded behind them, were streaked and chipped with layers of darkened varnish, but sturdy and beautiful nonetheless.

Each door had a glass panel teasing a sneak at the contents it guarded, though the view was restricted by the adornment of a protective brass grate, which boasted a highly elaborate and ornate tree design. It was highly polished, like the rest of the yellow brass jewellery that adorned the wood of the doors in the form of knobs, kick plates and a plaque that read *LIBRARY*.

Inside, the library was by far, in Alex's opinion, one of the school's most redeeming features. It was an opulent labyrinth of shelves laden with volumes upon volumes of books amidst tall stone columns that raised the vaulted wooden ceiling high above the room. It was among the oldest parts of the school and every bit as beautiful.

The desks in the main chamber had several boys huddled in their cherry red leather seats, ploughing through the various compendiums taken from the enriched shelves, whilst under the private light of their individual green glass desk lamps. Marble busts of historical greats monitored the room from wooden columns, with white eyes glaring and keeping the peace.

Alex savoured both the smell of knowledge branded upon musty reams of ageing paper and the thick layer of polish that intoxicated the air with an amorous lace of heavy perfume, all of which were complemented by the naturally warm wooden base notes.

Remembering himself, Alex stood sheepishly at the main desk and humbly offered the books, accepting the trivial penalty for his late returns. From behind stuck-up scolds of the clerk, he also received an excessively disappointed look of the busy-bodying prefect. Leaving the crosshair of judgement, Alex backed away with the caution of somebody having walked into a potentially dangerous or awkward situation, like a couple rowing, not wanting to bring attention to themselves, and made his way into the maze to get lost among the shelves.

The library was awkwardly quiet, as libraries often are. In the main room, which hosted the librarian's office, several study areas and the main desk, there was comfort in the company of many silent bodies. Out here among the forest of leering shelves you were on your own. The library, despite its charm and beauty, evidently could be a scary place.

As with most schools, or generally any kind of old building that children frequent, there were many whispered legends of ghosts that roamed the corridors; each fable passed down from one generation to the next. And it was around the month of September, when the intake of fresh students embarking on their educational careers at Kingswould, that the stories were most rife. Such ghastly tales would have most students, at one time or another, second-guessing that second pair of footsteps that followed them down the corridor on late evenings.

Alex's favourite myth was that of a vengeful headmaster whose spirit, if any of the fables were to be believed, was an astral resident amidst the Dewey decimal system of this very library. The legend goes that the head of the school, from some long time ago, had been a spiteful and wicked miser who hated everyone, especially his pupils. The wicked teacher had been the master of the sciences; Alex imagined something akin to alchemy or potions since the stories were hazy with times.

Boys would be punished for the most mundane of things, be called to his office and then never seen again; gone without a trace. For example, the boy in question would be mysteriously *expelled* or *sent home for an emergency*, or the family had *gone bankrupt*, etc.

Following the unexplained departure, the horrid headmaster would present a mystery organ to his class some days later and relish as he cut it to pieces like some gruesome parlour trick.

Of course, the number of missing boys eventually grew to the point where it roused enough suspicion to bring a lynch mob to the grounds of the school. The headmaster was shackled and stripped of various, non-vital organs; the mob pulled out his tongue, gouged his eyes and broke his fingers, sewed them together and plucked his teeth out one by one. He was tarred, feathered and buried alive behind one of the walls of the then newly built library.

Years later, after an excavation of the ancient bibliotheque, a mysterious chamber was uncovered by the workers where they found a series of scattered human teeth and blackened feathers.

Of course, the faculty would readily debunk such stories and even the savviest detective would take decades to find anything in the archives or on the internet. Rightfully, Alex gave little credence to stories such as these and was normally one to brush aside such superstitions and local folklore, dismissing them as urban legends. However, when alone in a large room with nothing but shelves and paper for company, one's imagination can't help but start to get the better of you. With this in mind, he made his way through the labyrinth, cautiously.

Met with the hostility of the muted atmosphere, each footstep was a dismal whisper on the carpet. As he delved deeper amongst the vast chambers, Alex heard the distant clip clap of footsteps on the large tiled floor of the main room. The central area was the only tiled area, with the main library itself being carpeted for soundproofing. He could picture a naive first year flying across the chamber with new shoes that pounded the tiles. An older student would shoot death-glares at his immaturity and insolence, whilst the dictator/librarian would hiss a vicious "shush" at her unsuspecting victim.

Alex could make out the hushed whispers of some boys from the year below. He could not see their faces, but they were speaking urgently and the sneaky tone of scandalous gossip was unmistakable. Fortunately, Alex arrived at his destination. Idly fingering the spines, he half-heartedly searched the shelf for his required Shakespearean text. With a cocked ear, he tried to listen to the juicy conversations going on between the salivating scandalmongers.

"No, you don't get it – it *wasn't* murder," said the first boy.

It was Geoffrey Turner from the year below; a vicious little gossip who had inherited his investigative journalist skills from his prominent columnist mother. Both had a reputation for having an insatiable appetite for sticking their nose where it was not wanted. The words she had written about Alex's parents were imprinted in his memory.

"What? You mean it was an accident?" The disbelieving accomplice was John Mackintosh from Alex and Lars' year. John had been in Lars' Latin class and Alex thought he was OK as far as the school elite went, though a bit of a non-entity in the hierarchy of school life nonetheless.

"Nope," said Geoffrey with a resounding voice that implied he desperately knew more about the story.

"What? You're saying she... killed herself?"

"Yes – she stabbed herself! With a knife." He revelled in leaking the scandal, especially to those who resisted at first. "She was there in her room for ages. One of the lower year girls had woken up in the early hours of the morning to the dripping of blood on her face as she slept. Apparently, her screams woke up the entire dormitory. The body above had bled out entirely. It went right through the floorboards and found its way to the room below."

"You're lying. And how do you even know this?" John was sweetly surrendering to the gossip as it became more and more enticing. Geoffrey was waiting for this question, and in quick succession, fired his answer, and stage two of the story.

"You know how it goes with things like this; they spread like wildfire. Of course, Mother has followed the family for years, especially after... well you know, since the *other* death." Geoffrey stressed 'other' by saying it in a quieter tone as if to even mouth the word would see him shot on the spot. Alex rolled his eyes but had found that he had stopped what he was doing, allured by what they were saying, much like John.

"That's awful," said John. Alex could not decide if he was disgusted at the gossip itself or how much Geoffrey salivated over sharing this news.

"The headmistress has come all the way here to break the news to him. They haven't been able to find their father. Apparently he's wanted for questioning in conjunction or something. *They're* calling it a suicide, but between you and me..." he leaned in "... there are rumours of murder."

"You just said she killed herself? Was there not a note then?" John tried to counter with an intelligent question. At the very least he wanted to get the facts straight. Alex silently commended him.

"Oh yeah, but after the incident a few years back it's a bit suspect that he disappears." From between the cover of several hardbacks, Alex could see that John looked unconvinced, but enthralled nonetheless.

With that, another boy from Geoffrey's circle whizzed along the lanes to greet the two clucking gossips. "Oh my god, have you seen the policewoman?"

At this point, the penny dropped and Alex felt his stomach drop as the pieces came together and he realised whom they were talking about.

Leaving the book, he dashed through the aisles knocking over a second-year student and tripping over several chairs along the way. He did not pay attention to the furious huffs and poisonous glares of the clerk and prefect.

9. A Friend in Need

A short and sharp succession of violent clangs from a distant alarm yanked Lars from the morbid realm of his dream. It took him several moments to adjust to where he was and appreciate that he and his surroundings were real and solid once more. He sprang to attention with elastic reflex and darted urgent eyes about the room for signs of danger. Everything seemed fine, but there was a distinct smell that lingered under his nose, which dragged him back to the familiarity of the ghastly vision from his dream.

The disturbing draft of the ancient dormitory was cool as it caressed his clammy skin and tickled the dewy beads of sweat that had transpired across his forehead and left his golden hair feeling thick and tacky. Lars was awash with the reality that he was alone and that for now, in this exact moment in time, he was back in his school and perched on the bed in his dormitory.

Nightmares have a spiteful way of getting under your skin, making you feel uneasy about yourself and you no longer trust your thoughts because they took you to a dirty place of shame and fear. This particular dream had hit him in the gut and made him question the lengths that his warped and wicked mind would go.

Lars brought his attention to that screaming clang that had boisterously retrieved and rescued his astral form and had forcibly placed him back within this reality. It wasn't his phone, but something further away – the lunch bell.

How long was I out for? What do I do? What did Lilah do?

The alarm ceased and silence fell upon the school momentarily. Then, within moments, swarms of hungry souls rolled out and amassed the campus like a plague as bustling bodies searched for replenishment after a morning of studies. From the confines of his dormitory, the hustle was distinctly feral. The world outside was loud and busy and Lars noted how much the hungry howls and jeers of the boys of his school sounded like the beasts of a wildlife documentary.

For a moment, Lars might have also been hungry. He had not eaten since yesterday and his own stomach started to sound as savage as his peers. Lars desperately tried to dismiss the nightmarish visions, but that damned disgusting scent lingered under his nostrils quelling any hint of an appetite he may have had.

He closed his eyes and visions of his sister, suspended within the decaying vacuum, punched through his memories and burned onto his eyelids like morbid photo negatives. He also could not shift the vicious smell that lingered throughout the dream realm and around his sister's rank corpse.

He ran his tired fingers through his sweat-matted fringe and craned the muscles of his upper body in an agonisingly sweet stretch. Having spent the morning physically fighting for his life and fleeing the scene of a horrific crime, his experience of the last few hours was painted as cuts, grazes and bruises all over the canvas of his aching body.

Everything hurt. Lars winced as he arched his neck, trying to ease the tension caused by the death grip of the demonic creature that had clamped her hand around it so tightly earlier. He was suddenly very aware of his body and how much pain he was in; his muscles hummed with the urgent pump of blood, his feet throbbed and his legs were like dead weights. His face was tender in patches around his jaw and forehead, and his eyes stung with fatigue. Never had Lars wanted to cry so much and yet been too tired and frustrated to actually physically do it. Lars silently contemplated how the final, most painful blow left no physical wound or blemish.

His sister was dead.

Right now, Lars needed a lot of things; he needed to scream, he needed to cry and he urgently needed to punch something. Lars really needed to eat, but he also needed to know the full story.

Enraged, he threw his legs off the bed and strode across to his desk, which he swiped his arms across and up-ended, leaving a chaos of papers and trinkets at his feet. In his rage, Lars failed to see the mysterious wooden box skid under his bed.

After a succession of short painful breaths that burned his chest with every sharp intake, he stood silently and tried to tame his tempestuous energy. He needed to find Professor Lenton and the other two and hear what they had to say.

First, I should call Dad.

Lars and his father had never been particularly close in the traditional father-and-son sense. In fact, they had never been close in any sense, but right now he was the only person in this miserable universe that he could think of speaking to. He somehow knew with a raw instinct that he would know what happened and have an explanation for his grieving son.

Retrieving his phone he dialled his father's number with anxious thumbs. Lars lifted the handset to his ear carefully and waited as the tone purred. He didn't realise that he was holding his breath.

With some slight relief, Lars was disturbed by three sharp thumps that rattled his door. The line to his ear had not connected and he hung up with silent gratitude. There was a pause of tense silence and Lars considered ignoring the fiend at the door. A harder succession of three more bangs followed suit...

What the– ?

Opening the door with cautious apprehension, he was nearly punched in the face by the frantic fist of his best friend.

"Jeez, Alex. What the hell!"

"Blimey, Lars. You look like shit."

"Thanks."

Lars could read the face of his friend with ease. Alex was a map of deep concern and fear. "Lars, are you OK?" he asked with mild apprehension, not quite sure if he even wanted to know the answer.

Alex's face was sincere and soft. The look of empathy in his haunting blue eyes made Lars uncomfortable with the prospect of his own fragility and choked involuntarily on a lump of overwhelming sadness that had been garnering at the back of his throat. Lars fought desperately for words to respond to Alex's question, but instead, all he could do was sob.

With that, the sad, broken boy caved into the arms of his friend and cried the tears he needed to. Alex's shoulder was warm and laced with the scent of day old cologne and hot skin. It was soothing to Lars and his spirits lifted slightly.

Lars pulled away from the safety of Alex's arms with a sniff of his nose and a deep breath for composure and looked his friend square in the face. Alex wore a perpetually concerned look at the best of times, which is unsurprising after a lifetime of tragedy and upset, but his current gaze was intense and immediate. His eyes were devoted and sheltered by a concerned brow. He looked to Lars patiently and expectantly.

Lars opened his mouth but Alex broke the silence.

"I heard what happened. Sort of," he paused to construct what came next so that his half-facts were delivered with care. Lars remained silent, prompting Alex to continue.

"I overheard that moron, Geoffrey Turner, telling John Mackintosh about something in the Library and I wouldn't really have known had I not seen Professor Lenton and his police escort outside your room earlier. I kinda put two-and-two together and figured it had something to do with you." Alex looked away to the floor. "Are you OK?"

There were no two ways about it, Lars just had to say it – out loud: "She's dead, Alex. My sister is dead."

Alex already knew this, but seeing reality come to life right in front of him was excruciating. Lars was a manifestation of pain to the point that Alex couldn't bring himself to look at him for too long.

Lars paused. He then ushered his friend into his room, shut the door behind him and sat on the bed. Alex followed him and perched alongside him on the bed. Alex was polite enough to not mention the mess on the floor, although his sympathetic eyes were locked onto it with awkward intent.

"Alex, I'm not having a very good day," was all he could muster.

Alex turned his head and sniggered with genuine sincerity. At this gesture, both boys smiled sadly at Lars' misfortune. There was nothing that either of them could say or do at this stage. They paused for a long moment, each collecting their thoughts. Lars tried to make sense of what was happening to him, whilst Alex just sat on standby, waiting to offer his shoulder or advice. It was then that Lars noticed the strange, contorted expression on his friend's face.

"Lars, what the hell is that god-awful smell?" Alex darted his eager head in various locations in an attempt to locate the source of the wretched stench.

Lars gave a feeble, but genuine snigger as he contemplated the relay of all the sordid, horrific and painful details from last night's escapades.

"You're not going to believe this, but I need you to listen. I figure if I say it out loud it's not just with me – not just in my head – and I'm somehow not going out of my mind. Do you promise you won't think I'm crazy – in fact, even if I am, please help me."

Alex simply raised an eyebrow, pursed his lips tight and contemplated making a joke but instead just nodded apprehensively.

"So, I arrived late at the bar last night and couldn't find anybody. Nobody answered their phones or texts and just as I was about to leave, I made some new friends... anyway, one thing led to another and... you know... *we had a sleepover.*" Alex blushed with a disapproving shake of his head.

"Anyway, when I woke up, I went to get my stuff together and they attacked me. Literally. Like, they tried to actually kill me – look at these bruises." Lars pulled the collar from his neck to reveal the distinct choker tattoo of fingerprints under his jaw.

"Lars, that's awful! What did you do? Did you report it? I'm calling an ambulance, and the police–"

"No! No police. And I'm fine, I didn't do anything – just let me finish." Alex continued to look unfavourably as to where this story was going but Lars continued regardless. "Anyway, there was something wrong... they were... dead. Sort of. They were dead-ish, or kind of zombified or possessed."

"They were *what*, sorry?" Alex interjected. "*And* they attacked you?"

"Yes. Anyway, I managed to escape after they exploded and their bodies erupted all over the apartment. But, yeah, anyway. So then I'm running, and I get hit by a car, but I'm OK, and I just kept running and running until I came to the woods just outside of town and I hid. I hid in the woods. Then, when I thought it was safe, I snuck back into school, and the headmaster knocked on my door and then I fell asleep and now... well, Lilah's dead." He paused for breath, which allowed the weight of his words to sink in. "And that's about it really."

Alex was silent. Lars stared back with a weird sense of vulnerable pride.

Alex went to speak, collected himself, and questioned Lars with a slightly accusatory tone, "Did you, by any chance, hit your head throughout any of this?"

Probably.

"Yes, Alex, but it's all true. That smell, it's the guts and entrails from the couple. You need to believe me."

"I believe..." Alex broke off. "I think... Well, I mean... What's important right now is that some really horrible things have happened to you. And I can't even imagine what you're going through, but there are three people downstairs who hold a few answers that might shine a little more light on your current situation. I can't explain the... " he hesitated, "... *zombies*, but let's take one thing at a time and at the moment, finding out about Lilah seems like the place to start."

I hate when he's right.

Lars felt the resurgent sting of bitter tears once more. Wiping his teary eye, Lars quickly pulled himself together. Alex was right.

"I know you're right, Alex, but I'm scared and confused, and I don't know what I'm doing."

"No one does. But go and see Lenton and I promise we'll sort the... zombies... out when you're back. Are you going to be OK?" Alex asked as Lars laboriously shoved his feet into his battered sneakers and tied the laces.

"I'm going to have to be." Lars grabbed a jacket and threw it over his arm. In a moment of sure composure and certain clarity, he braved the realm of the outside world beyond his dorm in search of the two headmasters and the policewoman, leaving an overwhelmed and confused Alex alone in his room.

10. Revelation

It would appear that word of Lilah's death had spread fast throughout the school, which was no doubt thanks to that little shit, Geoffrey Turner. Little did Lars know at this point that the waiting headmistress would be devastated that word of her charge's death was beginning to spread, despite it being considered hearsay and speculation at this point. Suspicious faces unabashedly contemplated his infinitely personal ordeal and each look was deafening, speaking louder volumes than any of their whispering conjectures.

Lars ploughed through the masses of uniformed bodies, feeling each beady eye from the gangs of boys around him. Like leering grotesques of humanised CCTV, their stares penetrated his skin so blatantly, scrutinising and probing him with their emotional x-ray vision.

The Thurstons are an old and prolific dynasty; an English family of high nobility that dated back many centuries and as such, the Thurstons proved to be a topical conversation in all circles at any given time. Lars had long grown used to people talking about him for all manner of reasons and in his younger years, could not understand why people acted as such, neither could he appreciate what was the truth and what were lies. The older he grew, the less he cared.

The family's patriarch, Lord Jude Thurston, was an undeniably powerful prominent figure within the ranks of the country's elite. Besides being a noble aristocrat and the head of a very old and wealthy family, Lord Jude was also a tenacious businessman, a savage politician and occasionally a not-so-keen philanthropist. Jude's wife, Evelyn, and their children knew more than anyone that such accolades often came with their fair share of gossip, conjecture and scandal.

When it came to the Thurstons, no topic was out of bounds; whether it was the purchase of an undiscovered Picasso or Monet, the acquisition of failing businesses which were readily enveloped in the Thurston's already thriving empire, or even the tragic death of Jude's wife, Evelyn, there was always something that piqued the attention of High Society. It would now appear that Lilah was on her way to being everyone's latest scandal.

Growing up, Lars and Lilah had been indifferent to their ardent celebrity status with contrasting attitudes. In life, Lilah had easily brushed off what people thought of her because, quite frankly, she did not care. Her confidence and exuberance were fuelled by the mantra that people were simply interested in her and her family because they were admirable. People are drawn to pomp and tradition because it reminds them of where they are from. Lilah believed that families like the Thurstons were coveted because they were in touch with something greater and it stood to reason that their family were better than everyone else because they had it in abundance, alongside money and prestige. Lars had rolled his eyes when she elaborated with an example of tigers not losing sleep over the opinions of sheep.

In many ways, Lilah had been like a tiger; beautiful and strong, ferocious and like most apex predators, had little regard for the lower beings that crossed her path. Lars had not been entirely on board with his sister's attitude, mainly because it was not her attitude. It was their father's. It pained Lars to see an element of truth in their way of thinking.

Unlike his twin sister, Lars was slightly more uncomfortable with the status and reputation his family name afforded him. Lars did not want to think that he was better than anybody; he just happened to be born into a privileged family. Yes, he both recognised and appreciated that he could be a little ungrateful at times and that he may have a warped sense of the world because of the opportunities life presented him, but Lars believed that he should play the hand he was dealt and that he should play it for all he could.

Lars knew full-well that he had not earned anything that he called his own; from his good looks which were the luck of genetics, his exclusive education, which his father had insisted upon, right to the expensive shoes on his feet, all of which had been given to him. Lars knew he was lucky, and he figured that as long as he wasn't ignorant to his privilege, he was fine as he was and that there was no need to flaunt it like his sister. He was not better. He was lucky.

Somewhat hypocritically, Lars guiltily felt entitled to the right to a private life. For what it was worth, he was uncomfortable with the way the world saw him and a lot of it had to do with the actions of his father. Anyone that knew Jude's son well knew that the apple actually does fall quite far from the tree, but that said apple actually gains momentum and rolls a long way away too.

As much as he wished he could be as blasé as his sister when it came to what people thought, Lars was just too sensitive. Every discussion about his family, every slanderous word and every vicious whisper was a stab to the chest. A notion that was especially true when pointed towards the death of his mother, Evelyn.

It was no secret that Jude Thurston absolutely worshipped the ground his wife, and the mother of his twins, walked on. It was also no secret that after a long battle with mysterious ill-health, Jude took the death of his wife very hard.

The less miserly and somewhat romantic aristocrat soured and withered into a hardened and beastly crone. He withdrew from high society and became tyrannical, ploughing his efforts and resources into more and more secret projects. Lars, or anybody for that matter, knew very little about what went on in the study. Towards the end of Evelyn's life, Jude could not bear to see his beloved suffer, and so he withdrew from the family and secluded himself to his projects.

Lars blamed his father for not being around more at this point. The death of their mother had been especially hard since the twins were alone for the majority of the time. Lilah made excuses for her father, stating that he found it hard to see their mother suffer. The twins would then row, clashing like fraternal titans since Lars made no secret of the fact that he thought their father was selfish and cowardly. Although he did not blame his father for the direct death of his mother, Lars certainly thought that she would have been around a little longer, had he been more present and supportive in her last days.

Sadly, Evelyn believed that her illness had driven a wedge between her and her husband. Jude could not face seeing his wife suffer, and as he distanced himself from her more and more, the worse she got. In Lars' unprofessional opinion, it was a broken heart that killed Evelyn Thurston and her sickness was just the catalyst.

Meandering amongst the drones of people in the old corridors, the gaze of passersby continued to bore into him with little sympathy and ample judgement. Lars remained composed with his eyes ahead, ignoring the looks and whispers as he passed his school peers. He tried to channel Lilah with each painstaking step. Their hushed words skimmed over him as he tried to take no notice. But really, each breathy tone was like a stab with a blade, forged in the fires of scandal and quenched with the icy hush of tempering whispers.

Trying to concentrate on precisely anything else at this point, he listened to the steady thump of his shoes, which mimicked the thud of his beating heart as he marched up the polished parquet flooring. He could feel his chest tighten and his cheeks flush while the blood whirling in his ears whistled a private high-pitched screech. Lars tried to steady his nerves with a deep breath but the paralysing wave of sudden anxiety caused his lungs to seemingly stiffen, which permitted him nothing more than a succession of shallow pants.

Lars was surprised at how suddenly he found himself outside the broad door of Professor Lenton's office. His secretary, Mrs Lomax, was a bug-eyed old woman with ratty hair that was loosely forced into a limp and lopsided bun. Her hooked nose peered from behind her monitor and she gave an awkward smile upon realising who was about to disturb the headmaster.

"Go straight through. They're expecting you," she quipped from across her desk with little sincerity.

Lars acknowledged the command with a solemn nod and grasped the brass handle of the door. It was cold under his fingers. He tried for another deep breath and prepared to open the floodgates. Nervous, he paused a little further and tried to decipher their cryptic hush from inside the room. Making no sense of their words, he wrapped his fingers across the door with his free hand to announce his presence and strode right into the room to try and catch them off guard.

Lenton's stuffy old office was exactly what one would come to expect from the stuffy old headmaster of a stuffy old boys boarding school. The parquet flooring of the corridor bled into the room but was covered by an oriental carpet that was once rich in crimson and jade colours, flecked with faded gold and cream-coloured pile. Only now, it was limp and faded and worn with the paces from decades of tread – not to mention the ample cigarette burns and brandy stains, most of which Lars was sure were earned during Lenton's tenure alone.

The office felt like one of those village museums you find in the arse end of the English countryside. The kind of museum that is filled with local treasures and trinkets that don't necessarily mean a great deal to the rest of the world and humankind, and where the only member of staff is the curator who had taken his post a long time ago and predated many of the artefacts on show.

The walls of the office were adorned with various portraits of what Lars assumed were pompous old twits; each very serious, self-assured and certainly superior-looking. Lars had no idea who any of them were but at some point in their life at Kingswould they had undoubtedly meant something to someone. Mahogany cabinets guarded the room like wooden sentinels while exposing dated old treasures through their glass doors. The shelves were crammed with archaic ornaments, awards for goodness-knows-what since the engravings were long worn, and vintage whiskey that would probably put a large horse into a coma, as well as a few personal photographs all lined for show. Lars eyed the stacks of tattered leather books in their washed out emerald greens, oxblood reds and cornflower blues. They adorned the mighty shelves and were dotted about the room in piles of paper columns with frayed pages and exposed sinuous spines.

The adults had not noticed Lars and he could not bear to disturb them. He cleared his throat.

The trio stopped mid-conversation and fell silent as soon as they realised they were no longer alone and unable to speak as freely as they had been. The two women perched on a bottle green Chesterfield sofa, whilst Lenton filled an armchair awkwardly with his robust figure. His face looked even pinker than it usually did in contrast to the green of the studded seat.

"Come now, sit down."

It was his sister's headmistress, Beatrice Barty, rather than his own headmaster who motioned for him to come and sit in the only other free armchair. He did as he was told and lowered himself into the supple seat of the green chair.

"Lars, Ol' Bean–"

"–If you don't mind, Headmaster," the silver-haired woman interrupted, to which Professor Lenton unceremoniously subsided and cradled his cup and saucer. Barty leaned forward and overturned an upside-down teacup so that it sat correctly within a delicate saucer. "Tea?" she invited.

Without waiting for Lars to respond, she took the pot by the handle and placed her other hand under the spout, giving the contents a swirl to excite the amber brew within. Delicately pouring a cup for Lars, she then proceeded to add milk and sugar. She stirred four times anti-clockwise, making sure not to touch the dainty bone china with the spoon, and then dragged the delicate silverware across the Royal Dalton rim, before handing it over to Lars with a forced, but seemingly well-meant smile.

I don't take sugar.

"Lars my dear," she started, "Firstly, let me tell you how sorry I am to have to break this awful news to you first." Taking her own beverage, she leaned forward to Lars.

"First? You mean my father doesn't know?" Lars interjected. This interruption obviously annoyed Barty. She placed her own cup and saucer down with such decisiveness and then ran both hands down her lap to straighten her dress as she pursed her lips and briefly considered her next words.

"Unfortunately, we've been unable to get a hold of your father. And honestly..." she paused, considering another choice of her next words "...we didn't want to be the ones to tell you, but in these circumstances, we had no other choice. Her being your sister and all, we thought it best, that is... you have a right to know."

"Tell me what happened." Lars pleaded to his sister's grey-haired headmistress.

The trio paused what they were doing, each not entirely sure if or how to respond. Lars eyed Lenton as he awkwardly downed the remainder of his brew and inspected what Lars assumed were the remaining tea leaves that must have been left in the bottom of his cup as a way of avoiding to look Lars in the face. Turning to WPC Shilling, he saw that she was absentmindedly distracting herself with her dry cuticles.

Beatrice Barty continued, "Lars, there's no easy way to say this..." Another awkward pause "...but your sister... well," she coughed lightly and then struck with the vital information, "She... took her own life. We found her this morning." She paused again, longer this time, horrified by what she was saying.

Her blunt words laced with a sickeningly sympathetic tone stabbed him like knives to his soul. Despite an earlier head's up from Alex about the rumours of his sister, Lars still could not believe what he was hearing.

The silver-haired lady was waffling on whilst the ever silent WPC Shilling continued to do very little, having still not looked up from her cracked nail beds. The WPC had not said a word since meeting for that matter. But Lars did not care. He was not listening right now.

He cast his stingingly tired eyes across to Professor Lenton, who sat rigid, unable to get comfortable in his chair. The ambient temperature was cool and pleasant, yet Lenton had gathered a sticky sheen across his fleshy brow. The way the headmaster had kept calling him "son", "chap" and "Old Bean" was normally endearing, but today it was grating on Lars far more than usual. He stared idly at his once proud and jovial headmaster in a newfound and all-too-bright sudden light. The now nervous and sheepish headmaster was a glistening mess of passivity that was annoying Lars. The grief-stricken boy was using every fibre of his moral being to hold himself together and was let down by the way Lenton had willingly bent in submission to the stuffy old woman. She was a stranger to him; she was breaking his heart with her wicked news. Lars felt betrayed and disliked Ms. Barty with a passion.

Admittedly, Lars did not have run-ins with his headmaster over the past seven years of attending Kingswould Academy, but Lenton knew Lars by name and he knew the Thurston family. Now at a time when a familiar face would make the world of difference to a bleak horizon, Lars had been let down. What little contact the professor had previously had with his pupil, Lars knew that whatever news he needed to hear was much better coming from a familiar figure, rather than this sickeningly considerate woman with her cold, sophisticated manner.

"...And so you see my dear boy," Lars zoned back into their conversation and Ms. Barty was still speaking, "That's why I have asked WPC Shilling to accompany me on this."

Lars realised he had been staring uncomfortably towards Professor Lenton for quite some time. He turned and looked to the uniformed officer, who perked up, equally caught off-guard, upon the mentioning of her name. She flicked the crusty remains from her chewed fingers and gave the most insincere grin in Lars' direction.

Subtly spitting through her pursed lips she asked, "Where would your father be Lars?"

He didn't like her vulgar mannerisms, and neither did an unimpressed Barty judging by the sour face she was pulling. Lars did, however, appreciate being called by his actual name rather than a ridiculous and uncomfortable term of endearment like the other two had been doing.

"I don't know." Was an honest answer. "I've neither seen or heard from him since before school started a few weeks ago. He had gone away for work before the start of term, but my father is often away.

"He coordinated the arrangements for mine and Lilah's return to school. Our things were taken to our respective schools separately, ahead of our arrival. I left earlier than scheduled as I wanted to see an exhibition at The Louvre in Paris."

"The loo?" interrupted the policewoman.

Barty was obviously not impressed. "The *Louvre*; it's a gallery. Lars, please do continue."

"I returned by Eurostar and got the train back from St Pancras straight here. Lilah was still at home when I left... That was the last time–" he coughed and composed himself.

"The last time I saw him was some time before; a few weeks ago. I'm not sure." All three adults were captivated by this story, staring intently for Lars to continue as though he were about to divulge some vital nugget of information, a secret clue or even the meaning of life. In reality, Lars had little else to say on the matter.

Barty's gaze was the most intense. Her icy eyes leered right throughout the boundaries of politeness and comfort. Their unusual colour almost vibrated and shimmered with an odd blue that looked almost violet as she leaned forward into the light. Despite how awkward her intense gaze made him, Lars did not – in fact – could not look away.

He continued talking.

"I mean, I was worried about Lilah." His audience nearly fell off their respective seats, each hanging on to every word that left his mouth. "She hadn't been too well over the summer and had gone to stay with friends in the country before returning to school." Lars thought this had been funny since the regal Thurston estate sat proudly in the rolling landscapes of the sleepy Kent countryside, a short distance from the sea with plenty of fresh air and open spaces.

"With whom had she gone to stay, my dear?" probed Ms. Barty.

"I don't know. Despite being twins, my sister and I aren't particularly close. We said our goodbyes when I left for France, and that was the last I spoke to her."

"So you're telling us that you think your sister went to stay with *friends?*" The emphasis on the last word sounded like an accusation from the WPC. "At a destination *unbeknownst* to you?" The tone was definitely not a question.

Taken aback, Lars considered his next sentence carefully. There was something that the trio was probing for. He was unsure what it was, but was certain that he wouldn't be of much help since he did not know of anything out of the ordinary. Something was definitely off.

"Yes, with friends. And, no. I don't know where she went. The decision was made last minute. That and, as I just said, Lilah and I have never been particularly close.

"Contrary to popular belief, Constable Shilling, twins aren't born with some telepathic bond. At the very least, they never manifested between my sister and I. We are fraternal twins – not conjoined ones – she and I never saw eye to eye on many things. In fact, as much as we loved each other, she will..." He paused, correcting himself. They had struck a raw nerve and he had to reign his emotions back into a calm place.

"... She would have told you herself, that we didn't really get along. We may have shared a womb, but that's about it as to where our similarities lie. That and our resemblance."

The room fell silent. Lars had never said that to anyone before, despite it being something he had felt for as long as he could remember.

"The thing you have to understand, if you know my father as well as you say you do, is that he thinks the world of Lilah." WPC Shilling shifted awkwardly in her seat, whilst Lenton adjusted his immense weight in the chair and Barty still stared with a burning intensity. The silence forced Lars to pose a question before the tribunal himself: "Is my father in trouble? Do you think he's involved somehow?"

An awkward pause.

"We're just trying to ascertain what was going through your sister's mind, and see what events lead up to..." The constable broke off, seeing that Lars was uncomfortable. This was obviously a horrible conversation to be had for anyone.

Wiping his deep-set brown eye with the cuff of his jumper, Lars cleared his throat as he fought the urge to cry in front of these people. He needed to be strong. Falling apart right now was not an option.

"Honestly, I don't know what to tell you people. Lilah wasn't herself all summer. But was she suicidal? I couldn't tell you."

Was she suicidal?

"I mean, over the last few weeks I was with her, she was quiet and spent a lot of time by herself locked away in her room. I just assumed she was moody. She wouldn't take phone calls from her friends and hardly left the grounds. I think she might have lost weight over the summer? And when I did see her, I think she hadn't had a decent night's sleep in weeks"

This got their attention.

"When he was around, my father was concerned and had tried to spend as much time as possible with her. People came and went and I would ask after her. I even tried to see her, but she either wouldn't answer her door, or father would tell me that she wasn't up to visitors."

"Are you saying that you went a whole summer, having hardly seen either your sister or father, all whilst living under the same roof?" Asked Shilling, the disgusted tone was far from subtle. Lars had to snigger but wiped his eye again before rolling it.

You obviously don't know how big our house is.

Sensing their frustration by this point, Lars knew that the most of whatever they wanted to know had been garnered by now or that, most probably, the answer they were looking for did not actually lay with Lars.

Ms. Barty took the opportunity to tactfully lead the interrogation once again, shifting the power back to her side of the court. "We have a few of your sister's things; belongings she probably would want you and your father to have. Speaking of which, there was one item... Have you received any parcels or packages?"

His heart stopped. The wooden box on his desk.

"Nope. I don't think so," he said.

"Very well. But if you do, you must tell us. It could be evidence. Do you understand?" She barked.

Lars was glad he trusted his gut earlier and decided to hide the box. He nodded silently.

Taking a large breath, he looked up and said to his hosts, "Are we done? I think I have a lot to think about right now." With that, the three adults, somewhat begrudgingly, stood and gestured the boy's leave as though they were not yet finished with him.

"Of course, Ol' Bean. Take all the time you need. Your professors will have already been advised of your bereavement, and you're not expected in class for a day or two."

Lars gave a tight smile through pursed lips and made a very swift exit out of the room. The three adults remained standing, speechless and pensive for the stupefied minute of his absence.

"Do you think he knows what's going on?" Asked a curious Lenton.

"I'm not sure, but everything is ruined now that the selfish little trollop took her own damned life. And where the hell is Jude!" Snapped Barty. The headmaster and the policewoman shied away, continuing to once again inspect their tea leaves and cuticles respectively.

11. Exodus

Lars mercilessly found himself at the haven of his room for the second time today and once more relished the ability to lock himself away from the rest of the world. Desperately closing the door, he placed his head on the wood, shut his eyes and momentarily took stock of all that had happened while he desperately tried to catch his breath.

His heart fluttered rapidly and he took deep breaths to try and control his anxiety. He turned to face his room and immediately realised that he was not as alone as he had initially thought. Lars was a little startled to find Alex still there, curled up on the small armchair in the corner of the room, strategically nestled amongst a pile of what Lars couldn't remember was possibly clean laundry or not.

Lars' room was a mess before his outburst on the desk an hour or so ago, but amidst the chaos of his life, there, snoozing amongst a fraction of it was his best friend. Despite the surprise, Alex's presence was actually a welcomed intrusion but Lars could not shake the envy that Alex could sleep so soundly and without a care in the world.

Lars could not help but admire Alex; a boy who should have grown up with all the privileges and opportunities afforded to him. Instead, his life was drenched in tragedy. Furthermore, Alex could have quite easily gone off the rails – Lars supposed to himself – but he possessed a seniority and knowledge about him that meant his friend was mentally and emotionally a lot older than his actual age.

With that, Lars slid his back down the door and squatted where he once stood. He huddled his legs tightly to his chest and wept silently into his kneecaps.

Many moments passed before Alex stirred, stretching one arm and contorting the other to rub his eye before noticing his broken friend.

"Hey, are you OK buddy? I didn't know whether to stay or not? I figured you might have wanted somebody to talk to after..." he trailed off, realising that his best friend was still in a bad condition.

"It's true Alex... it's all true. She's dead. My sister is dead." The silver streak of a tear shimmered down his sandy coloured cheek. Alex rightfully thought Lars looked pretty pathetic. Lars lay his head back upon his knees and continued to sob gently to himself. Alex paused, not really sure what to do with himself because emotional people made him uncomfortable. Nonetheless, he prowled over to his friend, slid his back down the door and plonked himself next to him.

He considered putting his arm around the crying boy's shoulder but instead, offered, "Do you want to talk, mate?"

Lars took a moment to respond. "Not really if I'm honest." he offered. "Sorry Alex, but I can't be here. I could maybe do with getting away for a bit... Go home, find Dad – I don't know – but anywhere is better than here right now."

Alex nodded and could see the sense in his plan. Lars paused, he was deliberating something.

"Want me to come with you?" offered Alex.

Lars pondered, trying to be cool, but in this sorry state, it was obvious that he needed the companionship. Alex did not judge him for this.

"Please. I just have to get out of this school and away from everyone. It's suffocating here, and I can't be around these leeches any more."

"Sure thing. I need to balance my perfect record with something and truancy is a good idea." He smiled with a genuine warmth as he spoke. Alex would never know this, but his kindness made a dent in Lars' mood and for a moment, Lars forgot how wretched he felt.

"When do you want to go?" Alex offered.

Contemplating, Lars returned with, "Let's get an early night; I've had a long-arsed day. Pack some things and we'll go back to mine first thing."

"Are you going to be alright?" Alex dropped his brow, and his watery blue eyes darkened under the stern shadow of his own sincere expression.

"Yeah. Right now, I just want to sleep and never wake up." Lars felt pretty sure of both statements at this point.

Alex was unsure about that comment but heaved his limber body up from the floor in one swift movement. He gave a silent nod and placed a gentle hand on Lars' shoulder and left. For the first time, Lars felt relieved.

It wasn't dark yet, but he did not care; the allure of his bed was lulling him like a siren.

He locked his bedroom door, undressed quickly and jumped straight under the covers. The cool sheets felt crisp and soft against the surface of his naked skin. He wriggled his body into the contours of his mattress, fluffed his pillow and relished the subtle scent of his bed linen.

Staring into the abyss of his consciousness, multitudes of ideas and recollections whirred like fireflies around the menagerie of his mind. Each spark of a notion rushed at the speed of fireworks across the map of his consciousness. Pulses of memories would ebb and flow into manifestation as he thought back to summers in the family grounds when his mother was still alive. Their picnics under the trees and water fights in the pool before demonic flashes of a tired and weary dream-Lilah burned on his mind's eye, accompanied by the flaring face of their hostile father who scowled at a defiant Lars.

Next up in his reel of thoughts – a cameo from the trio and the murderously foul creatures from the morning. All of which ignited his senses with disgust as the wretched stench teased his nose, and the glistening yellow goop revolted.

Finally, thoughts of sweet Alex who had shown kindness and friendship arose to the forefront of his dreams. Like a herald of goodness, his smiling, and caring face was Lars' final thought before he drifted off to a somewhat peaceful state of rest.

Lars closed his eyes and quickly nodded off to sleep. Again, he failed to notice the single peering magpie perched upon the branch of the tree outside his room. A gentle breeze tussled her feathers, which caused her to shimmy her body and correct the wayward plumage. The monochrome bird dotted along the branch, flexed her wings and tilted her head; looking contemplatively at Lars while he slumbered.

***

Thrust from the Land of Nod and firmly thrown into the Realm of the Living, Lars had the desperate need for the toilet. Despite the excess of dreams, Lars had slept surprisingly well for the most part and was, therefore, most annoyed when he woke up with a startling bolt in the early hours of the morning.

Trudging with heavy feet, he plodded stiffly yet quickly with a thick pitter-patter to his en suite toilet and urgently alleviated himself within, what felt just like, the nick of time. As he relieved himself in the white porcelain, minute little pimples flexed across his skin and brought his awareness to how very cold the air was across his body. From beneath his nose, the ghostly wisps of condensation from his breath danced in the air in front of his face. He shuddered as the temperature seemed to plummet by the second.

More awake now, Lars leaned over the basin of the sink and ran the hot tap with a full turn. It spat and hissed, and the pipes moaned as they summoned hot water from the bowels of the school boiler room. Plunging his sedated hands into the pool of molten water sent waves of sensation up his forearms. He cupped a precious handful of the crystal broth and doused his face with an invigorating splash, then patted it dry and examined the contours of his face.

Lars looked tired – not just physically but emotionally – and he wondered if people could see the sadness and guilt behind his eyes. He quickly dismissed such thoughts, pulled on a nearby t-shirt and hugged his arms across his still-aching chest.

The twilight of the morning left a grey hue across the murky bedroom meaning that his dorm wasn't particularly dark at this point but it was awash with a sketchy charcoal complexion.

The wind outside was barely moving though it still caused the spindly branches of the leering outside tree to gently brush the window glass with softly scraping slow sweeps. Lars looked out through the dancing twigs that scratched the window pane to assess the time of day according to Mother Nature. The half-light of the early morning meant that the outside view was also an ashen pallet of dull white and pale black, much like it was inside.

Lars could decipher the bulbous shapes of turgid topiaries and the jutting squares of the honed hedges, both of which were shaped with military precision and the sloping grey mounds of the far-off hillsides resembled the pallid curves of a nude model from a dated black and white photo.

Below his window, in the charcoal courtyard that joined the boy's dormitories to the dining hall were the various statues of nameless Greek women. Among the leering statues and greying marble figurines stood a particular figure, distinguished mainly by the depth of its black hue in contrast to the other figurines around it.

Upon first glance, Lars mistook the shaded figure as one of the statuesque figures; arms poised elegantly, with carved contours of her billowing robes etched perfectly in the cold stone. He pressed his face closer to the window, trying to peer down and decipher the strange figure below.

With his curiosity getting the better of him, Lars tried to place this sculpture — one he would probably pass on a daily basis, never really taking notice. The ornaments themselves were far from Renaissance masterpieces and not particularly noteworthy, neither were they very ostentatious for that matter.

About to give up and step away, Lars could have sworn the strange appendage moved in the peripheral of his line of sight.

It was the sort of movement that you would have to rub your eyes and possibly ask a bystander if they saw it too or when you're not sure whether or not you've seen lightning, before that rolling crack of thunder and torrential downpour that confirms your initial sighting.

His heart raced, but the figure stood perfectly still and Lars had to admit defeat and put it down to the god-awful hour and that his eyes were playing tricks on him. He stepped away from the window and rubbed his eyes. Before committing to his next task, curiosity got the better of him one last time and Lars stepped back to the pane, just to be sure.

Lars essentially pressed his nose to the glass and looked further into the courtyard from his dorm with an intense gaze to decipher which statue it was. Upon second glance, it was gone.

He looked harder, as though his mere sight would compel the strange shape to reappear.

Lars cursed under his breath.

Had it been there? Did it move?

I'm just seeing things.

The last day had been strange, but on this occasion and in the grand scheme of things he dismissed what he thought he saw and retreated. His jittery shudder at that particular moment was not due to the cold atmosphere, however.

Lars felt the ache of every muscle as he now lowered himself onto the floor by his bed, which was littered with the mess from his desk. In the grand scheme of things, this was something that Lars could deal with immediately and proceeded to do as such.

Lars winced as he reached to gather pieces of paper and was reminded of the various cuts and bruises that were still tender and served as a constant reminder to his suffering. He reflected that upon seeing WPC Shilling at his door earlier he had panicked, thinking that she was there to arrest him. He shrugged it off.

Since sleep was now well-and-truly out of the question, and while he was on the floor, he had intended to retrieve his holdall from under his bed and pack a few days' worth of items for the trip with Alex back home. That was where Lars remembered – *but was just as equally surprised to find* – the mysterious box that had found itself on his desk yesterday.

Lars had forgotten about it.

Peering from the darkness was the polished surface of what Lars suspected was a simple jewellery box. He clocked it and reached awkwardly to try and grab it. He ignored the pang in his ribs and manoeuvred the box in front of him.

He placed his cautious fingers upon the sides of the wooden box and assessed the carcass, which was in his unprofessional experience, a very old and beautiful antique. The box was the richest colour of red wood and wore deep, bold veins of darker browns that streaked its surface like tiger print. It was highly glossed and elaborately decorated with swirls of brass leaf and the entire artefact was perfectly smooth, except for an intricate engraving of what looked like Art Nouveau foliage upon the lid.

On the corner of the box, where one piece of wood met the other, he noted the crusting brown substance that tarnished the side. He realised that the same layer of crust tarnished a little of the top on the polished surface. Thinking it was the scarred grain of the wood, he scratched at it gently with his nail and reddish flakes flecked away.

He instinctively licked his other finger and cleaned the substance from the box. It was not a lot, but enough to determine that it was, in fact, dried blood. Lars felt his stomach drop at the realisation of receiving blood-stained gifts.

With a deep breath, he made the decision to continue inspecting the wooden box. He had got this far now and figured that he couldn't get in any more trouble.

The front latch glistened under the half-light of the room. Far from your traditional lock and key mechanism, the strange design was nothing like Lars had ever seen before. That being said, despite its complicated-looking security device, Lars merely brushed his soft thumb across the metal and the latch relieved a delicate sigh, "Click".

The lid of the antique box squeaked gently as he tilted it to reveal it's contents within. Prising the lid open further, Lars was met with a waft of old wood, warm velvet and the rushing scent of his sister's lingering perfume. The fragrant exposure was like a breath of memories and emotions that caused a lump in Lars' throat.

On the inside of the lid itself, Lilah had placed a photo over the mirror, which drove the guilty knife in a little deeper into Lars' chest. It was an old picture of them both from when they were younger. Taking the photo for closer inspection, he held it in his tender fingers and admired the looks on their faces. There was an imprint – he flipped the photo to reveal blue words, written in his sister's handwriting. It read:

> Sorry, I couldn't do it – my destiny was too great – hopefully, you'll do what I couldn't. Always remember that my gift is just a loan and that you won't keep it forever. This isn't and never was meant for you.
>
> Lars, beware the Seven. Beware the Fold.
>
> Love always,
> Lilah

Lars read his sister's note and then read it again. He then read it one last time and decided that it made absolutely no sense to him whatsoever. He noted the smudges – were they tears? – and realised that the message was not any less important, even if he was not quite sure what it was yet. Lars placed it back where he found it and made his way through the rest of the box, feeling closer to his sister than he had done in a long time.

He fingered the contents sensitively, feeling a little uneasy about going through what could be his sister's most treasured possessions, especially when they were quite possibly one of the last few things she could have touched. It all felt too personal. Lars somehow wanted to preserve her spirit, and rummaging through her possessions in some way exorcised her memory, making her essence disappear into the ether like dust from a stale rug, or leaves caught in the shimmering autumn breeze.

This box had answers though. It was meant for him.

Foraging through the inside, he ruffled papers and noted his sister's favourite necklace; a gift from their mother. The box stored a few other trinkets and random bits and bobs, all of which probably held sentimental value to his sister — what exactly they meant to her, he would probably never know now.

About to put the box down and leave this ritualistic sorting, he caught sight of an artefact that he had long forgotten and had not realised that his sister had been in possession of. Under the items lay one part of a small cylindrical item; the lid to their mother's ivory pen.

Lars recalled that the pen belonged to his mother, who had given it to Jude. Some years ago, Jude then passed the pen to Lilah so that she could give it to her husband one day and they could then gift it to their child, or something.

Lars recalled how in his youth he had not realised what ivory was. Upon his father enlightening him shortly after the receipt of this beautiful but strange tool, Lars had rightly thought the procurement of the material cruel and vile. Lars was not particularly keen on animals, but the thought of an elephant or rhinoceros giving its life so that some pompous old colonial could have a fancy pen to write cheques and sign documents with was disgusting.

Searching for the other piece of the writing instrument, he ruffled more of the items within. Fingering through her personal items, he noted the pictures and odd little bits of paperwork, some with her own handwriting others with doodles and sketches. With urgent movements, he brushed his hurried digits eagerly over the contents. In one quick movement, something brushed violently under the tips of his discovering fingers. He felt a short, sharp stab and retracted his hand with lightning speed.

"Mother f—" He cursed, instinctively putting his injured fingers in his mouth and stifling the rest of his curse.

A moment passed and he withdrew them for a closer inspection to find a thin blue strip had been slashed across the tips of the three middle fingers of his right hand. Peering closer, the inky blue evolved into brownish purple as blood began to emerge from the thin gash. He sucked his fingers again to quell the bleeding. The sweet ink and metallic blood made for a strange tasting concoction in his mouth. The small strip was also incredibly sensitive under the soft brush of his tongue that he winced in pain. With his other hand, he gently searched for the culprit, eager not to make the same injury.

Under a photo of them both, lay the weapon in question; the vicious ivory fountain pen. The golden nib was stained with the dried blue of the ink and accentuated by the fresh, vibrant red of his own blood. Awkwardly, he tried to place the lid back on the pen to keep it from causing more harm but gave up in favour of keeping his bleeding fingers in his mouth. Instead, he placed them side by side next to the rosewood box.

Licking his fingers, he felt a wave of nausea sweep his body. His fingertips grew numb under a peculiar hot burning sensation. Upon inspection, the blood had now stopped and the blue ink had been washed away under his saliva. Now clean, the slash was no wider than a paper cut and it wasn't particularly deep, though heavier than a graze whilst the burning sensation persisted, growing hotter and hotter by the second.

The room had begun to take on the quality of an ethereal consistency, almost blurring like the heat that dances off the tarmac on a hot day. His throat grew tighter as the alarming temperature and distorted sense of reality began to constrict both his mental and physical states. He broke out into a sweat, yet shook violently as the temperature appeared to drop drastically.

Looking around, his attention was fixed upon the lethal golden nib of the spiral pen as it appeared to leak profusely all over the wooden floor. At first, Lars thought it was the remnants of ink, however, the liquid was a thick, black treacle colour, glossy and slow, whereas the ink on his fingers had been blue. That, and the amount of fluid was far too much for the capacity of a pen to hold.

Lars tried to stand but buckled and lost his balance, falling awkwardly and hitting his head on the corner of the nearby desk. Landing with an almighty thud on the floor his vision was blurred and a searing pain throbbed between his burning fingers and freshly pounded skull. As his sight adjusted, the room spun sporadically with every short inhalation of breath. Once again he clocked the dirty white pen with its shimmering golden nib. The air hummed around it, to which Lars thought he could also hear a droning buzz emitted.

Laying in a soggy patch, Lars panicked at the thought of his bleeding head. Frenzied, he touched the bump to find it was bone dry. The moisture was, in fact, the leaking fluid that seeped from the pen. Thick black gloop continued to spill slowly, and constantly in his direction.

His instincts were to get up and move away from the creeping slime, but the ability to roll over or lunge upwards had been stripped from him. Both his injured hand and now the good one that had inspected his injury, seemed to numb under contact with the mysterious black liquid.

As the feeling drained from both legs it also spread up his arms, making them feel heavy. Weighed down by this mysterious sensation and his own sense of paralysing panic, he could feel the black gunk sweep his body, causing debilitation all over. From the shoulders down, Lars was weighed down by his own inability to move.

Like a serpentine streak of tar, the fluid had a life of its own. Just inches away from his face, it sat collected on his chest and hissed as it darted up and reared like a striking cobra.

The burning cold sensation on his skin was electrifying – both terrifying and oddly exhilarating. In a brief moment of clarity, whilst the poised liquid head of this ghastly serpent swayed in contemplation, Lars realised what was about to happen. Stripped of movement, but also the ability to scream, it split in two and lunged savagely into his eye sockets.

No noise left his mouth, as a surging agony violated his face and penetrated his insides. At that moment Lars remembered nothing more and passed out into the surrendering bliss of unconsciousness.

Part Two

12. Mrs Heath

The news of Lilah's death came knocking at the Thurston Estate when three figures arrived unannounced, wishing to speak with the master of the house. Naturally it was the housekeeper, Mrs Heath, who answered the door on that fateful morning and was the first of the household to be blown down with news of Lady Lilah's tragic death.

Mrs Heath, as the family respectfully and affectionately called her, had started her day like any other. Her alarm dutifully sounded at the same time of 5:30am every morning, though being organised and alert, she was always awake before it. She would wash her face, apply modest makeup and neatly pile her wavy brown hair into a tight bun at the nape of her neck just above her collar. Her uniform was always freshly pressed from the night before, and her humble shoes were immaculately polished.

She would proceed to the kitchen at 6am to brew an intensely strong pot of English breakfast tea. Whilst allowing the leaves time to infuse the water and fragrantly bleed their dark amber extracts, Mrs Heath prepared two slices of toasted granary bread, oozing with dribbling yellow butter that she would either enjoy with a generous lashing of honey or a smothering of shredded marmalade; dependent on which she fancied that particular morning, with the latter usually meaning she was in a good mood. Today, unfortunately for her temperament, was a marmalade day. Placing her favourite bone china cup and saucer on a tray, along with the now perfect pot of tea and two sumptuous slices of toast, she would sit down at the faithful oak table and enjoy twenty minutes of doing nothing, other than to eat her breakfast.

As housekeeper to the Thurston estate, Mrs Heath oversaw the running of the family's stately home, a job she had always relished, despite having to answer to the perpetually sour and equally temperamental master of the house. Her job inevitably kept her busy and no doubt was met with its challenges, most of which centred around Lord Jude himself.

Rarely did Mrs Heath and Jude Thurston see eye-to-eye, which equally was what brought the pair together on many-an-occasion or dispute. Jude was bombastic, self-indulgent and exceptionally selfish. In every aspect of his life, his way was always the right way and he asserted his opinions as facts as far as he was concerned. If you did not like it, or agree, then there were employees to replace you or personnel to take care of you in a not-so-personal manner.

That was until Mrs Heath joined the Thurston staff.

Her first day had been some fifty-something years ago, when Jude Thurston had been just a young lord. Despite now being well into her sixties, the stout woman vividly remembered how much she had detested the Thurston boy. He had been an acerbically tempered young gentleman, and an exceptionally spoilt child with an over-inflated sense of entitlement.

As the eldest of eight children, and the only sister, Mrs Heath knew about pulling her weight and the importance of family, not to mention the sacrifices we make for those we love. Master Jude knew nothing about these, and had made no attempt to do so in his life.

Mrs Heath's mother had been the Thurston's housekeeper before her, as had her grandmother, and in turn, her great grandmother. In fact, for as long as there had been Thurstons at the Thurston Estate, there had been a maternal ancestor of Mrs Heath, running the household. Her mother had explained that all the women in their family had an important job of looking after the Thurstons. It was her duty to take the reins one day and look after them, just as she had done.

So on her first day, an unusually frosty September morning, a very young Mrs Heath – a girl somewhere in her late teens – was instructed to take the young master Thurston's breakfast to him and see that he got ready for his first day of boarding school. Dutifully, she had taken the polished silver tray in both hands and ascended to the west wing of the opulent manor house. She had never had the pleasure of meeting the boy at this point, but was certain that the stories of a brattish little brute with spiteful manners could not possibly be true. How naive she had once been.

Mrs Heath remembered how nervous she had been. Looking after her seven brothers and father while her mother looked after the Thurstons meant that she was more than adequate to learn the ropes. That aside, Mrs Heath had heard such stories about the Thurston family. Despite a rich and colourful history filled with tales swathed in murder and superstition, it was the stories of the spiteful son, an impish little creature that was as a vicious as he was calculating, that worried her more.

Reaching his door, she had placed the breakfast tray upon the sideboard that stood sentry just outside his room. Breakfast was a stodge of greyish porridge, a slender glass of warm water with a slice of lemon, and several brightly coloured fillets of pungent smoked haddock. The waft of fish was not the most appetising of smells so early in the morning and she remembered turning her nose away with little effect.

Her instructions had been to knock twice and call in to see if the young boy was both awake and decent. Should he reply, then she could proceed. Failing that, she was to knock once more and enter the room, announcing herself.

A young Mrs Heath wrapped the door with her knuckles making two distinct and clear knocks, which had reverberated along the silent corridor. Nothing.

A young Mrs Heath had prepared for this. She waited a moment longer and considered knocking once more. Then, just as her hand reached the stern dark wooden door a direct and stern voice hollered from within the room.

"Go away you stupid little bitch."

Ever so slightly taken aback, the fledgeling housekeeper had not been prepared for that response.

With a decisive huff, she straightened her white pinafore, clicked the handle and slightly pushed the door open so she could enter the room. She then turned to collect the tray, gathering it awkwardly with one hand. From this point, she half-crossed the threshold and then made her way entirely into the young boy's chamber.

It was then, with an almighty crash, that Mrs Heath fell backwards into the hallway, covered in the boy's would-be breakfast. The porridge was tacky on the floor as the warm water merged with the greying oats, causing a foul-looking puddle. She had not seen where the fish meat landed but the stench was still strong, which meant it had not landed far.

Dazed, she was roused back to her senses to see a sharp-featured eleven-year old standing proudly over her from the arch of his doorway. His spiteful face was sniggering a vicious little grin of pure satisfaction. The impish little fiend was immensely more than pleased with himself, having just launched his body at the door and making his house-servant fall flat on her backside.

What the boy did not anticipate however, was that this was a new maid and he had underestimated her comeback.

Not to be humiliated by a spoiled little boy, she flew to her feet and grabbed the precious urchin by his ear, dragging him to the mess he had caused on the hallway floor outside his bedroom.

"Tidy this up immediately." The stern tone of her voice was not one that she heard from herself very often. Others that had faced this side of her often did not come out this confrontation well.

"No. You're the servant, you do it." The command was not so threatening under the wince of the painful submission he was experiencing.

"I am nobody's servant, young man, least of all yours. Now pick this mess up immediately."

"No. My family owns you, so you have to do whatever I want," Mrs Heath had to give the boy credit for his stubbornness, but he was just adding fuel to her fire. She proceeded to twist his ear even tighter. "Ow, you stupid bitch, you're hurting me!"

"This can end one of two ways now, Master Thurston; either you pick this up, apologise, and I'll fetch you another one, or you find out the hard way what it is to mess with me." Her voice remained even and stern, despite wanting to throttle the little shit. Then the boy spat at her feet. "Right. I take it you want to learn the hard way," and with that, she forced the boy down onto all fours by his ear. With her free hand she grasped the boy by the collar of his neck and forced his disgusting face into the sloppy lukewarm mess on the floor.

"Now that you've eaten, I suggest you get washed and dressed. You've wasted enough of both of our time already this morning and you're off to boarding school in a few hours. You need to prepare your things and say goodbye to your family." She expected a snappy retort or spiteful comeback but his actual reply was not one she was at all prepared for. The boy suddenly looked very pathetic and much smaller in the half-light of his dusky bedroom.

"They won't care when I'm gone. They're not even here, you idiot. No one cares if I'm here or not"

"Well that's not true," she offered, before he cut her off.

"Yes it is!" He insisted. "Have you even met them? Have you even seen them?"

He had her at this one. She had done neither, but within the first 3 minutes of having met this child, she knew instantly that this was not the behaviour of a well-adjusted and happy boy. He began to sob, and with the smothering of lumpy porridge over his face the boy looked pathetic and helpless. Seeing such a poor creature brought tears to her eyes, though it could have easily been the ripe smell of haddock.

"Tell you what, young man, if you get yourself washed and dressed, I'll clear this up and fetch you bacon and eggs. A growing lad like you needs something a bit tastier before his first day at a new school. I'm here, and I'll see you off later if your mother and father can't."

"OK," he decided "And stop calling me young man; you're not much older than me."

"Righty ho, Master Thurston. Now come along, we haven't got all day. I want you washed and ready before I'm back with your breakfast." She ducked down to clear the mess, where he involuntarily offered to help.

Mrs Heath smiled fondly at the memory, though with disappointment, as glimpses of kindness and sincerity from a now much older Lord Jude Thurston were still few and far between still.

A small blessing to come from their first meeting was that Lord Jude had never forgotten the encounter and from that day on had shown Mrs Heath the courtesy and respect he should have shown everyone. Whether it was the small act of kindness or the way she stood up to him, she did not know, but a combination of the two had left a lasting effect on their relationship.

Years went by and frequent news from Jude's school, The Kingswould Academy for Boys, would reach his mother and father about his spiteful and bullying behaviour towards some of the other boys. Most, if not all incidents were either forgotten or unpunished upon the young Lord's return.

Some fifty years on and Jude still has a wicked way with people. None so much felt his wrath as much as the boy, Lars. For whatever reason, Jude was exceptionally stern with his son. Of course many saw it, though Mrs Heath was the only one to pull Jude up on it. Lord Thurston would no doubt deny it vehemently, but it was obvious that Lord Thurston had a favourite child and he made no secret about the fact that it was his daughter Lilah, and not his son Lars.

It was for that reason that Mrs Heath was drawn to Lars. Lilah was every inch her father's daughter, in looks, personality and demeanour. Her twin brother was the quieter sibling; an unassuming and somewhat gentle soul, much more like their mother. That being said, the twins had their moments as children. Both were powerfully clever and wickedly headstrong and had unashamedly kept Mrs Heath on her toes for the last eighteen years. Now three people stood at the door of the family home with news that Lady Lilah was dead.

Mrs Heath had not recognised the motley crew of characters at the door, though she knew two of them by name. Besides being friends of Lord Jude, Ms Barty and Professor Lenton were also the twins' respective headmasters at their schools. It was the strange policewoman who had asked to speak with Jude, though after discovering his unexplained absence, had then divulged the devastating news to Mrs Heath.

It was at that moment that she had forgotten herself, and sat down on the burgundy chaise lounge in the foyer. However, at times like this, people ought not to judge one's manners.

"How? When? Why?" Mrs Heath assessed that all three questions were logical and relevant, though didn't know which to ask first. "Where's Lars? Does he know?"

"He has been informed, yes. We're having a difficult time locating the whereabouts of Lord Thurston. At present, he is not a suspect, though due to the suspicious nature of his disappearance, we will be looking into this also." Chimed WPC Shilling.

Mrs Heath was astounded, yet instantly jumped to her master's defense, "Lord Jude has been away..."

"Where?" cut in the stout little policewoman with the country lilt.

"I– I don't know." Mrs Heath answered. "I know what you're insinuating, and I can inform you that you are barking up the wrong tree. Jude would never harm a hair on Lady Lilah's head. He dotes upon the girl and thinks the world of her."

"We're not insinuating anything, Mrs Heath, we just need to ascertain Lord Thurston's whereabouts. You can surely understand why we would need to be in touch," interjected the taller, more charming of the female duo. "This is truly devastating news and, being such dear friends, I wanted to be here to console darling Jude."

Mrs Heath, feeling overwhelmed by the barrage of traumatic information, glared at Ms Barty, assessing her demeanour. The headmistress was cool and rather nonchalant about the whole scenario and Mrs Heath could not help but wonder why such a close friend of Lord Jude would be relaxed about the whole situation – especially one that claimed to know Lady Lilah very well. After an uncomfortable silence Mrs Heath piped up.

"What of the boy? I'll endeavour to locate Lord Jude and make the necessary arrangements for Lars' return." In reality, Mrs Heath knew more than this trio suspected and that her first response would be to instruct the Arête to locate Lars immediately before the wrong people got to him first.

"No matter. We already know that Lars plans to vacate the school and make his way here," said Barty.

13. The Great Escape

Alex swung a laboured arm across his bedside table to silence his phone's whinging alarm. It had not actually woken him up since he was already wide awake after having endured a painfully restless night, one that was spent tossing and turning under his now twisted and crumpled sheets. His waking hours had been spent churning a relentless amount of guilt and sympathy towards his grieving friend. So, after a night of idle mental marathons, Alex was ready to focus his energy on something productive, like escaping the school.

Ever the boy scout, it was barely five o'clock and he was already packed, prepped and ready to make a run for it within the next half hour; all that remained was for him to get out of bed and throw on some clothes. Alex had initially planned to throw an overnight bag together upon waking but in an attempt to preoccupy himself and do something constructive during his tediously restless night, he had already packed, unpacked and repacked several times. What was finally in his holdall, he was not entirely sure, having grown frustrated with the arduous task some few hours back. The result was an eclectic mix of junk and possibly life-saving necessities alongside the usual pants, socks and an array of tops and bottoms.

Now opting for a staple pair of trusty converse, skinny jeans and a sweatshirt, he dressed quickly in the chill of the new day, brushed his teeth – remembering to pack the paste and brush in his holdall – and threw the duvet over his bed to leave the place looking moderately tidy. He turned off the lights, grabbed his bag and keys, put his phone in his pocket and shut the door in swift silence.

The murky corridor was submerged in one part vacuous silence with a generous dash of morning darkness; the perfect atmospheric combination to make your hairs stand on end when you're doing something sneaky. The escape was mutually, though silently, agreed to be a clandestine affair; one that, given Lars' current circumstances, went without saying.

Alex fought back a yawn as he stood at the door of his friend's room before knocking with a quiet urgency. He waited intently for the clammy pad of footsteps before being welcomed by his accomplice but there was just silence on the other side of the door.

During the moment's wait, he conjured the reflections of his own sleepless night and was reminded of his unfortunate friend on the other side of the door and how his own night might have compared. Alex knew of pain and suffering, especially the high-profile kind that appears to be public knowledge among total strangers, having rediscovered only too recently that the primary party is nearly always the last to find out.

The humiliation, as flocks of vulturous third parties peck at the carrion of your soul, exposing all your deepest and darkest fears, laying bare and magnifying your most shameful indiscretions and flimsiest of follies, is crippling. Whether you unintentionally added fuel to the fire or the gossip is ironclad fact, the only garment that's left to cover your naked body and protect your modesty is a polyblend blanket of hurt and shame.

Alex wrapped his knuckles a little louder this time. Still, nothing stirred from the room on the other side of the door.

From a few doors down, something else stirred instead.

The loudest click of a releasing latch gave way to a tawny beam of light that sliced the corridor in two halves of darkness. Spinning quickly, Alex pressed his back to the wall in the small alcove of the door where he stood. It was probably Terrence Wooderson; the annoying busybody who always seemed to pop up when you didn't want him to. He was hated among the rebels of the school for snitching on those who enjoyed smoking behind the bike sheds or those conspiring to steal the answer sheet for next week's mock exam.

Alex held his breath, stifling puffs of air through his nostrils. In those few short moments, he spent what felt like hours wishing and praying to some nameless deity or higher power that Terence would bugger off back to bed. He counted the time away in his head, fearing even then that the obscenely observant kid would somehow hear the numbers being recited in Alex's own thoughts. Terrence stepped back, his shadow bleeding back into the recess of his room, closing the door slowly but silently, which diminished the yellow spotlight and immersed the hallway back into the safety of darkness once more.

A different, more drastic approach was needed now.

With the stealth of a jungle cat, Alex silently retrieved his wallet from his bag and removed his oldest credit card. For the many centuries that the school had stood here, Alex relished a minuscule moment of gratitude, thankful that the locks on the dorms were the relatively modern, Yale, versions. Having spent many-a-night off campus with Lars, the boys had often needed to drunkenly break back into the dorms. It had been Lars who had the knack of breaking and entering, which Alex now tried to mimic. He slid the plastic card between the door and frame and proceeded to fumble aimlessly until, "snap," the card broke.

Discarding the piece in his hand to his pocket, he abandoned the other half as it fell onto the floor somewhere in the swamp of darkness at his feet. Retrieving his Amex, he tried once more but with less force. He slid the card down the crack of the door where it kissed the frame, a little higher than the actual door handle itself, right down until it came level with the lock. With the slightest breath of a push, the latch connected and gave way with a whisper. In a moment of disbelief, Alex forgot himself and comprehended how easy that had been before remembering his actual purpose.

He proceeded through the door.

Scanning the dormitory in the morning twilight, Alex was annoyed to find Lars still sound asleep, only fully clothed and on the floor. He entered the room fully, drawing the door to a close with such precision and silence so as not to alert Terrence and his radar ears down the corridor. Alex marched over and tapped his sleeping friend on the shoulder, whispering urgently into his ear.

"Lars. Wake the fuck up. Lars, we have to go."

Alex was taken aback, having felt something tacky on his fingers, which he immediately lifted to his face and quickly realised was blood.

His stomach dropped.

Alex tried again, only this time he jabbed rather than tapped, and the urgent hush of his voice was more of a desperate whisper, "Lars, get up for Christ's sake!"

Still nothing.

Do I call an ambulance? Yes, Alex. Of course you call an ambulance – he could be dead.
Alex fumbled for his phone, noticing the compression of his friend's chest.
OK, he's not dead.

His gut was to abandon calling the emergency services. Instead, with the alert of a watchful cat, Alex sprung upright and urgently surveyed the room for anything that would make for a successful rousing aid. Nothing jumped out at him, so Alex instinctively grabbed Lars by the shoulders and shook him vigorously. His head rocked with a lazy sway and still did not stir. He dismissively dropped Lars, who flopped back onto the floor with a thud. There was something to be said about Alex's bedside manner.

Oops. Sorry, Lars...

Panic set in as Alex placed his ear next to Lars' slightly pursed mouth to check that he was indeed still breathing. Lars' balmy breath was warm and lazy and tickled the downy hair of Alex's cheek. His stomach lurched with a twisted pang of nervous guilt and planted a swift slap across Lars' face.

Lars opened his eyes.

"What the f—! What was that for?" Lars was oblivious to Alex's efforts to wake him. "My head is pounding. And now my face feels like it's on fire." He retaliated and shoved Alex with a boisterous push that was uncomfortably playful. The swift and sudden attack caused Alex to roll backwards and land flat on his back in the middle of the floor.

Alex looked directly up to his friend, who somehow appeared older than he had been when Alex said good night only a few hours before. He could see that Lars desperately needed rest, and it was obvious that even the sleep he had had was not peaceful. Lars must be exhausted, but Alex eased his own conscience by remembering that skipping school and hiding away for a few days was Lars' idea, and that it was now or never. The school's housekeeping staff would soon emerge, followed not long after by the faculty. And before you knew it the entire student populace would swarm the corridors and bleed onto the surrounding school grounds, meaning that their escape would be impossible.

"You're bleeding," said Alex.

Lars peered over the side of his bed, raised a hand to his enraged cheek to caress the hot skin, before fingering the spot on his head that was bleeding. Upon seeing a dishevelled Alex, Lars began to giggle uncontrollably.

Alex pulled himself up, straightened out his jumper, adjusted his jeans at the waist and brushed off his knees. "Keep it down, Lars. We have to go soon, remember?" Alex hushed, "We don't have much time to get out of here now, and we have a train to catch in 20 minutes." He noticed the vicious handprint gradually became more prominent as he spoke to Lars. The cruel claret of his cheek was in stark contrast to his unusually pale skin and tired grey eyes. "Are you OK? We should get your head checked over."

Lars dismissed his uptight comrade's nagging, stumbled up and gathered his belongings, throwing them into last night's holdall. He undressed without shame or modesty, which threw Alex into a state of distress. He amused himself with several trinkets and artefacts that were strewn about the place, trying desperately not to look as uncomfortable as he felt. In the corner of his eye, he could just make out Lars' slender frame covered in a patchwork of bruises and scratches.

Now decent, Lars frantically gathered a couple of day's worth of items and shoved them into a duffle bag. Alex caught sight of the small wooden box on the floor by Lars' bed. He strode over with curious indignation to retrieve and examine the beautiful and expensive-looking item. It was slightly unhinged and a few of the contents were spewed from the opening.

He gathered them up whilst Lars was hurrying about the bathroom. There was a strange white pen which went straight in the box, several papers and a photograph of Lars and his twin sister Lilah. "You don't really look alike, do you?" he called out. Lars could hear the smile in his jovial tone but was not in the mood.

Lars flew from the bathroom, snatched the photo and the wooden box from Alex's hand and stuffed them into his overnight bag as well. "Those are nothing to do with you." Sheepishly, Alex perched on the bed and waited for his friend to finish gathering his belongings and to ultimately be in a better mood.

Before leaving, Lars forgot to dispose of his bag of discarded clothes after his incident with the couple. He never paid them any mind after that and would never know that they were already taken by a mysterious figure.

***

The walk to the train station was uneventful. Neither boy came forward with an attempt at small talk after this morning's earlier run in. Alex felt awkward around the tempestuous Lars, whilst Lars, in turn, felt guilty for snapping at his friend.

In mutual silence, they agreed to leave the school grounds via their secret skiving route. This took them on a muddy shortcut through the leering forest that enveloped the grounds of the school.

It was significantly brighter than it had been when Alex first woke up but the half-light of the chilly morning cast the imposing trees in elongated shrouds of darkness. The crevices and cracks of the trees promised eternally vacuous wormholes, whilst every overstretching branch and vascular twig reached out with claws of hostility against the grey sky.

Alex marched on strong legs that powered through the growth of the forest. His converse became sodden with exposure to the silvery dew strewn along the floor. Lars half-heartedly traipsed on ahead. His once athletic and powerful stride seemed lazy and forlorn. Lars seemed jumpier than usual, where every crunch of the mulch underfoot or snap of a twig would conjure some imaginary attacker to jump out from behind a gnarled old tree and attack him.

The condensation of Alex's wispy breath danced in the exposure of the chilly air. He recalled trudging through Kingswould Forest on numerous occasions previously and never once felt unnerved by the eerie surroundings they were both subject to now. Alex could not shake the feeling that they were not alone and strode a few longer steps to keep up with his friend.

More than once, Alex swore that footsteps besides those of his own and Lars' were joining them and for good reason. He was right to be suspicious, since they were indeed being followed by a hooded figure, darting amongst the trees. But, the boys were oblivious.

Several minutes' more walking, a few trodden-in puddles and a snag of Lars' sweater, the boys emerged unscathed from the forest, right on the outskirts of the village of Kingswould. Neither boy noticed the other's shudder at the thought of a mysterious figure looming from the forest, surveying their departure.

The roads in the village were quiet but for a tractor and the odd car every now and again. The train station was deathly quiet at this hour and several of the cars parked outside were dressed in a film of moisture that shimmered under the amber light of the flickering streetlight. A dusting of mist swayed over the platform, as a large magpie cawed from a nearby tree.

The ticket office was closed and a self-service ticket machine was far too modern for this neck of the woods. Looking on his iPhone, Lars scrolled through his train app, breaking the silence to confirm their next move, "It's on platform 2, in about 5 minutes, so we need to cross over the bridge." Alex agreed with a nod of his head and shrugged a gesture that looked like after you. The boys lazily climbed the steps over the platform, where each plodding foot orchestrated a loud metallic clang that resonated throughout the skeletal structure of the bridge.

The platform was covered in the shade of an overgrown hedge which shimmered in the whisper of the hushing breeze. The mist parted, and under one of the benches lay a crumpled heap of khaki and grey. It lurched gently in an up-and-down motion. Alex nudged Lars on the arm and nodded in the direction of the pulsating lump under the bench. Both boys peered closer, getting a cruel waft of the now discoverable puddle of vomit. The heap erupted in a violent cough, which startled them and made them edge away toward the other end of the platform. Goosebumps ran up Alex's neck.

"This isn't the type of place that gets homeless people." Lars said, breaking the silence.

It was an obvious comment but Alex could see the olive branch peeking out somewhere between the lines. "He must have been thrown off, coming from the City. It's sad."

"Then why did you creep away from him?" Lars' tone changed to one of teasing, which was further confirmed by a playful nudge with his elbow.

"Fuck. Off." was Alex's most educated retort. "I saw you leap out of your skin when he coughed his guts up."

The train stretched around the corner in the distance with two blurry cream lights that smudged their way through the thickening morning mist. It rolled past and groaned to a scratchy stop. The doors beeped and opened with an automated sigh. They hopped aboard, placed their bags on the compartments above their heads and sloped into a pair of facing seats with a table in between them. The train was practically empty, with the front end being dotted with several commuters. The homeless man got on further down, just in time before the carriage rolled away, and sat amongst the suited and booted.

From the opposite direction, a stoutly old man with bulging and puffy features that gave him the repulsive bloat of a drowned frog waddled down the carriage. His eyes protruded and his fingers were swollen like sausages. He was friendly and smiled, but his little stumpy white dentures looked like milk teeth. "Tickets please?" he sang to Lars and Alex, causing the former to whisper "nobody is this friendly before 6.am," making the latter snigger.

"We got on at Kingswould," said Alex, composing himself, whilst trying to not to laugh at his friend's rubbish, and horrible joke.

"I know you did. Only a true Kingswouldian would pronounce it properly. The number of people that say *Kings-wood*," issuing a pair of tickets to the boys as they handed over their credit cards. He continued, "I say to them think of it like King's Old, but with a 'W' – funny thing, place names and geography. Anyway, you boys have a good day now." He sauntered down the aisle and disappeared into the next carriage.

The train journey was long and uneventful. Alex fell asleep, whilst Lars surveyed the blurring landscape as it rushed past outside. By now, the carriage had acquired a few more additions: A strange looking woman in an oversized coat, with wild salt and pepper hair who painted her nails while surveying passers-by with indignation; a hooded boy wearing oversized headphones that blared loud music and a builder who mindlessly scrolled through his smartphone.

It was while staring out the window, admiring the patchwork of grey hues from the mish-mash of concrete structures as they blended with the green and brown of the affronted environment, that Lars failed to notice the homeless man traipse up the aisle and join their carriage. He stumbled and swayed with the motion of the vehicle and fell upon a passenger or two, who were most indignant to their guest.

Lars was brought from his daydream when the homeless man grabbed him by the collar and pulled his defenceless face up to his own. His breath was toxic and his face was dirty; mapped with the lines and creases of sleeping rough. Without warning, staring Lars dead in the eye and between intervals of insane giggling, he started chanting:

> *One for sorrow,*
> *Two for joy.*
> *Three for a girl,*
> *and FOUR FOR A BOY!*

He sang in a dreary babble that was laced with alcoholic breath. Each breathy pant of the chant was a layer of warm and stagnant moisture that barraged his face. He cackled hysterically as he continued the rhyme:

> *Five for silver,*
> *Six for gold...*
> *Seven welcomes you to the Fold*

He released another cackle, doubled over and coughed a viscous fluid from the depths of his lungs. He paused, cleared his throat, and pulled Lars even closer, who in turn was paralysed with fear and shock. Their noses practically touched as he spat each word as if his life depended on this message being relayed with the utmost accuracy:

> *Seven. Welcomes. You. To. The. Fold.*

14. Ambush

Alex was roused from his nap by the commotion Lars and the homeless man were causing from across the carriage table. Through blurry eyes, he half-yawned and muttered to his travelling companion, "You got the words wrong. Everyone knows the magpie rhyme– "

It was only then that he realised there was a dishevelled homeless man pinning Lars to his seat and aggressively shouting nonsense into his face.

Lars struggled; the tramp was insanely strong and his vile hot breath prickled against Lars' cheeks and made his stomach churn. He desperately craned his neck away in an awkward position to avoid getting a face full of sticky saliva as the tramp continued to vociferate violently in his face.

From the corner of his eye, he could see Alex edging out of his seat ready to pounce on the sizable assailant. His eyes were no longer lazed and puffy but instead were wide and intense. Lars could see from the tension in Alex's broad shoulders and tight long arms that he was ready to leap across the table that separated them both. Then, within the breadth of a second, everything changed. For as soon as Alex had fired up, the concerned friend's tension subsided quickly and he eased back into his seat. Lars then realised that the aggressive man had relinquished some of his grip and eased off slightly.

Alex sniffed once and choked into his sleeve as a way of stifling the sound in an attempt to avoid unwanted attention. Most importantly, it was a vain attempt to protect his sensitive sense of smell.

A putrefying stench had wavered through the atmosphere and seeped through the carriage. At first, Lars thought it was coming from the aggressive homeless man, though it was stronger and more intense. If it was possible, this new stink overpowered even the damp smell of the tramp's sodden jacket, which was equally laced with the woody scent of cheap booze.

The homeless man had now completely paused with his eyes glazed. He took several short sniffs of the air, like a dog on the hunt, and surveyed the intoxicated atmosphere through his nasal senses. He stopped chanting his interpretation of the magpie rhyme, loosened his grip around Lars completely and turned away slowly, enamoured by the revolting stench.

Awash with a sudden wave of senses, Lars remembered the putrid whiff like a slap in the face. It was no longer the offensive smell of urine and whiskey, but the same rotting stench of the couple he left yesterday.

Alex was none-the-wiser to what was going on and still delirious from his short-lived power nap so, with concerned and confused eyes, he looked to Lars for a desperate explanation. His attention was soon grabbed by something else and he displayed the surveyed caution of a cat on the hunt towards a commotion that came from down the aisle. Lars and Alex watched eagerly as the homeless man edged from their vicinity and plodded slowly towards the door that separated the compartments.

Through the glass, the lights of the adjoining carriage flickered, wherein the brief moment of light, the boys could just about make out some sort of commotion in the next car. The vagrant eased his way to the door in a hypnotic state that had Lars equally captivated.

Lars held his breath with every step the man used to edge away from them. His heart pounded against his ribs as the enthralled homeless man peered cautiously through the glass to ascertain what was going on next door. Placing his hands around his eyes to gain a better view, he moved his face closer to the glass. Lars felt his heart thumping so hard that he thought he could even hear it as he helplessly watched the beguiled vagabond, who continued to leer through the glass with avid determination to identify what was happening in the next car.

The lights flickered off and nothing could be seen for a painful moment, whilst the chug of the carriage ticking over and over was the only noise that could be heard. The air was electric with tension and it seemed the slightest movement would be the catalyst that would cause an eruption of fire and incinerate the entire atmosphere.

Still, the boys continued to watch.

At that moment, a thick, dark streak of yellow gunk ejaculated across the glass. It rolled down the pane in a slow and disgusting movement, leaving gloopy mustard remnants as it dripped under the force of gravity. The man jumped back in alarm and looked around behind him for reassurance of what he just saw.

Without warning or explanation, the man's demeanour suddenly changed. Lars saw it happen like a flipped switch in the vagrant's consciousness. Humanity seeped through his facade and he grew a fiendish aura. Slowly, the man released a slow and menacing grin that was followed by the unadulterated release of a sinister chuckle that caused the few other passengers in the carriage to move away in terror. Right before dislocating his jaw and releasing a roaring howl, in the unholiest of voices he bellowed, "Seven welcomes you!" and pointed straight to Lars with a grubby finger and piercingly glazed eyes.

The window behind the vagabond smashed as a greying and decrepit hand forced itself through the glass and pulled the homeless man through the jagged cavity. Blood etched the shards of glass as piles of mauled flesh and grubby coat bordered the window frame.

Lars noted that his insides smelled a whole lot worse than his outside.

At this point, the boys had leapt to their feet in an attempt to try and help the victim, only it was too late. As they stood in the aisle, each looking to the other for an explanation, they slowly craned their necks towards the doorway to see the chagrin of the characters in the next carriage who were clawing at the damaged doorway trying desperately to get through.

Several of the other human passengers in this cart hustled over seats and clambered away from the door, though could not get very far due to being bottlenecked by the seats.

Whilst neither Lars or Alex knew what was happening, one thing was certain; the monstrous beings were baying for the blood of people in this carriage. The boys instinctively edged away in an attempt to escape to the carriage behind. "What the hell's happening, Lars? We need to get off this sodding train!" exclaimed Alex through a rushed, but level voice. He was, however, looking a little green in the face.

Not again! What is this? I barely escaped last time and what if I'm not so lucky – what if they get Alex?

"I don't know, but stay with me – I can't explain, but these things are dangerous. We have to get off this train, now!"

"No shit, Sherlock! What do we do?" said an oddly composed Alex.

Lars scrutinised the carriage for a weapon or some necessary means of escape but nothing was blindingly obvious. The nearest exit was crowded by overwhelmed passengers, whilst the other was keeping crazed passengers at bay.

Lars felt a wave of shivers trickle down his neck and roll along the length of his spine like tiny razor blades. He suddenly noticed that the panicking passengers of this carriage were no longer struggling to escape, and were now eerily still. Their hysteria seemed to have subdued and they stood, backs turned and motionless, all but for the sway caused by the rocking train.

One by one, each figure turned slowly to face the boys; their faces no longer plump and fleshy, but sallow and lifeless. Their eyes had been drained of all colour, leaving milky lenses that gazed emptily towards them.

Once passengers, the people were now demonic shadows of their former selves. Their skin grew withered and papery in a matter of moments, whilst their hair became limp and wiry. Handsome men dressed in finely cut suits were now waif and thin, ageing and rotting right before their eyes. A pregnant lady and some other commuters plodded closer in a sluggish and heavy swagger, each with the same laboured gait. Emotion, warmth and life all leaked out of their bodies, causing the gaunt yet surprisingly ferocious creatures to become lank and wispy replicas of human beings, who craved Lars' blood and flesh.

Lars felt his stomach lurch as memories of yesterday's rendezvous came flooding back, only on a much bigger scale. He surveyed the carriage, looking at the individual faces, and was overcome with both fear and sadness by what had just happened. His guttural sense of dread elevated when he considered that Alex could be at risk of this contamination.

I must keep Alex safe. But how? I don't even know what's causing this. We must get off this damn train.

As if by magic, the moving train was already beckoning to a sudden stop. Lars then realised that pragmatic Alex had pulled the emergency cord above their heads. Whether out of panic or practicality, this did, after all, seem like a pretty big emergency.

Lars was relieved to find his companion mysteriously unaffected by the mysterious disease that was killing the passengers and turning them into bloodthirsty zombies.

This is the second time this has happened now. How come we're immune... or am I the cause? Why is Alex not affected? Or is he already infected and it's just delayed?

The ageing train screeched under the pressure as it rolled and juddered to a slow standstill. By now, the festerous creatures were upon them and eager to devour them. Clumsy but determined hands grabbed at their hair, clothes and even the bare flesh on their arms and faces.

Alex managed to punch one in the face with surprising force, causing it to fall back and take several others with it, giving Lars a brief opportunity to grab their bags. Alex shoved another attacker out of the way, which allowed the boys just enough manoeuvrability to get themselves to a better vantage point down the carriage.

The zombified humans got up one by one and edged after Alex and Lars. The disgusting creatures scrambled towards the boys who were now desperately trying to open the exit near to the internal door where the original creatures were still vying for entry to the cabin. Lars launched his already aching body into the door, shoulder-first, to no avail. Alex tried to prise his fingers between the crack of the door but it was sealed shut.

"A credit card won't help with this one" he muttered under his desperate breath, but Lars did not get the joke.

Lars continued to try the handle of the ancient door that would release from the carriage and allow them to leave the train, but it was jammed shut. Hands grabbed desperately from the shattered window that swallowed the homeless man and Alex tried to fend off each new deathly assailant as they approached. "Hurry up, Lars! They keep on coming!" Lars punched the door over and over, and as he did so, he heard the eerie magpie song repeating through his subconscious, knowing and recognising the strange version from his dream.

Lars was brought back from his daydream by a rapid, yet faint spark, which he thought he may have imagined. Did he see a snap of little white light jump from his hand to the door handle? It did not matter now. He clasped his desperate palm around the metal and it gave way. The door beckoned a welcome escape and he leapt out of the carriage onto the temporary safety of the grass verge.

Alex was not far behind. He was pushing and shoving several attackers back and successfully managed to kick one in the face as it was crawling along the floor trying to bite him. Alex successfully rolled out of the door and onto the grass, although did not manage to clear as much distance as Lars had. Barely getting to his feet and before he could catch his breath, more demonic commuters tried to pile out of the door, fortunately, though, Alex was quick and pushed the door shut to lock them inside.

Lars grabbed Alex by the arm and ran along the track a short way before ducking into the protection of a nearby copse. Neither spoke as they ran nor did they have an inkling as to which direction they were going. The instinct to survive was mutual and fierce, and safety was a destination that was far from here right now.

The air was cold but clean and burned Lars' throat as he dived through the trees with his friend close behind him. Oddly, it was the homeless man's rhyme that was the focus of Lars' attention. Over and over he mulled the song in his head, rolling it around with the frustration of a boiled sweet that's lost its flavour.

Lars knew that chant from somewhere before. But where?

He continued to sing it in his head with each aching footstep. Then it struck him, much like Alex's slap in the face earlier – he knew exactly where he had heard that eerie version once before – "Of course! Lilah, she sang it in my dream!"

15. If You Go Down to the Woods

Lars and Alex had stopped running from the demonic train some time ago and had not spoken a word to each other since they made their narrow escape from the possessed passengers. Fortunately, the copse at the railside had shortly turned into full-blown woodland and provided the boys with ample cover to get them away relatively safely.

Lars could not shake the feeling of being followed but simply put it down to the harrowing events and how eerie the woods were.

Neither said anything to the other, but both Lars and Alex were marooned in their own silence as they each relayed the hauntingly hollow and lethal glares from the stomach-churning creatures from the train carriage. Stunned and pensive, the boys individually clawed with silent urgency for an explanation as to what had just happened to them.

Lars obviously had something of an upper hand, having dealt with a similar situation after his experience following his rendezvous the other morning, although this time on a much bigger and far more dangerous scale. Lars knew that Alex was in a state of shock. Ever the pragmatist, Alex could deduce a logical and reasonable explanation out of any situation. His so far never-ending silence indicated that he was still trying to fathom something logical and reasonable.

Lars punished himself by recalling the people he remembered from the train carriage. There was the homeless man, then the number of passengers who fell prey to the 'thing' itself, among them a pregnant woman.

What happened? What do I keep doing to these people and why are they after me? That poor woman. That poor baby.

Lars silently battled with his emotions as he toyed with the idea of what could be affecting the innocents within his vicinity and was still none-the-wiser as to what was happening to the people around him.

Was it airborne? Perhaps some kind of virus, like the Walking Dead? Is it mind control or even a magic sodding spell? I don't know.

The two survivors continued walking with heavy strides, getting as much distance between them and the train track. Lars had used the map on his phone to navigate through the forest and head in the right direction towards his ancestral home. They were still a long way off. He contemplated sidewinding to the nearest town, or ordering a taxi from the nearest point of civilisation, but dismissed those notions on the grounds that it was too dangerous. He did not trust himself to be around the public for fear of zombifying an entire population within minutes. As it was, Alex could well be in danger and turn at any moment for all he knew. The only thing that deterred him from sending his friend to safety was the fear of being left alone.

Besides, Alex seems to be immune like me. Or is also the cause...

Lars was stolen away from his thoughts with the cruel whisper of an icy breeze that licked against the clamminess of his own blood on his jumper. His thoughts quickly receded back to poor Alex and how he had been caught up in the attack. Lars looked out of the corner of his eye with a huge pang of guilt, to survey his friend's own injuries and see if he could determine whether he was all right.

On the right-hand side of Alex's face glared three red scratches that spread from above his firm eyebrow and traced down to his cheek, luckily missing his piercing blue eye. Lars could see the combination of fresh and crusted blood that was smeared across his face. From this angle, he could also tell that his sleeve was sodden with browning blood.

"Alex, you're bleeding," he stated rather flatly like he was thinking out loud.

The usually mild-mannered Alex had proven to be a force of nature in protecting them both and securing a successful getaway. Lars could not help but look at his best friend in another light to what he usually did because something had now shifted in their dynamic and that caused him to feel differently towards Alex in that moment. It was a feeling that he had trouble defining. It wasn't romantic but it was intimate. Fighting for your life and being saved by someone adds a new layer to a relationship, one where you become indebted. Lars felt grateful, inspired, scared and overwhelmed because Alex had not paused for a second to secure their safety and this made him feel awkward, like looking at a whole new person entirely.

"Oh yeah. So I am bleeding," he replied hoarsely and rather quite astonishedly. He cleared his throat and continued, "I didn't even notice, to be honest..." He paused, as though trying to find the right thing to say. Naturally, Alex wanted to ask a question, but determining the right one out of a long list was proving to be overwhelming.

"Lars, what was that? I've never seen anything like it before. It was awful. We should phone the police and tell them what happened and warn everyone. What if there were survivors and what if others got off the train."

Alex continued to rant, probably spilling everything he's been stewing on since the incident.

"I mean, there was the thing with the homeless man, the blood, the screams... and that smell. Jeez, those people too... I don't know what to think. Were they zombies?" He subconsciously felt the wounds up and down his arms. "Oh God, am I infected?!" Then Alex paused. His expression dropped from wild panic to a flicker of realisation.

Lars remained silent, not knowing which question to answer first, or if he even had an answer for any of them. Alex's good eye squinted with a focused accusation towards his friend. "You've seen this before..." The tone in Alex's voice was slow and processed.

Lars broke eye contact, headed forward and picked up the pace to avoid the confrontation. A swift Alex caught up immediately and grabbed his arm forcefully, spinning him on the spot.

"You've seen this before, Lars. What is it? What did you do?"

"Me? I did nothing... Oh, I don't know, Alex... I don't know what it is. I don't know what they are. I don't know what's happening. I don't know anything, except that I'm in danger. You're in danger." Fear, panic and sorrow all flared in Lars' eyes. He clenched his fists and kicked a yellowing tuft of grass. Indirectly or otherwise, Lars was responsible for those people's deaths and felt powerless in his frustration.

Alex continued to stare with urgent patience, waiting for an explanation, to which Lars conceded.

"Yes, I've seen them before, but not on this scale. It's like what happened the other night, before I found out about Lilah. The truth is I don't know what any of this is. But I ran into these things the other day – the night I didn't come home – the couple at a bar and... you know..."

Alex dropped his glare to his feet.

"When I woke up they seemed fine. They were asleep but fine. So I gathered my things and made for a swift exit. Then, they just attacked me. They were all possessed and murderous, with the yellowing skin, stinking of rotten eggs and their eyes – Alex, their eyes – they were horrible. The couple tried to kill me. I didn't want to, but I had to protect myself. They just..."

"How are you feeling, Lars?" Alex asked, not sure what to say, or wanting to relive his friend's story.

"They exploded, Alex! How do you think I feel?" he snapped, "They fucking exploded and I ran... ran like a fucking baby. And now it's happened again and I'm so sorry. I didn't want to bring you into this and I just want it all to stop. We can't go to the police – how do we explain all that? And besides, Shilling is involved. I don't know how, but she is and I don't trust her."

Lars felt a lump in his throat. It was suddenly hard to swallow and he was short of breath. Another sharp breeze cruelly caressed his face to unveil the bitter tears streaming down his cheek. Alex just stared. It was a tactic to encourage Lars to keep talking, and whilst Lars didn't want to, he involuntarily succumbed and kept going.

"And then Lilah goes and kills herself and now I'm left here, all on my own; Dad's out of the picture – Lord knows where – since this whole thing happened and the undead is trying to kill me. We're in trouble – I can't be near anyone. I'm dangerous. All I really have in this world is you and this box of crap." He pulled the wooden box from his bag and gestured it to Alex who received it silently.

Alex prised open the lid and gently surveyed the contents with his fingertips.

"She was really pretty," Alex remarked as he retrieved a photo of Lilah. "Are you sure you're even twins?" He grinned the widest grin, exposing his most sincere smile.

Lars wanted to be upset. He wanted to cry and scream and kick and punch anything he could. Ultimately, he was fed up of being fed up. Lars could not contain his misery any longer. He released the tension and let out a snigger.

Alex lowered himself to the floor and sat cross-legged on the grass to continue inspecting the contents of the rosewood box. An off-white stylus peered through the various treasures, which Alex liberated in disgust, "Ewww... Is this bone?"

"Hmmm... ivory, I think? Be careful with that, though."

"Why, is it expensive?"

"No. I mean, probably, but that's not what I mean. I had the weirdest dream about that last night."

"Really?" Alex brought the pen closer to his face for a better look, as though it would somehow enlighten him or secretly reveal Lars' dream to him.

"Yeah, I cut my finger on the nib and this weird black goo possessed me. It went through my eye sockets and everything." Lars rubbed his temple, remembering how real the experience had been. Instinctively he looked to his fingers, remembering the pain of slicing them open on the golden nib of the fountain pen. He was shocked to remember that the pen did actually cut him, as he stared at a crusty black scab that scored the breadth of three fingers.

A twig snapped nearby and both boys looked up to the direction from where it came. The sun was low and the sky was awash with streaks of yellow and blue that bled together on a lilac canvas. The boys looked back to each other, scrambled and jogged out of the woodland with each step carrying them a little faster than the last. Once they cleared the leering trees, they were surrounded by golden fields.

Lars peered back after hearing a louder, more pronounced crunch that came from behind them. He stopped and surveyed the brush they had just run from. Streams of yellow light pierced the clouds and illuminated a small patch of the woods. Another crunch, as though a large branch fell from a tree, came nearer.

Lars and Alex stared ferociously towards the trees in a bid to locate the origin of the snapping branches. Lances of light cut through the mysterious vista as the crunches turned to marching. Then the greenery parted in several places as the branches swung back and forth, giving way to invisible bodies.

More and more invisible creatures came forward and emerged from the trees. The boys were dumbfounded by what they were seeing. When a cloud parted in the purple sky, allowing an abundance of glorious blades of light to partly illuminate the clearing further, for a brief moment, Lars swore he saw a huge creature become visible under the gentle autumn sunlight.

It was big and covered in what looked like thick brown fur, which Lars mistook for something like a disfigured bear. Lars grabbed for Alex.

"Did you just see that?"

Alex nodded nervously. "... A-and there's more." he pointed out.

One by one, the iridescently invisible creatures stepped through the rays giving Alex and Lars a brief glimmer of their otherworldly and brutish appearance.

Without question, Alex and Lars ran as fast as their legs would take them.

Then, without warning, a huge explosion erupted from behind them that caused Lars and Alex to stop in their tracks and look at what was happening now.

A wall of fire now magically snaked its way across the field separating the boys from the beasts on the other side. An ear-piercing howl came from the forest as more, though smaller, explosions forced the monstrous bear-creatures back into the forest.

Hooded figures on horseback came galloping across the field, driving the beasts away, each one lobbing strange missiles that continued to bombard them with more and more mystical explosions. The hooded figures had strange attire and were dressed in purple cloaks with their faces covered by black cowls that made them resemble twenty-first-century contemporaries of Robin Hood and his Merry Men with black armour that looked like highly advanced riot gear.

Their weaponry was as equally strange to Lars and Alex. Many of the figures bore swords that sat at their side, whilst the majority had bows with arrows that rippled and exploded upon hitting their target, which in this case, seemed to be the floor. Those riders that did not have arrows were using slingshots to lob small white pouches in the direction of the bear-creatures, much to the same effect.

Amidst the commotion, Alex was captivated by the mystical battle plucked straight from a Peter Jackson trilogy and failed to see the stray ball of light from a rogue pouch come hurtling in his direction. The pre-exploded pouch was misfired from one of the hoods and the dangerous remnants were making their way through the air ready to cause some serious damage. It spun and hissed, crackling loudly with the static of lightning but hot and yellow like fire. Lars immediately clocked the glowing sack and instinctively leapt in front of his friend, forcing him out of the way.

Alex flew several feet and rolled into a clearing. He looked up and instinctively snapped his knees to his chest and covered his ears with hands, staring in horror at the sacrifice Lars had just committed while bracing himself for the oncoming explosion. Lars stood, paralysed in the crosshair of the approaching fireball. It whirled and roared, getting louder and louder as it approached. Alex was only a short distance away but could feel the heat as it flew closer.

Lars raised his arm to shield his face and squinted his eyes tightly, preparing for the worst.

Then, something clicked in Lars' atmosphere. The air hummed and his ears popped. He could taste that metallic tang in his mouth again, like chewing tin foil with a filling.

The oncoming missile, stopped in mid-air, suspended in the sky several meters above Lars' head. Alex watched in disbelief, before the flaming ball dropped straight out of the air as though it had hit an invisible wall of water, where it hissed, rolled to the floor and imploded on itself at Lars' feet. He eased his eyes open, checked himself over and grabbed an equally stunned Alex by the arm to run away, leaving the beast and hood battle in their wake.

Based on his track record, Lars did not want to hang around and see whether these riders were friends or foes. "We need to hurry and get out of here, now!" urged Lars.

Until now, Alex wanted to insist on phoning the police, but after their morning, he also knew that they would have a hard time explaining this. He also knew that deep down, his friend had something to do with what was happening.

"Yes", he agreed. "But I think we should avoid as many people as possible until we get to yours.

16. Thurston Manor

Lars and Alex took the entire day to make steady progress ploughing across the countryside with desperate determination to get to the safety of Thurston Manor. It was a voyage that now took them into the night and although they were already over halfway into their expedition to Lars' ancestral home, it was dark and late and Lars knew that there was still a fair way to go, especially on foot.

"We should rest," Lars said, breaking the long, though not uncomfortable silence. "Look, Alex, there's an old pillbox over there that we can sleep in for a few hours. You look knackered, so I'll take the first shift to keep watch while you rest up."

The hexagonal concrete structure sat in the middle of a vast field with views for miles around its loci. Alex had questioned if it was a good place to hide since it stuck out so deliberately on the landscape and that seemed like a bit of an obvious place to stop. Fortunately, the six individual loopholes that were once intended for rifles, meant that Lars would be able to spot trouble in the distance. The white moon was low and illuminated the entire sky in a rich swirl of blue and purple, giving the empty landscape a grey hue and making for relatively substantial visibility.

Inside, the floor was sodden and littered with browning foliage. Aside from some graffiti on the walls and scorch marks on the floor from what looked like a previous fire, it was relatively cosy. Its most recent inhabitants were probably pre-teens exploring the countryside during the summer holidays. There were still sweet wrappers, coke cans and BMX tracks scattered around the vicinity. Lars initially feared it was home to junkies or murderers, but remembered that this was on the outskirts of a sleepy little village in Kent, where nothing exciting ever happens. *Aside from the odd mass-possession of two train carriages, mysterious ghost creatures and mystical bandits, that is.*

Alex kicked a clearing in the tidiest of the six corners and slumped down the wall into a secure crouching position. He surveyed the damage of his arm, which was still bleeding, though it had calmed down quite significantly since earlier. Lars watched out of the corner of his eye as his friend retrieved a bottle of water from his bag and squeezed the contents over the various cuts, bites and scratches.

Lars had initially shared Alex's concern at the prospect of being bitten by one of those creatures earlier. However, despite his lack of experience, many hours had passed and Alex was not showing any signs of *weird shit.*

He continued to watch as Alex riffled through more of his things, which apparently proved quite difficult due to the poor lighting inside the pillbox and using his one, better arm. Taking a clean garment from the bag, he wrapped it over as much of his forearm as possible. Once he was cleaned up he cradled his bandage and got comfortable.

"Are you OK, Alex? How's your arm?"

"Yeah, it's fine thanks. A little tender, but the damage is just superficial and better now I've cleaned it" he affirmed. "Wake me up in an hour or so," to which Lars nodded in acknowledgement.

Lars stared out of each one of the loopholes for a few long moments and once he felt moderately happy with the apparent lack of danger, he stepped outside for some fresh air.

He sparked up a much-needed cigarette. The orange glow glimmered between his fingers and offered him the sweet release of doing nothing but focusing on taking one breath at a time. He gazed through the miles of vast open space that surrounded them, enjoying a chance to let his mind go blank for the moment.

At this hour the atmosphere was laced heavily with the salt from the not-too-far-off sea, a smell that he had always associated with coming home. The air was also spiked with the fragrance of fresh leaves, leaving Lars with an overwhelming head rush and a strong sense that they were not far from sanctuary.

Lars took another puff of his cigarette and quietly laughed to himself as he recalled the prospect of returning home in order to get away from the stress and drama of school.

How wrong that had been.

Satisfied with the apparent level of safety, for the time being, he made his way back into the pillbox and slumped down the wall, across the way from Alex. His friend was blissfully peaceful in his sleep. Lars looked him up and down in the greying light and saw that his shoes were muddy and his clothes torn, not to mention covered in bloody wounds of various severity. His black hair stuck to his forehead in moist clumps, and his breathing was heavy but pleasant.

Lars continued to watch until the room blackened under the submission of his own lazing eyelids. Neglecting his duty, he opted for some rest and fell asleep.

***

Lars dreamt of magpies, bobbing in and about the carrion of a train; an obvious regurgitation of the day's previous events. The greedy birds scavenged about the deserted carriage, plucking and pecking at the greying flesh of each lifeless corpse. He paced up the aisle, disgusted by the birds' grotesque behaviour. The faces of the bodies were hidden; either face down, covered in some way, or mauled by the relentless feasting of the magpies. A splutter of coughs echoed from the far end of the carriage and caught Lars' attention. He forced his feet into an ethereal run and located the victim. Lars placed a hand on the shoulder of the body and rolled it over to see his face. As he did the body exploded into a fleet of magpies, all fluttering and squawking as they emitted his chest like some twisted nursery rhyme. When the last bird fluttered away, the eyes of a familiar face burst open and his mouth moved to pronounce: "One for sorrow, two for joy, three for a girl and four for a boy, five for silver, six for gold, sev-"

Lars soon woke up, with no recollection of the dream.

***

The boys roused at the break of dawn, where the sleepy sun had already emerged over the horizon and painted the sky with glorious red and orange streaks. A thin layer of mist had been spun along the ground of the surrounding field, like iridescent webs that twinkled in the waking day. It was eerily peaceful.

Alex and Lars had fortunately endured a much needed full night of sleep and both felt much better for it. The pain in Alex's arm had eased, though a little itchy, it otherwise felt good. Plus they had not been ambushed, kidnapped or murdered in their sleep after neglecting their watch duties, which was a big bonus.

"Right, let's get a move on. We'll be at the manor in a short while," commanded Lars.

"I know it's early and we've been a little preoccupied, Lars, but have you thought about phoning home to let them know we're coming, or even about sending someone to pick us up?" Alex offered lazily.

In the harsh light of day, this seemed like the most obvious course of action but Lars still was unsure about whether Thurston Manor would be the haven they needed. Despite this, he felt sheepish and kicked his toe slyly into the dirt. In the heat of escaping for their lives, his primary concern had been with immediate escape on foot and not beyond that.

"No, I'll give it a go now. At this time, Mrs Heath, our housekeeper, will be up."

Lars retrieved his phone from his bag, scrolled through his contacts and called home. He held his breath as the phone kept ringing, over and over, into his ear.

"Hmmm... No answer; I'll try the other line," he said flatly. There was no answer again and the line was dead this time. "I think we should hurry... something feels off and no one's answering."

"It *is* still early." Alex offered, rhetorically.

"Thurston Manor has a staff of twenty-something people – gardeners, cleaners, cooks, security – someone would have answered the phone. Something's wrong." Lars said matter-of-factly, trying not to sound pretentious.

"Lars, why on Earth would your Father have so many people working for him?"

Alex knew the answer as soon as he completed the sentence, to which Lars just raised an eyebrow in response. Alex nodded, accepted that it was the ostentatious necessity of a narcissistic aristocrat, grabbed his belongings and led Lars out of the pillbox into the morning.

They marched on a short while coming across little more than a murder of magpies every now and again. Lars paid little attention but Alex silently nodded to the largest of the birds, whom he could have sworn nodded right back. The morning up until that point was unnervingly uneventful.

If the last few days are anything to go by, someone or something should have made an attempt on my life by now.

And now I've got Alex involved in this mess too.

I just need to get us home.

Soon the glorious architectural structure of Thurston Manor pierced the rolling idylls like a whale breaches the ocean surface. The ancestral family home was the grandest building Alex had ever seen. Its presence demanded dominion over its surrounding landscape and was seen from a great distance. Even from here, he could tell that the manor house was ginormous and incredibly beautiful. Alex was in awe. Lars, on the other hand, remained incredibly silent and kept his eyes to the ground as he marched onwards.

Alex was well and truly in awe of the magnificently regal structure from the moment he clapped eyes on it from across the grass sea. His father has been in a rock band and his mother had been a famous model, so he was used to ostentatious and flamboyant things, but this, however, was on a whole new level.

He deduced that Lars' home was actually more of a castle or fortress, and certainly not far off from the size of one. As they drew closer he could also see where the original, ancient part of the building had seen many additions to the structure over the course of its long and rich history. Lars had never spoken much about his home, but Alex had learned that parts of the Thurston Estate went as far back as the Roman Empire, and the stewardship of the house and grounds had been with the Thurston family from about the same time.

The house was a Medieval mash of historical parts; some gloriously Gothic, others brazenly Baroque and nearly all of it awesomely ancient to produce a creation of the most beautiful and terrific architectural features. Its style resembled that of an elaborate cathedral, monastery or extravagant private school; Lilah had once told her brother that she thought Hogwarts an appropriate moniker, to which Lars had scoffed "minus the magic and giant snake in the cellar". From this distance, the looming towers and turrets gave the building a strange skeletal appearance, which was emphasised by the shadows cast upon the niches and archivolts.

Most distinguishable from this vista was the Great Hall, which sat in the middle as the main body of the building with the buttresses looking like the ribcage of a great leviathan. The Great Hall was most discernible from the south side due to the huge stained-glass rose window that had captivated a young Lars and Lilah, how the light would cast through it all day long, projecting a kaleidoscope of reds and blues across the interior.

On the other hand, while Lars could not deny the terrifying beauty of his ancient home, the appeal of the building was tainted by sad and painful memories. It was the shrine to his mother, the chamber his father then ignored him for the years after and Thurston Manor was also the place where he and his sister became strangers.

They had been on Thurston land since way before they left the train but as they approached the grounds proper, the boys followed the huge red-brick wall that surrounded the immediate property. They reached the main entrance, which Lars was shocked to find wide open.

"This is bad. The guards would never leave the gate open." Lars then immediately realised that the security team may not have had a choice. "Look at this – what do you suppose did this, Alex?" Upon closer inspection, they found that the once majestic wrought iron gates had in fact somehow been bent over and warped before eventually being blown off their hinges with some great force. "Are these... melted?"

Lars' stomach suddenly dropped at the realisation of imminent danger again.

The third time's the charm.

As they neared the building, both recognised instantly that something was wrong. Many of the ornate windows on the ground floor were smashed through, leaving jagged gaping holes in the walls. A huge cavity had been blasted in the wall to the side of the Great Hall that had obliterated the once glorious stained-glass rose, which had caved in on itself and spattered gem-coloured debris all over the floor.

At that moment, Lars was about to run in before Alex immediately grabbed his arm, which in turn mentally pulled him back into the realm of practicality.

"Wait, Lars! Look at these," he said, gesturing to the mud on either side of the gravel path, "they're hoof prints; probably from our friends on horseback. And they certainly seemed to have this kind of firepower yesterday."

"What do we do?" Lars paused and surveyed the area. "It seems quiet now."

"Is there another way in?" Alex offered, "The front door has been blown wide open – I don't think it's safe – what if they're still here waiting for us?"

Lars nodded in agreement. "Follow me – we'll go through the servants' quarters."

As they ducked through the foliage towards the west of the building, they noticed that many of the haunting features had been destroyed. Casualties of some ferocious ambush, the stone grotesques and gargoyles that once leered over the grounds from the house now lie in crumbs on the floor. Mighty trees that dotted the gardens lay in scattered splinters across the gravel driveway, and of course, many more gaping holes had been blasted through the walls of the house.

"Lars!" Alex's voice was hoarse and urgent. "Is that..." he struggled to complete the sentence. "...Is that blood?" Perhaps one of the few remaining windows was smeared in a glorious splatter of crimson. It took a moment for Lars to realise that it was indeed a huge blood stain and not stained glass.

It was strange for Lars to be walking through the grounds like this since every step struck a whirlwind of emotions for him. He kept thinking how oppressive this place had always been for him, feeling more like a luxurious prison than stately home. But now, seeing it beaten up and defenceless, having been unable to provide security and protect its inhabitants as it had done for centuries, left Lars feeling angry and unusually possessive. Most of all, he felt guilty for not being around to defend it and for having taken it for granted over the years.

The Servants Quarters, an affectionate moniker since the Estate now had employees, were sealed by a knobbly studded door with archaic black iron features. As children, and unbeknownst to their father, Lars and Lilah would run around and pester the kitchen staff for treats during the summer holidays. They would bang on the heavy metal knocker, wait for the clunk of shoes on the stone floor and then the clink of the latch. As the door squeaked open, Mrs Jones the cook or Mrs Heath the head of housekeeping would slyly meet them, sending them on their way with a handful of freshly baked goods or biscuits from the pantry.

This same door now sat ajar with a collage of bloody handprints over the age-bleached wood. Lars pushed it wide open, chilled by the same squeak that had only moments before invoked warm memories. His stomach churned with disgust as he stepped over a fresh pool of crimson blood, wondering whose it was.

Once inside, they stood in the servants' kitchen horrified by the scene, silently absorbing the massacre that lay before them. The kitchen resembled an abattoir rather than the heart of the home. Faces Lars knew and grew up with, now slaughtered like animals, were violently dashed about the quarters. Among the victims were the once generous Mrs Jones, several kitchen staff and Oakley, the butler, who looked morbidly dapper on the floor. All of their throats had been slit; a far from merciful execution.

To Lars, it seemed that hours passed in the few moments it took him to realise what had happened.

The boys were unceremoniously brought back to reality when an old oak panel aside of the oven revealed itself to be a secret door. Lars felt the hairs on his neck stand on end and Alex jumped back at the sound.

Like many old houses, the Thurston Estate had many secret passages and rooms. Typically, they were used for the servants to move about the house quickly and quietly without making themselves known to the gentry in the main house. This particular one was new to Lars and definitely lived up to its clandestine name.

From inside came a wheezing cough and a hacking splatter as someone struggled to clear their throat. The boys braced themselves to fight the creature from where the noises came. When Lars peered around the corner, he found an injured elderly woman sloped awkwardly on the floor. She fought to catch her breath and looked awful in blood-stained clothes and her face was covered in bruises. To be fair, she was far better off than the rest of the staff.

She looked up and new life warmed her complexion, "Thank heavens, Lars, you're safe!" she coughed with sheer joy.

Lars recognised her at once and was elated to see a cherished face. He could not believe it; so many emotions whirled around his body and he had so many things to say. So, he said the first one to spring to mind, "Mrs Heath..."

17. The Truth

"Yes, boy. Stop gawking," the housekeeper jibed from down on the floor.

"Are you OK, Mrs Heath? What the fuck happened here?" Lars forgot himself in the excitement of finding a safe and familiar face, not meaning to swear in the presence of someone he respected so greatly.

"Mind your language, young man," she snapped, "for all that money your father spent on your education, I'd hope that you had a wider vocabulary at your disposal. A young lord shouldn't speak so profanely. Take it from me – you weren't raised with a foul mouth and you most certainly aren't too big for me to wash your mouth out with soap. Now, be a dear and help an old lady up."

Lars awkwardly half-laughed at her joke knowing good and well that Mrs Heath was half-serious and definitely not one to make idle threats. With her beaten and bloody face before him, Lars struggled to see the funny side of life right now. Though, he appreciated her spirit in spite of the tragic circumstances.

"Excuse me, but who did this to you? Was it the Hoods? We saw them yesterday morning, firing arrows and throwing bombs at sh-, we saw them throwing bombs at shtuff," interjected an impatient Alex, who successfully recovered from almost cursing in front of the injured woman. Alex was standing amongst the latest wash of horror, having experienced more first-hand inexplicable danger since leaving the school with his friend than he ever cared to in his life. Right now he had perspective and did not see the sense in small talk and hanging around. If they were in danger again he wanted to know and he wanted to know how to get everyone to safety.

Mrs Heath smiled towards Alex through her bruises with warmth and serenity before turning to Lars to ask, "and who might this chap be?"

"Mrs Heath, this is my friend, Alex, from school. Alex, this is Mrs Heath," said Lars as he surveyed the room for danger, obviously sharing Alex's concerns for their safety.

"Oh my! Alex, aren't you handsome," she coughed. "You look so familiar. Have I seen you around here before?"

The question made Alex feel awkward. He looked like his mother and she had once had one of the most recognisable faces on the planet for the best part of two decades. She stared at him, not knowing where she could place him, before hacking a cough into her fist. Alex did not like the sound and suspected that her state of health was worse than it initially looked, which itself was very bad. He faltered in his response, which prompted Lars to clear his throat and in turn, clear the atmosphere. He then spoke slowly with heavy words to his old friend and carer.

"Mrs Heath, we've had a weird few days and I think I could be in trouble."

Lars had failed to get her up and move her properly so instead settled for sitting Mrs Heath in a more comfortable position, still on the floor, as she could not move due to her indeterminable injuries. She was definitely in a bad way.

"I should call you an ambulance – Alex, go get help!" he barked but Mrs Heath bit back, causing Alex to pause in his tracks.

"No. There isn't enough time. I'm old and I've been blessed to spend this brief moment with you. Tell me, Lord Lars, what's happened to you?" she soothed.

Lars proceeded to pour his heart out. He told her about his 'sleepover' and how his 'friends' had attacked him. He assumed that hearing about his threesome was not something that would sit very well after the comment about his swearing.

The Innocent Generation and all that.

Lars then went on to describe how the homeless man had shouted at him about magpies on the train, which in turn led to the two train carriages being possessed in the same way as his 'sleepover friends' and how the two of them had barely escaped with their lives. Lars then explained their cross-country hike to Thurston Manor, their run-in with the weird ethereal creatures in the wood and how the Hoods had intervened with fireballs and horses. Alex clocked a brief flare of her nostrils at the mention of the semi-invisible beasts but she otherwise sat wheezing and listening intently with little expression.

"... And at the heart of it all, Lilah killed herself and I don't know where Dad is..." He paused to catch his breath, choking on the tears that presented him with a painful lump in his throat. "And... you're not fazed by any of this, are you, Mrs Heath?"

In return for his story, she gave a sad, knowing smile before making a heartfelt admission. "Lars, I sent those *hoods,* as you call them. They are my people and I sent them to watch over you.

Well, it turns out I was being watched. I bloody knew it!

"I had scouts stationed at your school to escort you back when the time was right, but you had already left before they could approach you safely. And when I got word of that attack on the train, I knew that bad magic was afoul. Again, my people were too late to assist and you were already gone. You were both too quick for my clanspeople."

The boys sat and listened intently, as though they were hearing a bedtime story from Mrs Heath, who in reality was giving the boys some much-needed answers.

"Wait a minute – you said *magic?*" Lars questioned, although appreciated that it oddly made a lot of sense in light of his experiences over the last few days.

"There are things you need to know my dear Lars; there are powerful forces at work here, most of which are greater than you, and equally want to do you great harm.

"You see, I am a Gypsy and I come from an ancient clan, known as the Arête. My family, like yours, is very, very old and our sacred duty has been to watch and guard the Thurston family for many centuries. I don't really know how to explain this, but Lars, your father – and your mother, in fact – both come from supremely important and powerful Witch dynasties."

"Hold on." Alex interrupted. "Gypsy soldiers... Magic spells... Exactly how hard did you hit your head, Mrs Heath? Lars, do you believe any of this?"

"Alex, as crazy as this all sounds, there's a part of me that sees that this is the only stuff that makes sense so far, and at this point, I have to be open-minded. Even if it sounds insane..." Lars retorted.

Commanding her audience once again, Mrs Heath continued, "I must come clean..." taking a brief moment to gather her thoughts and think about how she was going to enlighten the boys. They needed perspective. "First, I need to start at the beginning. You're ignorant and that's your father's fault. And mine, I suppose."

The boys just glared towards the wise woman.

"We've all heard the Bible's Genesis – the story of creation – and how everything in the beginning was dark, God said: "Let there be light" and there was light, and so on. Well, this is only half true. There was indeed darkness, but it was certainly not the beginning of everything.

"My people tell Genesis slightly differently. When the Earth was new, it was a far different place to what it is now and it was a paradise. Earth, Pangea, the Universe – we were all created by the immortal beings, and they lived among their mortal subjects on the terrestrial realm. Life was good and harmonious. The mortals would tend to the earth and waters and in return, the immortal beings would provide everything they needed to sustain their lives. Their treaty was one of power and loyalty.

"Unfortunately, the brightest lights cast the longest shadows and dark forces threatened a plague upon the new universe. These *Daemons*, were the darkness personified. They are the ancestors of the beasts my people tried to ward off for you yesterday. Back then, they were titanic creatures of pure, undiluted evil; brutal and merciless beasts that would act without remorse or regard for consequence. They wanted the new world for themselves and would stop at nothing to destroy the work of the Immortals and mortals.

"They waged a war that lasted millennia, leaving the universe violated as it was shredded and torn to pieces under the brutal destruction of these powerful forces." Mrs Heath paused to let the room breath.

This is nuts but would make a great film.

"To preserve what was left of their precious creation, drastic action needed to be taken. The story goes that the most powerful of the Immortals used their most dangerous magic to summon a portal and banish the Daemons into the great abyss that lies far outside of this dimension. It worked but came at a great cost, something our people know as The Immortal Sacrifice.

"While mortal blood is true and pure, it's frail and ever-fleeting. Immortal blood, on the other hand, is miraculous and the price to rid the universe of the beasts would cost many immortal lives.

As always, the Immortals gave willingly and generously. They gave their immortality for us and banished the Daemons to the netherworld and its huge abyss. By this time, the remaining Immortals had to take leave of this realm and retire to the dimension they themselves came from since their power was a collective and their sacrifice had left them diminished.

"However, before leaving, the remaining Immortals had a parting gift. Two mortal clans; the most faithful and strongest allies were blessed by the deities. First, the Witches, the clans who had been the most favoured and faithful to the Immortals, were entrusted with the secrets of the universe and their women could bend and manipulate the laws of nature to their will. This became the birth of Magic.

"The second of the clans were the Gypsies and their gift was to respect and guard the immortal secrets of nature, blessing them with the most powerful of knowledge and the ability to cast spells. While Magic is in their blood, they themselves are not innately magical and do not have magic in their soul.

"Urgh, but you know what people are like. Humans in general always feel hard-done-by and want what someone else has. We fight, we wage wars, and even to this day, Witches and Gypsies are sworn enemies, each jealous of the favouritism shown by the Immortals."

Mrs Heath sighed, as though she knew of these troubles first-hand.

"Who knows if that's how it went down, though? I think that the Immortals probably watch in disappointment as both Witches and Gypsies abuse their gifts and each other."

Lars interjected, having many questions following this story – one that he had heard as a child, but had long forgotten. "But what has this got to do with me? You said witches were women; does that make my father a wizard – am I like Harry Potter or Gandalf now? Do I have powers, because I'm not sure if turning people to zombies counts."

"Not quite." She interrupted, "You and your father are indeed witches, but like Gypsies, you don't have *powers,* as you put it. You carry the gene to your children, meaning that your son will carry the gene and your daughter will have a magical gift that often manifests as a unique power or ability. Your mother and father were both witches, meaning that your sister is... was... capable of performing magic. Like Gypsies, you can perform spells, but your father was never keen on sharing that knowledge with you..."

Lars had never been so hurt by such a statement. A whole history – a legacy – and a heritage lie before him, and his father had point-blank decided to deny him of it. "So, Lilah died not knowing any of this?"

Mrs Heath's sudden wash of guilt was unmistakable. "She knew everything, Lars. Her power manifested after the death of your mother and she was trained and raised in the craft by your father."

This was a low blow. Your parents are not supposed to have favourite children, but Lars had always suspected his father's favouritism towards Lilah and this was the punch in the gut that painfully confirmed everything.

"What was her power?" Alex chimed in, breaking Lars' concentration.

"I don't actually know. Lord Jude kept Lady Lilah under strict lock and key. He was a suspicious man and suspected Gypsies were living amongst him."

He wasn't wrong.

"So, you're saying that you're an actual spy? I'm so confused right now..." Alex scratched his head, trying to make sense of this fantastical soap opera situation.

"Yes," she coughed, unfazed that blood had appeared on her hands. "You heard the story, our people are mortal enemies. Your father is a powerful and dangerous man and what's more, he's unstable. More so, since the death of your mother. I was charged, as was my mother, and her mother before her, to watch your family's ancestors. Prophecy tells that something dangerous will be born out of the Thurston bloodline, and it is my sacred duty to stop it."

At that moment, something – a mirror or window – crashed from the top of the stairs that led to one of the manor's many corridors. They were not alone and Alex and Lars both came to attention like a pair of dogs on the hunt, looking to one another with urgent desperation and painfully knowing what they had to do. They had to fight. The boys leapt up from Mrs Heath's side and made their way out of the secret corridor from which they were hidden, back into the kitchen.

When this part of the manor was built, the kitchen was placed slightly underground with the rest of the house built on top of it. The idea had been that the heat from the kitchen would warm the rest of the house, which it did. From the kitchen, there was a large wooden door that guarded a short spiral stone staircase that connected it to the rest of the house. There was also an identical door at the top, which had just creaked, indicating that it had been opened. Small but precise steps gently careened down the stone stairway.

Lars edged towards this kitchen door, grabbing a rolling pin from the large oak table in the middle of the room as he walked past it. Alex followed, pulling a huge carving knife from the rack which hissed as it left its dock. Their hearts beating and their blood rushing about their bodies.

Lars paused to the side of the door in order to be out of sight when the intruder walked in. He could hear the approaching sound of shoes on the stone stairs that lead to where they were standing in the kitchen. He looked back to his friend, raising his rolling pin over his shoulder like a rounders bat, ready to take a deadly swing. Nodding a silent gesture, which Alex understood as the command to attack when ready, he dutifully positioned the knife in an offensive position.

The descending steps edged closer. Lars' heart pumping against his chest and hearing the throb of blood rushing in his ears.

Suddenly, the figure rounded the stairs and saw Alex first, but Lars jumped out from around the corner and brought the full force of the rolling pin down on the figure that now appeared before them.

With the speed and precision of an adder, the intruder grabbed Lars' arm with incredible speed, twisted his hand and disabled the rolling pin in a matter of seconds. As if that was not enough, the figure then squeezed his arm and contorted it into an even more uncomfortable position that brought him to his knees before the hooded figure.

Alex was about to charge when the figure pulled off their cowl and pointed towards him. "Quick – Behind you!"

Lars looked up and Alex spun one-hundred-and-eighty degrees to the secret passage they had only moments ago left Mrs Heath.

Slowly and deadly, the injured old lady now crept out as an unrecognisable figure. Her complexion was instantly sallow, her eyes white with death and she stunk that immediate and hideous smell of festering flesh and rotten eggs. Lars and Alex were devastated to see that Mrs Heath was possessed.

18. Girl Trouble

The grotesque Mrs Heath waddled into full view with her greedy arms reaching straight for Lars.

This was the first time he had seen the magic take control of someone he knew and loved. What happens to the body when it is possessed is an instant transformation; an eruption of decay and a manifestation of all that is physically vile. To see this woman – someone who had practically raised him – now reduced to a hideous creature, was the most devastating thing he ever had to witness.

He stepped back several paces, shaking his head in disbelief at what was coming towards him. *No! This can't be happening, not to her. We literally just left her side... We walked away and then this happened... But how? Why?*

Lars was not concentrating on what he was doing and in stepping backwards, he knocked his leg on the arm of a sturdy oak chair and stumbled awkwardly. He fell and on his way down, knocked his head on the corner of the mighty oak table, which caused streams of searing red liquid to trickle down his face.

The sight of blood procured the beast from within the former housekeeper who savagely lunged forwards to Lars within the blink of an eye. In life, which was literally just moments ago, she would not have been capable of such a feat. Lars cowered under the protection of his arms, thinking he was done for. At that moment, Alex vainly attempted to throw the oak obstacles out of his way. He wanted to dive-tackle the crazed Mrs Heath to save his helpless friend. But he was stopped in his tracks and pipped to the post by the once-cowled newcomer.

Alex barely got a look in but could tell that their defender was a girl and that she was similarly dressed to what he now understood were gypsies, although her garb was different in some way and he could not yet decide how.

He watched as the powerful girl flew across the length of the room, passing Lars, and landed a double-footed kick in the chest of the demonic Mrs Heath, temporarily knocking the now-hideous creature back out of the way. The Gypsy girl landed on her back but whipped her legs up to her chest before pouncing to her feet, a move that massively impressed Alex.

Like a riled rattlesnake or poised cobra, the warrior recoiled into a strong stance that was as equally defensive as it was threatening. Her gaze was ferociously determined; a look that radiated the confidence of someone who was about to slay a bloodthirsty monster and secure a rescue for herself, the Thurston boy and his good-looking companion.

Readying herself for a fight, she calmly unsheathed her xiphos; a small double-edged sword favoured by the ancient Greeks. Alex knew the type of sword from the various RPGs he played on his Xbox and was proud to have picked up something about historical warfare. He admired her weapon, which was seemingly forged with a strange and unusual metal because of the way it did not glimmer with the silvery sheen of a normal blade. Not that Alex was too familiar with ancient weaponry, but he had watched Game of Thrones and been to museums. In fact, her sword was a dense black, as though carved from polished stone. The blade was less than half a metre in length and tapered like an elongated leaf from an exotic palm. The girl held it with tremendous poise and strength.

Disabling Mrs Heath gave Alex the opportunity to dash to his friend's side where he landed a spontaneous hug around him. The demonic figure lay on the floor, though from the sounds she wheezed and spluttered, the boys could tell that she would not stay there for long.

Mrs Heath spun with both horrifying speed and monstrous agility as she landed perfectly on all fours before proceeding to savagely pounce towards the boys with all the menace of a deranged hyena. She specifically sidelined the girl who was nearer, who in turn had predicted the creature's move and anticipated a counter attack. Just as Mrs Heath ran past, the warrior gypsy streamed an armed hand through the air and sliced the head off the newly reanimated Mrs Heath, before she could lunge for the helpless boys.

Her severed head rolled across the room, landing at the feet of Lars. Milky eyes glared up to them for a moment of awkward grief. Just as Lars was about to move it, the eyes became pulpy and began to melt in their sockets. Within seconds the entire head started to melt and decompose right before their very own eyes. Finally, the body did the same thing, only from several feet away. The putrid smell of egg intensified with even more aggression as the body folded in on itself in soggy lumps, that fizzled and dribbled away on the floor.

Alex looked to the hideous decapitated figure that was spitting and hissing from across the room and emitting that disgusting odour of sulphur before whispering softly into his friend's neck, "I know what she meant to you."

Lars eventually looked at the tragic and horrific remains of someone he had called a friend, not knowing what to say or do. Just as he was about to spew the first thing that came to mind, which incidentally was the desire to spew, the walls of the room shook from an explosion from somewhere upstairs. Pots and pans rattled off the shelves and plates showered the floor with flakes of broken porcelain.

All three looked up and heard the rowdy voices of hostile bodies making their way down the stairs to them. The girl beckoned the boys through Mrs Heath's secret passageway, "We need to get out of here!" she hushed them urgently through gritted teeth.

Better the devil you know.

Without question they all bundled into the passageway, shutting the door behind them. It revealed itself to be a long cavern, where the boys instinctively retrieved their phones from their pockets to illuminate the darkness.

"Ooh..." The girl acknowledged and admired the fancy piece of technology that now lit the dank corridor.

"Do you know what this is?" Lars gestured, his tone a little patronising for someone that just saved his life, "It's a mobile phone."

Without warning, she punched him square in the chest, knocking the wind out of him. "Are you serious? Of course I bloody know what it is! It's the latest iPhone, you div. I'm due an upgrade. Do you think I'm from the effin Stone Age or something?" she objected.

Alex sniggered, though he would never admit that he would have made the same assumption, what with her Robin Hood ensemble complete with sword and riding boots.

It was upon closer inspection that they could see that her body armour was indeed 21st Century, like the ones the Hoods wore from last night. Though instead of purple, her hooded cloak was black.

She was powerful and strong. Not just in her physical appearance but in her posture, her aura and the face framed by her chocolate hair. The freckled skin across her nose and cheeks as well as her muscular arms were lightly tanned and weathered from what looked like a result of spending plenty of time outside among the elements.

"What happened up there?" Lars asked in a hushed tone. A commotion was unravelling just the other side of the door in the kitchen.

She placed her long finger upon his lips, keeping it there to silence him. Alex felt awkward. She retrieved a glass vial from her satchel, placed some powder into the liquid, returned the bung and shook it several times. The aggressive swirling caused the solution to radiate a brilliant yellow light, which she used as a torch. She then nodded her head down the dank shaft and led the way.

"Wow," said Alex in awe.

"It's a potion." her retort laced with a playful smirk. "Does your iPhone do that?"

Alex silently sniggered once again.

Yes, it's got a torch feature.

They walked in silence along the natural stone corridors that seemed to descend into the bowels of the estate's foundations. The air down here was stale and damp and made the atmosphere suffocating.

As though sensing the awkwardness, the girl piped up to address the boys.

"My name is Æleanir, but you can call me Ælla," she introduced herself, "You must tell me, because I'm having trouble understanding you both, why would you possess that old lady and most importantly, how did you do it – was it a spell or potion? Because I've never seen anything like it. Why would you do something like that?"

"Ella, we didn't do it. You did!" Lars and Alex chimed in unison with great contention in their voices. "Didn't you?"

"Firstly, it's Ælla, like AY-la. And secondly, I figured as much." She said suspiciously. "So, who did?" she chided, almost addressing herself.

"Look, I'm Lars Thurston, I live here," he started, "And this is Alex Wood. What were you doing–" before being abruptly interrupted by Ælla.

"Hold on, *the* Alex Wood? as in Roger Wood? No way! I love Silk Sword. I have posters of your dad on my wall..." Her awe at having met a celebrity was obvious.

Both were shocked by this response. Lars tried exceptionally hard not to use the "do you know who I am" line and not sound like a dick. Alex tried to play it down, genuinely not keen to discuss his family, especially with this stranger, even if she had just saved their lives.

"OK, I'll tell you what I know, which probably isn't a great deal in the grand scheme of things, but right now it's all we've got."

They dropped their pace slightly and walked at a more comfortable speed to catch their breath and take stock of what was happening. They were sheltered by the chalky walls of the tunnel, which appeared to taper out through various other routes along the way. It was dark, save for two phones and a potion but you could tell where tunnels led elsewhere in the cavern.

"Lars, I know exactly who you are. Your family is legendary in the magical world and just as infamous. Not unlike your old man, Alex." He gulped awkwardly and was grateful for the darkness that camouflaged his blush.

"I'm Gypsy – I'm guessing you know what that means?" They nodded, still heading to the tunnel's mouth which was still some way off since the light at the end was little more than a large dot. Behind them it was silence.

"I'm a scout for a neighbouring clan, the Fædan," Ælla continued, "I got wind of the commotion on the railroad and how the Aréte were caught up in it somehow and suspected that there was danger at the Thurston Estate. If there was magical trouble afoot, I suspected that your household would be involved somehow.

"When I arrived, the manor had already fallen and judging by the damage, I'm guessing witches are at fault. That much destruction can only be done with magic," she deduced, "I was searching the house for signs of life and it was only when I heard you two in the kitchen I suspected that you may need my help.

"Mrs Heath was a good woman," she reflected, "I didn't know her too well, personally, but the elders spoke highly of her. That's a shitty way to go." Ælla clenched her fists and her nostrils flared. "Whoever is doing this, must be stopped immediately."

The trio stood still under the chalk ceiling. It was quiet in the tunnel, apart from the dripping of water that cascaded down the slimy white walls. If you listened carefully, you could hear the crashing waves from the sea outside, but no one paid attention yet.

Ælla turned to face the boys, "I have to say, that was one intense possession up there. In fact, I've never seen anything like that before." She looked down and frantically darted her eyes as she tried to work out why or how this was happening.

"What does possession usually look like?" Alex asked with morbid intrigue.

"Well... it doesn't look like that. It doesn't really have that kind of effect, usually. I mean, the most you could usually expect is a bit of tinnitus or even a slight nose bleed. That – however – was full-on horrific. I've never known anyone to die from it before."

"You lobbed her head off! We might have helped her!" spat Lars. He was too upset for manners and rationality.

"I'm sorry, but she was dead the minute you left her side. I'm not the one who killed her and neither did you. It's hard I know, but we need to work together to fix this. Blaming me won't bring her back and I'm not sorry for saving your lives. My sword was a mercy, but I swear to use it for justice," she stated and Alex smiled.

"This keeps happening," Lars responded glumly, before going into detail about his previous victims.

Ælla offered a more sympathetic and practical approach upon her enlightenment to Lars' troubles over the last few days. Logic would help here and she had the level head to know that instinctively. She went on, "I'm no witch, but it would appear that someone is casting, or at least trying to cast, a possession spell either on these people – or on you..." She paused and clocked Lars directly, just as the penny seemingly dropped in the wishing well of her mind. "... But for some reason, you seem to be immune.

"OK," she began, knowing that this was a long-shot, but by far the best explanation she had at her disposal, "Someone seemingly wants to possess you, Lars, and if you are immune, which I believe is the case, then the charm caster is unaware of the effect you have and is using an incredibly intense spell to try and bypass your barrier. The result in doing so is something of a magical fallout that is affecting your loci and everyone in the vicinity. It would seem that your protection is impenetrable because the harder they try to possess you, the more dangerously disfigured the collateral damage is."

Ælla's analogy was beginning to make sense.

"Hold on, Alex has also been exposed, like on the train, and hasn't been possessed. He was even bitten by one. Also, you weren't affected either, come to think of it," Lars added, "In fact, how do we know that you weren't the one casting it in the first place."

"Hmmm... firstly, I don't think Alex's injury is anything to worry about. They're not ghouls or zombies and secondly, Lars, I'm a gypsy, not a witch. My people and I don't have anywhere near that kind of power. The best we could come up with is hypnosis, and even then, it's more of a guided dream sequence with some snazzy hallucinogens."

As they carried on walking through the secret cavern, Lars analysed his previous encounters, taking some form of bitter relief in believing that he may have finally found a few answers to the questions he had about these tragic occurrences happening around him.

So it was attempted possession. And when I streaked out the bedroom, they became affected. And the homeless man on the train, only once he left my side to inspect the neighbouring carriage did he become afflicted.

Lars toyed with the idea that he somehow acts as a magic repellent or protective totem since Alex and Ælla have both been immune also, thanks to whatever he was doing. He realised with a heavy heart that he is probably his friend's only chance of safety and that now Ælla would rely on him too.

Ælla's tone brought Lars back to reality from his train of thought. "It's obvious that someone is after you, Lars. Tell me more – there must be something."

He inhaled and looked to Alex for support, who nodded with an encouraging half smile.

"Well, we came here for safety, but that's now out of the question. I'm here for answers. My sister is dead, my father is missing and I've discovered that I come from a long line of mystical forces, most of whom are apparently out to hurt me. What's more, weird stuff just keeps getting weirder and people are getting hurt and it needs to stop."

"Let's get a move on then," said Alex, "I see light up ahead and we can figure out what to do next outside in the fresh air."

"Agreed." Stated Ælla with an approving air of authority. "Let's meet with my clan, the Fædan, and go from there. They'll know what to do."

"Wait a minute. How do I know I can trust you, Ælla? If my family are witches and yours are gypsies, aren't we supposed to be mortal enemies or something?" Lars asked out of genuine concern. Not for fear of betrayal or his life, but because he was genuinely beginning to like Ælla. She and Alex had been the only things to make sense in the last few days. Well, and Mrs Heath, but that was too fresh and he would need time to process his grief.

Later. There's always later.

"You can't trust me, not really, but you can only trust yourself and your decisions. That being said, I swear to the Immortals, a son of rock royalty is not dying on my watch."

And Alex blushed once again.

19. Negation

The triad of youngsters continued through the secret cavern that had led from the kitchen to a yet undetermined destination. From the cacophony of outside sounds that had flooded the tunnel as they approached its mouth, they could tell that they were reaching the sea. The crashing of frothy waves had echoed down the tunnel calling them closer with every lap against the rocks, while seagulls chimed in with their chorus of backing vocals. When the tunnel eventually broke and they were outside, the inglorious midday greeted them with an exposure of blinding glare from high up in the grey-white sky.

The trio emerged with blinking eyes that struggled to adjust after being submerged in darkness for so long. They looked back to see where they came from and were in awe of the leering white cliff that stood at least a hundred metres above their heads.

At the foot of the cliffs lay a small cove ordained with a carpet of polished black pebbles dotted with tufts of wiry silver grass that waved in the harsh sea breeze. Calmer waters lapped at the pebbles in the crescent bay thanks to the mighty chalk walls framing the land side, keeping it sheltered and private. Beyond the beach ahead of them, lay the huge expanse of dappled sea that rocked and rolled angrily ahead of them, where each wave pounded against the rocks in rapid explosions of white foam.

Lars took a moment to admire the unusual beach and appreciate how beautifully serene this private cove was. Ælla surveyed the surroundings to make sure they were safe from the mysterious attackers and the ever-inquisitive Alex made his way down the steps out of the tunnel for further exploration of the beach area.

Lars watched with a regretful smile as his companion clambered down the steps to the strange ruins. In a brief moment, he forgot himself and allowed Alex to go and explore the area ahead of them. Lars wasn't paying attention to the fact that both he and Ælla should not leave Alex's side for fear of becoming magically possessed by an unknown force that was trying to manipulate Lars. Instead, he angsted about how he was in way over his head. On the one hand, he felt guilty that Alex was now so deeply involved with this horrific mess. Yet, on the other hand, he wrestled with the deep sense of guilt he felt for being glad that Alex was with him.

He wandered slowly in Alex's direction in order to keep up with him. Lars pained over the innocent lives that lie amidst the destruction of his childhood home. He struggled with whom to trust. He had witnessed first-hand the weapons and destructive potions the Gypsies had at their disposal and everything at the Manor pointed to them, but they're Ælla's people and so far she's saved their lives and pioneered their successful escape.

It could be witches, but something did not sit right with that theory. Partly because he did not know what witches actually did. He had to take Ælla's word for the possession theory, but there was something missing.

Lars was yanked from his thoughts when a swooping black and white mass caught his eye. He turned to see that an overly large and incredibly boisterous magpie was watching him from the cliffside.

"Alex! Don't run off too far, it might not be safe." Ælla's voice boomed across Lars' train of thought. Alex seemed to not hear and continued making his way down to the crumbled stone ruins at the foot of the steps, which prompted Lars to move after him with more haste.

Several stone pillars, like remnants of an ancient civilisation, stood erect while the majority of the once larger structure lay on their sides amongst the grass and pebbles. Both of which had been weathered by time and nature, yet stubbornly adamant not to be beaten by decay. The ruins were much older than the Manor, but there were similarities in design and use of material, along with a general feeling that they simply used to be connected.

"Alex!" Lars called, his friend still not acknowledging him. The wind blew a spiteful chill down his neck as he called louder and more forcefully, "ALEX!"

Ælla stood a little way from Lars but immediately clocked why he started running to his wayward friend amongst the ruins. From where she was standing, Alex faced a wall with his nose unusually close to the grey rock as though he were concentrating or tranced by something.

"How far away had he actually been from Lars?" she muttered to herself.

With each desperate stride, Lars was quickly moving ever further from Ælla. The panic in Lars' voice was carried in the wind and she felt the same pang of fear at the non-responsive friend as she also dreaded the worst.

"LARS! ALEX!" she shouted, sprinting towards Lars, both to protect him and herself.

Lars picked up his own pace, finding his feet unsteady on the turbulent pebbles. "ALEX!" he blasted through burning pants of air. His throat was dry and his chest tight, Alex was within reach and still not turning around. Lars nearly fell into Alex before landing a forceful hand on his friend's shoulder and spinning him around abruptly.

Ælla's heart was in her throat at this point but she instinctively placed her hand on the handle of her sword ready to protect the Thurston boy, just in case.

Alex turned with an innocent smile and piped up with an equally innocent question, "What is this place?" enamoured by their coastal discovery. He could only imagine druids and pagans making sacrifices and worshipping ancient deities on this sacred Thurston land.

Without thought or hesitation, Lars proceeded to land a mighty punch on his friend's cheek. "Why didn't you answer me? I thought you were..." he trailed off, too angry to finish the sentence. At that moment, Ælla appeared at Lars' side, sword unsheathed and ready to attack.

"Woah! Jeez, dude – what the hell was that for – I didn't hear you. I was only trying to read what was on these walls." A thin stream of red rolled out of the side of Alex's mouth.

The trio stood in the decaying ruins of what appeared to be an old church or fort, which was only now apparent since back from the tunnel's mouth the ruins had melted into the landscape. Huge walls that once stood to offer fortitude now lay decrepit on the floor, covered in moss and barnacles. The two remaining stone walls still managed to provide adequate shelter from the battering weather.

Lars lifted his hand to Alex's face and nudged the blood from the corner of his mouth with his knuckle in a comfortable movement that was accompanied by a look from Lars that conveyed a thousand sorries, which caused Alex to turn away quickly out of embarrassment.

Ælla respected their tender moment by pretending not to notice as she ran her fingers over the stone walls. Lars remembered himself and quickly followed suit, running his own hand along the walls, reading the engravings with the touch of his fingers. Alex continued to nurse his fat lip.

Upon first inspection, Lars assumed the engravings on the walls were graffiti scars and half expected to see testimonials of undying love from local vandals encompassed in a wonky love heart, but quickly remembered where they were and how secluded this area was and deduced that it was highly unlikely to be such vandalism.

The stone carvings were unusual, ornate and elaborate; similar to something Lars had seen before, which he mulled over for several moments before landing the eureka moment. In that tiny moment of clarity, time had stood still while his subconscious rapidly trawled through the banks of long-forgotten memories until that bold spark of thought resonated with all the subtlety of a lightning bolt. He realised he had seen the etchings before... on the ivory pen.

Lars was instantly and painfully swept back to the mysterious night it magically leaked vicious black goo and violently penetrated his eye sockets. Lars pinched the bridge of his nose subconsciously at the memory.

Without a word, he flipped the bag off his back and unceremoniously started rifling through his things. Ælla and Alex approached and stood over Lars, wondering why he frantically needed to empty his belongings in such a manner. Lars retrieved the beautiful wooden box and haphazardly emptied the contents. A few odd papers fluttered in the wind, but their escape was foiled by an ever-ready Alex. With a delicate clunk against the stone floor, a heavy white cylinder rolled to Lars' feet. There it was, the ivory pen.

"Would you look at that..." Ælla was captivated by the writing tool.

"Do you know what it means? The engravings – they're the same as this," he gestured to the pen and then the wall in rapid succession. Lars could barely contain his desperation at this point, thrusting it maniacally in her beautiful face.

"I–" She was taken aback, "I don't really know my runic glyphs..."

"Dammit," Lars threw the pen and without thought, Alex, annoyed at his friend's brattish tantrum, ran off down the beach to retrieve the beautiful artefact.

"But... If you stopped acting like a brat to let me finish... I *do* know what's on the pen," Her voice was *matter-of-fact*, though Lars eagerly anticipated his companion's response. "In fact, you do too, or at least the common version," To which she sang an all too familiar nursery rhyme:

> "One for sorrow, two for joy, three for a girl and four for a boy.
> Five for silver, six for gold. Seven for a secret never to be told..."

Ælla continued, "Thing is, the inscription on the pen actually says the traditional version:

> "One for sorrow, two for joy, three for a girl and four for a boy.
> Five for silver, six for gold and seven... welcomes you to the Fold."

She rolled the pen between her two hands, exploring the intricate beauty of the delicate pen. If Lars could have seen his own face, he would have seen how deathly pale it was at the sound of this all too familiar and haunting rhyme, remembering the dream where Lilah had sung this to him, and most recently, the crazed homeless man from the train.

All the while she went on further, "Though, the one on the wall differs slightly; it's the lesser known variation:

One for sorrow,
Two for mirth,
Three for a funeral,
Four for birth,
Five for heaven,
Six for hell,
Seven for the devil, his own self."

She paused. The wind caressed her hair causing it to whip across her face. Her eyes narrowed, "Lars, what do you know about this instrument?" she gestured to the pen.

"Nothing much – why, should I? All I know is that it's old and that it's been in my family for years. I suppose it's mine now, but it's weird, like ivory or something?" he conjected.

Ælla pondered his brief description momentarily before deciding where to start, "Well, for one thing, it's not exactly ivory and if it's what I think it is, then it's actually bone... human bone."

Alex's face grimaced, snatching it from the girl to morbidly investigate the writing instrument a bit keenly for her immediate liking. "Urgh, that's vile," he analysed as he stared down the shaft bringing the nib close to his eye.

"Human bone?" Lars questioned, "That's disgusting and weird. Who even does that?"

"Well, your witch ancestors, apparently," she snapped sarcastically. "Tell me, do you know how witches got magic and who gave it to them? Do you even know what this pen is and what it means?" she quizzed.

"Yeah, a little. Mrs Heath told us about the Immortals, witches and gypsies, but she didn't know I had the pen. To be honest, I forgot I had it in light of recent events." Lars snapped.

Ælla pondered slightly before taking a deep breath and embellishing where her peer had left off, "Well, there's a bit more to that story... It's a myth, or at least, my people believed it was – but the story goes that once the covens were given their powers, the witch elders wanted to ensure that their legacy was immortalised, so they sacrificed their seven most powerful coven leaders and used their bones to forge seven wands. But no one's even seen them, the Seven Wonders are a thing of legend."

The boys' faces were a mural of disgust and fascination, but she continued anyway. "Have you noticed anything weird about it? Has it done anything strange?"

Lars' face dropped and went deathly white. He was suddenly aware of how cold and exposed he was. Without speaking, he grasped the pen from Alex's hands, who silently obliged in returning it to him.

"There was one thing," he said before clearing his throat, while Alex threw him a severe dose of side glance. "The day I found out about Lilah's death, this box – *Lilah's box* – mysteriously appeared in my room and whilst rifling through the stuff, I cut my finger on the nib, which is razor-sharp by the way, and..." He stopped, deciding whether or not he would sound crazy, "and, this weird black shit came at me and went through my eyes. Then it all went downhill from there really; weird attackers, hooded gypsies, strange invisible beasts, stories of witchcraft, immortals-" Ælla cut him off.

"Invisible beasts?" Her face was beyond insult or confusion but shook her head to dismiss the notion. Lars continued regardless.

"All I know is that since Lilah died, weird shit keeps happening. And things keep trying to kill me." He absentmindedly returned the pen to Alex who in turn put it in his pocket.

"And they'll keep coming until you surrender," offered a sharp, precise voice that cut over the trio.

The three looked to one another and then around to see where the fourth voice had come from. From the mouth of the cave emerged a tall, polished figure with wonderful silver hair in a neat bun. Behind her, a portly gentleman and scruffy police woman stepped out from the darkness of the tunnel.

"You!" Lars interjected, "What are you doing here? What do you want?"

Barty smiled sweetly, placing her fist to her lips before replying in her wonderfully overly-British accent, "We have come for you. It's time to see your father. I do wish you would come quietly, he's been expecting you."

"No," Lars said through gritted teeth. Ælla poised her hand over her sword ready to grab, and Alex stepped to Lars' side in support of his defiance.

I knew I couldn't trust them and that they were dangerous.

"I do wish you would not be stubborn. I will not tolerate your insolence. Now, I'll say it again; you can come quietly or we will be forced to use other matters."

I know that he'll have answers for me, but right now Father's more of a stranger than he's ever been. I don't know the full extent of his plan but he's a monster nonetheless.

Lars kept eye contact. He subconsciously clenched his fists and could feel Alex's body go rigid with anticipation. Ælla unsheathed her sword with a gentle hiss and stood in a defensive position. "No" he affirmed.

The headmistress narrowed her eyes, "I did not want to do this – Lenton, seize the other boy." Those same eyes shone with an ethereal violet, which Lenton's own mirrored momentarily, and he instantly took on the mindless autonomy of a robot.

Poor Lenton – she's controlling him.

The fat headmaster mindlessly made his way towards Alex with heavy movements on supernaturally nimble feet – speed and strength were a side effect that the troop were rapidly coming to realise quickly. Ælla leapt to her new friend's side, punching the possessed man in the face, which had no effect, other than a sore knuckle for her hand.

"Shilling, you know what to do," Barty commanded the officer.

Without a word, the stout little police officer snapped her fingers and they instantly ignited with crackling sparks of silver-blue. The air crackled and her loose hair that escaped the uniform of her scruffy bun stood on end under the static atmosphere. She too was a witch, like Barty, and had powers of her own.

So Barty controls minds and Shilling does what; conducts electricity? What about Lenton? Is he a witch or just a victim of the circumstances?

Shilling thrust her arm out towards Lars from several metres away, emitting a huge surge of electricity.

Shit.

Lars froze at the prospect of being zapped. He clenched his eyes shut and braced himself. He waited agonising moments, expecting the searing pain and heat from her attack, but there was nothing. Lars opened an eye with immense trepidation and then the other. Shilling's face was a picture of confusion. She did the same movement with her arms, only this time Lars kept his eyes open, still bracing himself for the pain of what he expected to be thousands of volts of mystical electricity. Nothing. She tried again once more, but the jet of silver volts crackled and fizzed away to nothing a few paces in front of Lars' feet.

Silently, she panicked. This had apparently never happened before. Shilling looked to Barty as though waiting for the next command. The headmistress had seen everything and was equally confused.

Somehow, behind Lars, Lenton had both Alex and Ælla slumped lifelessly over his broad and chubby shoulders, he had got the better of them and Lars feared the worst.

Approaching her baffled accomplice, Barty offered a pensive, "I see..." before continuing with her analysis, "Well I never, it seems the boy is immune." She walked up to Lars, who stood his ground for fear of endangering Alex and Ælla. Barty looked down, her thought process apparent, and threatened Lars with, "I'm going to try something. If you move, you won't see your friends again. Am I clear." It was not a question.

Lars stood still, ready to pounce at a moment's notice. His heart pounded in his chest as the older lady slithered uncomfortably close towards him, with Shilling several paces behind her for back up. She came face to face, leaned in and stared him square in the eyes. Her breath was warm and smelled of peppermint sweets or humbugs. Her perfume was thick and floral and her eyes pierced his own with a determined stare. Whether she was working magic or not, his senses were already bombarded but he would not be intimidated. The headmistress looked harder into his eyes as though she would see something imprinted on the back of his skull. Her gaze was so intense that Lars thought her eyes would pop or she would give herself a nose bleed.

"It can't be." She stepped back, almost with an amused smile she said aloud, "it's not possible." She looked back to Shilling, who simply shrugged nonchalantly like she was genuinely indifferent either way. Barty snapped her head back, placed both hands on the side of Lars' head and stared intently once again, speaking to herself, "If I'm not mistaken, I'd say that it would appear that we have a fledgling witch amongst us, but it's impossible. You're a boy," she spat. "I have only ever heard of one witch with this power and it was the stuff of myth and legend. But this should not be," she looked back to Shilling, "The boy appears to be a Negate."

A what? Does this mean I have powers too?

Ms Barty pondered for a slight moment and looked to Professor Lenton who seemed to be waking up from her enthrall. She backed away, edging closer to Lars' headmaster, conscious not to look weak or nervous. Lars noted that her ability to enthrall, or possess him, returned to strength the further she moved away from Lars.

"It would appear that I can't enthrall you, but I don't need magic to harm your friends, so I suggest you comply or they face dire consequences." She threatened.

"What do you want with me?" Lars could not control the panic in his voice, but he was as equally angry, which gave fire to his question.

"I don't want you... your father does." was her retort.

"But he's been missing..." Lars could not help his obvious confusion, realising how stupid he must have sounded.

"My dear boy, there's a difference between being missing and not wanting to be found, and with your father's power and wealth, one can make that very easy for oneself." Her voice was almost a hiss through spiteful teeth. "Now I suggest you come, as you know, Lord Jude doesn't like to be kept waiting."

With that, she held out a finger and whistled. Lars thought her a little strange until he heard the flapping of wings.

From over the clifftop swooped an unusually large bird for its species. At first, Lars had thought it had been a small eagle or falcon, but the distinct black and white markings were that of a magpie.

I'm beginning to see a theme here.

It landed on her forearm with effortless grace, ruffled its wings into place and twitched its head. "Avar, return to your master and tell him that we have the boy. Bring him here immediately. There's a good girl."

With that, the large monochrome bird flapped its wings and flew back over the clifftop. Lars' stomach dropped with the impending dread of coming face to face with his father.

20. Homecoming

Lars sat with his back to one of the crumpled pillars and stewed on the feelings he had about seeing his father. He was uncomfortable – mainly because he had stone ridges from the crumbling column digging in his back and a mottle of damp pebbles under his bum – but the reunion was unwelcome nonetheless. Lars needed to focus on something and instinctively looked down to his friends, both straining his eyes and cocking his ear in a vain attempt to make out what was going on down there.

Shilling and Lenton had somehow managed to incapacitate Ælla and Alex some way down in the lower part of the ruins nearer the water's edge. Lars knew that this was a tactic to keep Lenton under Barty's charm and to reinstate Shilling with her own electrical abilities, far away from him and his own newly released witch ability.

They'll be fine. Ælla's a badass gypsy warrior with more than a trick or two under her cloak, and Alex has proven more than capable of looking after himself over the last few days. I just need to stay calm, find out as much as I can from Dad and stop Barty or Shilling doing something stupid.

He shot a look at his snooty captor, who was sat upon a similar pillar with her legs crossed neatly at her ankles several metres from him so that she retained her enthrall over Lenton. Her hands folded neatly upon her lap. Lars thought she looked so unnecessarily poised and prissy, incongruous to her exposed and hostile surroundings.

Knocking out little old ladies was not something in Lars' repertoire but these were desperate times and if a good shove saved the lives of his friend and Ælla, he was open- minded.

Both physically and mentally, she literally has no power over me; if I were to push her over or knock her on the head, maybe that would disrupt her mental hold over Lenton – at least for a brief moment. OK, that's fine, but it does leave Shilling. Again, she wouldn't be able to harm me, but I can't guarantee that I'd be within close enough proximity to protect Alex and Ælla with my nullifying, or negating, effect...

"So, you're a witch," he posed rhetorically to which she smiled.

"Indeed, I am, and a very powerful one if I may say so myself. It would seem that your power really brings out the best in me," she gloated proudly.

"How does it work?" Lars was genuinely interested and she perplexed momentarily, deciding whether or not he was worthy of knowing the secrets to her craft.

"My gift is innate; it's as natural to me as the brown of your eyes or the curve of your nose," she started, "but it's more than that. To my people, my power, my gift, legacy – whatever you want to call it – is one that is revered. You might call it 'mind control' or 'persuasion', but its true name is Enthrall.

"Ordinarily, Enthrall would allow me to temporarily manipulate anyone I wanted. Of course, I have my limits and my ethics, but you, Lars, you are an exception. It seemed that no matter how hard I tried to enthrall you, nothing would happen. Zilch. So I would push. I would stretch my field of concentration harder and harder until something happened. Like nuclear fallout, the people around you would turn, intoxicated and poisoned by my power. It was magnificent to see.

"At first, I thought it was the work of Gypsies, but after the train and Mrs Heath, I knew that you were the reason I could turn ordinary people into powerful soldiers that will do my bidding – you're marvellous, Lars!" She was enthralled in her own hype and Lars was quickly growing to hate her even more.

"I'm not going to help you." He said aloud and quite matter-of-factly, "You and my father can shove whatever plans you've got for me and my friends. I want nothing to do with it. You make me sick." This really got her attention and was made apparent by the seeming look of disgust that furrowed across her stern brow. Her neatly drawn eyebrows gathered in the middle and she sharpened her gaze towards his own. Lars tried to keep eye contact but she was fiercely intimidating and he was thrown by the way her eyes changed colour, an indication of her gift, no doubt.

Over the course of being outside since escaping the secret tunnel, the temperature had dropped significantly as it did at this time of year. The headmistress pulled her cloak tighter around her shoulders as she maintained her focused glare upon an ever-increasingly uncomfortable Lars. Ms Barty's cloak was no doubt very expensive. It was bright red with a stiff collar that was pursed together with an intricate clasp at her papery throat. Said cloak was a fashionable accoutrement and nothing at all like Ælla's and the other gypsies whose seemed more practical and understated – at least as far as capes go in the 21st century. Lars thought she looked like a cross between a flight attendant from a high-class Asian airline and Cruella De Vil, minus the puppy fur.

After what seemed ages of contrived faffing, she responded to him. "Now you listen and you listen well – like your sister, you have absolutely no say in the matter–"

"What do you know about Lilah?" He interrupted, which no doubt annoyed her further. She was losing her patience but determined to keep her cool.

"I cared a great deal for your sister, but she was weak, just like your mother had been. Both of whom were tasked with a great purpose and couldn't handle the pressure."

"You shut up!" Lars erupted, choking on the anger in his throat. Thoughts of his mother washed over him in a nauseating wave of guilt that churned in his stomach.

Barty took no notice of his interjection and continued her dramatic speech with the greatest tone of condescension. "I'll admit, we thought that all was lost when your sister took her own life. But it would appear that the Immortals have given us a second chance... and in such an unlikely candidate." She paused for dramatic effect.

She's enjoying this far too much. I wonder how long she's been waiting to deliver this speech.

"It's ironic really. The forgotten child; the one nobody cared about, may well be the answer to all of our prayers." Her passion and spite were both apparent to the point that she was morphing into a pantomime villain. Lars was now struggling to take her seriously but knew that both her words and actions have had – and would continue to have – grave consequences.

"Ha! We were focused on the wrong Thurston child!" Lars pictured her rehearsing this speech, having waited for this educational confrontation with the boy.

"No-," he interrupted, only to hear Ælla's faint scream from down at the shoreline. His tone conveying the purest truth he had ever felt, "I swear that if you hurt them, I will kill you."

Barty stood up and made several severe steps towards Lars, then crouched down so that they were practically nose-to-nose. She grabbed him by his bold jaw, pinching the skin on his chin with her neatly filed, yet vicious nails. "It's not them I'd be worried about." She pushed his face away and turned to sit back down.

"I want answers," he said coolly, trying not to let his emotions get the better of him. "I demand to know what's going on."

"All will be revealed in good time." And just like that, Barty's tone switched immediately to a sing-song chirrup with the sweetest serenity.

"What? So, we just sit here in silence while your cronies hurt my friends?" He jibed.

Barty reached into her red leather clutch bag and retrieved a matching lipstick that she applied carefully in the reflection of her applicator. Her old lips wrinkled under the waxy caress, "Exactly."

"Tell me this, then–" Lars proposed, "did my father have anything to do with Lilah's death?"

"Of course not," she paused for a moment, closed her purse decisively and sat up straight, "you know your father loved Lilah."

"Just tell me what happened." Lars' desperation and frustration were getting the better of him, which he could see played up to Barty and urged her spiteful games even further.

Neither one of them saw the tall, sharp figure emerge from the cave behind them and were both shocked when it spoke with booming authority from over their shoulders and separated their argument, like a teacher in a playground.

"Lars, no one likes a snivelling little whiner. I didn't raise you to whinge, so do stop it."

Lars knew that rich, deep voice immediately. From out of the shadow of the cave mouth stepped Lord Jude Thurston himself, dressed in a sharp black suit with a white shirt and black silk tie. His ensemble was completed by a matching Avar, his magpie. She perched proudly upon his shoulder, making him look like an alternative, yet sophisticated and colour- coordinated pirate.

"You didn't raise me at all. Now tell me what's going on. This whole thing is fucking madness!"

Lars did not yet know the full extent of his father's betrayal, but he knew in his gut that Jude was somehow linked to his sister's death and possibly even his mother's. Lars believed wholeheartedly that his father's dubious actions had somehow orchestrated both of their fates, be it directly or indirectly. Furthermore, that guttural instinct, aching with danger and suspicion was shouting at him from his very soul and urging him that his father's plans were not finished, and that he himself was about to be entwined in this ever-growing plot of twists and turns.

Lars looked upon his father with pained and confused eyes. Rather than seeing the perfect parent, he instead beheld a pathetic and selfish creature who wanted nothing more than to further his own means in every way and at any cost. "What's going on, Dad?" Lars asked once more, only to be shot by Lord Thurston's sharp side glance and something of a proud and unsympathetic smile.

"Lars, our story is a simple one at its core. There are those with power and those without, and I wish to even the playing field." Lars saw something in his father's gait shift momentarily and he dropped the bravado to reveal something equally as pompous but slightly more heartfelt.

"Lars, I loved your dear mother with all my heart. I would have endured the most absurd cliches to indulge Evelyn's every whim, without question. To me, your mother was a goddess among queens..." He looked off momentarily and for a brief second Lars saw his face soften somewhere in the crevices of his weathered forehead. Jude instantly remembered himself and swiftly picked up with the story, seemingly not wanting to demonstrate any sign of weakness or humanity. "But, I'll be honest, that had not always been the case and our marriage, like most, had its ups and downs.

"I was the proudest man alive the day we married; right here within these very sacred ruins," he gestured with his eyes, probably painting his memories with his mind's eye, "our nuptials were a fixed arrangement and a union that had been predestined many generations before our own," he smiled to himself. "When I first beheld your mother – oh my – I had never seen such a beautiful creature! Oh, and her eyes..." His gaze met Lars and he stopped himself. Lord Thurston allowed his face to soften as it had done a moment ago, only this time, the sincerity was oddly intense. Lars could not decide whether it was contrived or genuine.

"You know you have your mother's eyes, and I'm ashamed to say that when she died, looking at you was like looking right at her..." His pause made Lars feel awkward, but he said nothing, which urged his father to continue.

"Alas, I digress," he said.

"Tell me, Lars, what do you know of witches?" Jude twitched his neck to one side, much like the bird that sat upon his shoulder had done. Lars cleared his throat and paused.

Is this a trick question?

"Not much... I just learnt that we, our family, comes from a long line of witches. Mrs Heath told me that the female members are born with *abilities*... And I figured out for myself that there's a load of bullshit going around."

Jude had looked mildly impressed until that last comment.

"Very good." He paced in front of Lars like a professor giving a lecture in class. "Tell me, do you think this is fair?"

"Do I think *what* is fair?"

"That women inherit the power, and we stand subservient?"

Wow. Dad's a misogynist.

Lars opened his mouth to interject but before he could answer, Jude continued.

"Did you know your mother betrayed me, Lars? She did. She knew that I wanted to bring magical equality to our people. And *she* knew how to do it.

Lars was already confused as his father apparently had trouble keeping to a linear storyline.

"Your mother had many gifts, Lars; the most enchanting being of the natural world and not the supernatural ones. I loved the magical blush of her cheeks, the melodic cackle to her laugh and the way she simultaneously tapped her fingers on her thumbs when she was anxious. However, that being said, her magical gifts were indeed among the most tremendous I had ever seen. She was an absolute goddess, one blessed with the gift of Sight."

"Sight? What do you mean, Sight?" questioned Lars.

"Evelyn was what you might consider a seer or someone with the gift of premonitions. In fact, she foretold the arrival of you and your sister, long before we ever consummated our marriage. What she failed to tell me at that point, was that your birth would also herald the dawn of a new age. An age that would see the balance of magic.

"When she told me I was over the moon! Our family was among the great covens but now, this would see us as absolutists amongst the witches and gypsies. Finally, I could take my true place at the head of the Thurston coven and rule the magical realm as I should.

"Evelyn did not need powers to see my obsession. She accused me of being consumed with your destiny and the lengths I would go to obtain it for us. But we loved each other and everything I did was for her.

"Remember how poorly your mother had been? She was cursed with a strong spirit that was imprisoned with a weak mortal body. You'll remember the times she would be bed bound?"

Lars remembered the long weeks when she would be too ill to see them because their father feared that he and his sister would tire their mother and make her worse. Lars and Lilah particularly hated those periods; the house had an intense atmosphere and one that was ruled with the hostile hand of Jude Thurston.

"Yes. And I remember the night she died." Lars offered through a dry throat, his eyes stinging at the memory. He had sat with his sister, outside the master bedroom as various people darted in and out, zipping past them both, oblivious to their existence.

"Yes," Jude remarked solemnly. "It was a difficult night. It was also the night she betrayed me." Lars felt a raging fire surge in his gut.

"Shut up! Do you know what you sound like? Mother didn't betray you. She probably saw what a monster you'd turn out to be and tried to protect us–" Lars burst out, only for Jude to scoff nonchalantly and not hearing a word his son just said.

"Her parting from this world came after her final, most prophetic vision. It pained me to watch her – it still haunts me, even after all these years, how her eyes glazed over and her already sallow complexion was whitewashed under the strain of her fatal premonition. When she came to, she gave me a look I had never seen from your mother before; one of pure fear. I begged to know what she had seen, "tell me!" I shouted at her, but she just cowered from me.

"Right before she died she kept saying that she couldn't trust me, it was dangerous and I was not to interfere. And still I begged, but she was relentless in guarding her secret. She kept saying she had to protect the Heir of Thurston, and that the balance would come with great sacrifice and loss. She feared for my soul.

"With her last breath, she escaped into death, taking that final vision with her to the grave."

Lars relinquished a solemn tear. It pained him to think of his mother being so scared that death became a sweet release.

What did she see?

"I was plagued by our final farewell and I was tormented by what she saw and what she had neglected to tell me. I couldn't let it go. I just knew that it was meant for me and she selfishly kept it and took it to the afterlife. The months turned to years and I know now that I was eaten away by this resentment. Most of all, I resented myself for not being able to help her or have the means to find out her dying vision. I sought seers, oracles... even Gypsies for a means to retrieve and unlock what she saw and came up empty every time."

"OK," perceived Lars, "But what does this have to do with Lilah? Where does she come into this?"

Ms Barty, who had been listening intently, was salivating over Jude's every word and absorbing his sermon, chimed in at this point.

"Now! This is where Lilah comes in," she all but giggled giddily with far too much excitement that was out of character. Jude shot her a severe glance before he continued.

She's drunk, off him. She's consumed with whatever he's got planned and is eating up whatever he says to her.

Jude looked back to Lars and started up once more, "Then, a remarkable thing happened and Lilah came into her own." He announced.

"Her gift was vastly different to your mother's, but equally magnificent, and I knew my prayers had been answered. Do you know what your sister's gift was, Lars?

Lars stared blankly.

Of course not, but he's losing his shit over whatever it was.

"Lilah was blessed with the gift of Resurgence! She came into her powers, as most witches do, around adolescence and just like your mother's, hers was truly glorious. She had the ability to grant vitality to the frail, and of course, to revoke it at will. It's a power that has been coveted by even the greatest of covens for millennia. Most importantly for me and my cause, she could bestow life to the dead and command them."

Lars knew where this was going, but hoped with every fibre of his being that Jude would not confirm his doubts.

"I'm not proud of what I did to my daughter, but it was for the greater good. Barty and I helped your sister hone her gift until we thought she was ready. I manipulated her to reanimate your mother's corpse and extract her final vision – you see – it was all destiny! The Immortals willed it so.

"And so I got it! I got what I wanted. Thanks to Lilah, I learned that in order to rule the magical realm, I had to first overcome the Fold and locate the ancestral relics of our peoples. I have to master the Seven Wonders. And it would indeed be the Heir of Thurston who finds and uses them." Lord Thurston paused and thought about his next statement but said it anyway, "Don't you see, my child, you both are my heirs! Oh, the irony that your mother had the gift of Sight, yet no vision, was astounding."

He paced up and down the stone floor, the wind billowing through his expertly cut jacket. The magpie surveyed the area and leapt off towards Alex and Ælla. Jude took no notice and continued his account.

"To find out that the bringer of magical balance would be brought about by the heir of Thurston, I was thrilled!

"Why your mother kept this from me, I'll never know. Maybe she thought she was protecting Lilah? Alas, she was no doubt right. Lilah was weak. She was not ready or strong enough to wield the responsibility of such power. Her gifts disgusted her and she could not live with what was expected of her, which is why I suspect she took her own life. Dead. My daughter and dreams of power, both dead."

The look of shame was unmistakable, but Lars could not lend his sympathy yet. He still knew too little, and what he did know was unbelievably painful and frankly downright selfish.

"You're sick!" said Lars. Barty sat enamoured, captivated by his father and his dramatic revelation.

"With Lilah's death, Barty and I thought all was lost. But then you, Lars, my unassuming little boy, come to me with your sister's borrowed destiny and what I understand are powers of your own – it's a miracle and testament to the power of my lineage!"

"The prophesied child was said to bring balance to the magical realm..."

Lars switched off and could not listen anymore. It was all too much for him right now as he felt nauseous with anger and disgust at this wicked man that leered above him, oblivious to his own vile nature. Perhaps, Lars thought, Jude is fully aware of his selfish and disgusting nature, which makes this scenario all the worse. Lars silently hoped this was a huge understatement and wanted to give his father the benefit of the doubt.

"You did it." Lars coughed out, "You're the reason my sister's dead. You made your own daughter so repulsed by herself, that she took her own life. You're disgusting."

He's genuinely lost the plot here. Dad, you're crazy.

"Lars, you don't understand – there's a bigger picture here. Your mother won't have died in vain, and here's your chance to give your sister's death meaning. You must now finish her destiny. Join me, let's wield the Seven Wonders and we can rule the Fold."

"But, Dad, what does that mean? What bigger picture? You're making no sense. What does wielding the Seven Wonders do? And why do you need the Fold?" Lars blurted.

Jude opened his mouth to explain his grand scheme to his son, but before he could answer, he was interrupted. Barty coughed, "Pardon my intrusion, but might you want to get a move on and perhaps take this upstairs and wait for your guest."

21. Ælla

Ælla and Alex could just about see Lars sat amongst the crumbling ruins up near the cave's entrance. From the angle of their current location near the shoreline, the basic structure of the once sacred building that stood at the foot of the cliff could be seen in all of its dilapidated glory. The vaulted arches of this crumbling temple now lay scattered on the floor like wonky teeth in a mouth of grassy gums.

Shilling was persistently brushing her fingers against her thumbs, which bore minuscule sparks that dashed and crackled from the light friction. Her eyes were pinned to Ælla with burning animosity. In turn, Ælla locked her own in retaliation. She knew this was a tactic to intimidate both her and Alex and a reminder of her power and that she could do them serious harm. That and something might also happen to Lars if they pushed their luck and tried anything stupid, like starting a fight or trying to escape.

Ælla sized up their female captor. The electric-policewoman was short and dumpy but had a muscular stature that alluded to her physical strength. However, due to her size and height, Ælla ascertained that she was not likely to be very fast and made a mental note not to take this for granted since looks can be deceiving and that she does possess an elemental ability. Ælla knew that elemental abilities were among the most common gifts in witches and were often the most dangerous. That being said, she most certainly was not going to be intimidated.

Ælla needed a distraction. Shilling was incredibly shiny and not the radiant glowy kind. Shilling had a greasy forehead that reflected light, even on this grey day. Her damp looking hair was slicked back off of her face and tied up into a scruffy bun. She wore little makeup and what she did wear was remarkably cheap. Ælla would not be intimidated by someone who wore clumpy mascara.

"Can I give you some advice?" Ælla piped up, "You should invest in a good moisturiser, one that works on your T-zone. I have a good solution that will help you out–" she jibed.

"Shut your gypsy mouth. I don't want one of your disgusting concoctions for my face. What do you use; cow shit and virgin blood?"

Clinique, actually.

In her peripheral vision, Ælla saw Alex straighten his back to the side of her and crane his neck in the distance towards Lars.

"Look!" Alex whispered to Ælla, "Who's that over there, with Lars and Barty?"

She too craned her neck for a better vantage, just about making out the lithe figure of a newly emerged body among the ruins.

"He's here, and it's about time too," said Shilling, though nobody was quite sure whether she was just thinking aloud to herself, telling Professor Lenton who by now was seemingly free of Barty's enthrall, or indeed warning her hostages. She walked to the Professor to say something they could not hear.

Ælla cast her eyes to Alex and with a silent look, asked him what he was doing with the stern but quizzical expression on her face.

Alex responded to her silent question with a hushed retort. "We're not tied up or anything, so let's do something. You can take her, easy. When she's not looking, jump her! The fat professor isn't going to be able to do much – he's not even possessed anymore – I could launch myself at him and cause you a diversion," he sounded both positive and eager. She liked his spunk.

"Agreed. But we must be careful because she's dangerous." Alex knew she was not talking about the policewoman at this point and looked to the headmistress under the cliff. "Now, listen, I may have a trick or two up my sleeve," Ælla urged, "But we can't be sure of the extent of the damage *this* bitch can cause us. For now, just follow my lead." He nodded with a definitive yes.

"The wait is almost over; Lord Thurston is here, which means it won't be long now. We just need to wait for the signal," Shilling addressed the Professor, who was breathing heavily. Lenton's sense of unease, now that he was regaining his faculties, was growing more apparent to an astute Ælla. He checked the time; straightened his bow tie; mopped his brow and cleaned his glasses simultaneously. She watched him, before attempting to strike up a conversation with hers and Alex's captors.

"I know what your plan is," Ælla jibed to the policewoman and professor. "My people won't stand for it."

"Well, it's more than I know." Alex quipped under his breath. Ælla noted the sarcastic tone and fought back a smile in this crucial moment of successfully goading a confrontation. She actually had no idea what the plan was, but calling the other woman's bluff was working.

"Your people are savages; they don't know shit. Now shut your mouth you gypsy scum." Shilling spat. Ælla reached into her cloak and searched for her blade. Her fingers found the cool handle of her xiphos.

Idiots – they didn't strip us of our weapons.

The sword was cold in her hands and memories of her father shot to her mind. The weapon itself had been a gift from him when she was training to become a warden, which was something akin to a scout or spy. The witch covens and gypsy clans had always trodden on uneasy ground and despite their last physical confrontation being some hundred-odd years ago, all gypsies were taught basic combat for the war that would inevitably come.

In training, the girls in Ælla's clan generally favoured the bow and arrow or daggers as their weapon of choice but for Ælla a dagger was small and clumsy, whereas the bow felt like a faff and it did not come naturally to her. Of course, she excelled in both, but neither were where she was most comfortable.

Ælla had been taller than most of the girls her age and had been for most of her life. Her love of sports and athletics had made her body strong and powerful. Furthermore, she had loved music growing up. Her talents did not lay in playing instruments, instead, she would listen to every kind and dance along, which enhanced her agility and made her exceptionally well-coordinated.

The natural hero, Ælla found herself in a lot of fights due to her size; mainly with boys. They would tease the other girls and she would inevitably stand up for them. The boys would not often pick a fight, but Ælla made sure that she finished the ones that did. She had a strong sense of justice and hated hostility, but above all she hated bullies.

The sword, which now sat in her hand as she poised to use it, was named Honour's Might. It had been something of a *coming-of-age* gift from her father, who had been the highest and most-trusted advisor to the coven leader. Quite rightly, he was a well-respected elder in the Gypsy community.

He had recognised how Ælla's differences were not something that brought her shame but instead were something she yielded like weapons in the name of good. He loved his daughter for having the strength and bravery to be herself and how she was relentless in getting her own way. Ælla was a true force of nature with a heart of gold.

When the time came, Ælla's sisters, all of whom had excelled in potions and natural remedies, were gifted with traditional mortar and pestles, Mezzaluna and foraging equipment. And whilst Ælla's affinity for the natural world was a divine gift from the Immortals, her passion lay in sports, particularly fighting, and her father bestowed what he knew was the most fitting gift; her sword.

At the time of gifting Ælla's mother had just scolded her for getting into trouble yet again. She had taken on and bested three of the other elders' boys and her mother was ranting about Ælla's actions bringing shame on the family, especially her respected father. When he returned from a council meeting, the passionate Ælla would not back down in arguing her case to her equally hot-headed mother. He separated the two head-strong women and sat his daughter down in front of the fire of their living room.

"Æleanir, my darling, do you know why your mother is angry?"

She paused, before answering; the look of shame apparent on her flushed face. "Because I'm not good like the other girls and my sisters."

"Nope." He chirruped.

"Because I bring shame on the family?" she asked, not sure if this was the right answer.

"Nope."He chirruped again.

"Is it because I don't do as I'm told?" She quizzed.

"Exactly!" He stated, to which her face dropped like a sack of stones, "But do you want to know something?" The young Ælla nodded eagerly. "Your mother never did as she was told and she never listens to me... and that's why I love her.

"She knows her own mind and has a strong sense of what is wrong and what is right. Just like you." His daughter looked unsure, staying quiet to permit him to continue his explanation.

"Æleanir, there are three types of people in life. First, there are the sheep, which is most people. They go about their business, mindlessly following the crowd and doing what is expected of them. Then, the second type of people are wolves. They're the vicious and selfish people who look to exploit and hurt people like the sheep. And then there are people like you and your mother, who make up the third; they're the fierce hound that wrangles the sheep and protects them from the dangerous wolves. You're ferocious, smart and a fiercely loyal young woman, and I wouldn't change you for the world."

He looked away to the fire as it danced lazily in the pit of the hearth, falling into a brief mini-trance. Remembering himself, he cleared his throat to speak. His eyes never leaving their searing gaze into the orange fire, his tone dropped and became more grave.

"Changes are coming, Ælla; I've seen it in the trees and the runes, and they all point to the same thing – you're going to play your part and it will be vital to the future of not only our clan but all the gypsy clans. What it is, I can't be sure, but you're the only one I trust with this mission.

"Ever since you were a little girl, I knew that you were different from your sisters and the other children your age; that's why I give you this:" He handed her a long flat present wrapped in a modest blue velvet cloth. "Her name is Honour's Might and she will serve you well."

The sword was relatively small and matte black in colour. In her hand, it was lighter than it looked, and the edges were so sharp that the air seemed to vibrate around it. Holding the handle between her fingers, Ælla felt the electricity of her father's words and knew that she wanted to serve her gift's namesake.

The coastal wind brushed across her face and whisked Ælla from her favoured memory before she heard the nearby squawk of a large monochrome bird that darted towards Shilling. "Here she comes, it's Avar, Jude's familiar. Ready the hostages." The Magpie's flight was the awaited sign that meant Shilling and Lenton were to start putting their plan in motion.

The latter of the duo seemed unprepared or unwilling, probably both, to action and keep up his end of the bargain. "What do you want me to do? You're the one with the power, and the blasted handcuffs." Said Lenton.

Without warning, Shilling motioned a fist towards her accomplice. Though he was several metres away from her, as she punched the air, her fist erupted in a ball of sparks and, like a mystical angle grinder, each white-hot dart flew like tiny electrical blades towards the Professor. Alex tensed his body and opened his mouth in a bid to shout. But he could not hear himself over the shriek from his headmaster. Lenton's scream was otherworldly. He howled demonically, with his head thrown back in sheer agony. He fell to his knees and pounded his fists to the floor. Ælla saw Alex turn his head and squint his eyes to avoid the horrific site. What came next was worse.

Ælla stayed fixed towards the tortured Professor; Shilling was killing him. Ælla could not steel herself from the diabolical vision. Under the searing heat of her electrical charge, Lenton's skin was reddening, blistering and melting off his bones. What little hair he had on his head singed instantly and blackened under the force. His glazed eyes bubbled and swelled before erupting and melting down his flaying cheeks. The smell of burnt hair and, weirdly, bacon, turned Ælla's stomach.

The savage attack felt like hours, but in reality, had only been a few moments. Shilling released her fist and the sparks ceased to a stop. The crouching remains of Lenton fell to the floor and shattered into a pile of scorched bones and burned flesh.

Alex gagged, "Jeez... I think I'm going to be sick."

Ælla took her eyes from the body and shot a threatening glare at the policewoman. She was adamant not to be intimidated by her.

"You two, get up and come with me. Try anything, and you'll end up like him."

Alex heaved himself to his reluctant feet and steadied his balance, reeling from the waves of nausea. Ælla stayed put, not dropping her eye contact.

"Do gypsy scum not understand English? Get up." Shilling swore through gritted teeth, brushing her fingers as she had done earlier to flick lazy sparks with the light friction. It is now apparent who had done most of the damage to Thurston Manor as she threw a fist in Ælla's direction.

In a deft swoop, Ælla leapt from the electrical current, released her sword from its sheath within her cloak and swiftly deflected the lightning force directed at her. She missed the full brunt of it, but was clipped on the leg nonetheless and released a painful howl. Had she taken a full dose as Lenton had done a few moments ago, she too would have met the same fate.

Quickly remembering herself and Honour's Might in her strong hand, she used the weapon to shield herself from the electric current and advance on the vicious little policewoman with the oily T-zone. With all her anger channelled down the black blade, she directly guided a swift blow and lobbed off the hand of her assailant.

Quicker than it had happened, Shilling curled up around her fresh wound, cradling it with her remaining hand. She wept and wailed before Ælla brought the solid pommel of her weapon down on her nose, which caused her to pass out and shut up. Ælla saw that Shilling's elemental ability had sealed the wound where her hand was severed.

Ælla looked to an awe-struck Alex who had watched the whole thing and was obviously impressed. He blushed when she threw her stern almond shaped eyes to him, which she then rolled and gestured her hand to steady him before he almost passed out.

"That, that was... that was... you're amazing." He stuttered.

Throughout the confrontation, Avar had darted about mindlessly, squawking and flapping at the commotion. Ælla and Alex looked up to see the black and white bird swoop off in the direction from which it had originally come. Looking beyond its perceived destination, they found that Lars, Barty and the mysterious new figure were no longer in the ruins at the foot of the cliff.

"Shit, they're gone," Alex stated the obvious. "What do we do now?" He had made Ælla the leader of this mission based on her demonstration, knowing now that if he had not trusted her before, he certainly did now. "Who was that man up there?"

She pondered, though she knew full well. "I think it was Lord Thurston. We need to find Lars quick. I don't know what his father's got planned, but I'm sure it isn't going to be something good."

"Will she be OK?" He gestured to the injured Shilling. "Will she die?" Alex noticed that her wound was not bleeding.

"Her arm will be fine. Between her electricity closing her wound and the ointment I use to treat my sword's blade, she won't lose any more blood," she stated.

"Ointment on your sword; what's that for?" Alex quizzed. He was learning a lot over the last couple of days and needed to soak up as much of this new world as he could.

She wiped it clean with her sleeve and responded, "It's treated with an ointment that seals the wounds it inflicts. Our job as Wardens of the Fold is to observe, not to enforce, punishment. I took an oath not to take a human life unless it is absolutely necessary. She's probably got a broken nose, though, if that makes you feel any better?" She jibed.

"Seems pointless having a sword, but hey-ho," he retorted

"Well, it seems pointless having a crush on a friend who's not interested," she snapped.

His face dropped and it was like she had kicked a puppy; a beautiful black-haired labrador puppy with sapphire eyes. She knew he was only joking and could tell that she had touched a difficult subject. Ælla coughed an awkward laugh in an attempt to skirt over the lead-like comment. He too laughed it off, as though not acknowledging what she had said. She could tell that Alex was in denial.

One of the first things she noticed about him, besides his famous dad, was his sadness. Alex was a genuinely sweet boy, and had proven to her that he had a good heart in the short time they had known each other. He was passionate and sincere.

She knew of his tragic childhood; growing up without a mother and having an absent father would be difficult for anyone. But she could not imagine having it blown out of proportion, scrutinised and speculated by the press. To have complete strangers know so much about your private life was heartbreaking, yet here he was. A strong, well-adjusted and smart guy, ready to fight for his friend; whom he may or may not be in love with. But that was his business.

"It's not like that–" he tried to explain, but could not muster the words and was grateful that she changed the subject.

"We need back up. And I know just the person; we just need to make contact." With that, she removed the satchel from her shoulder and started removing various contents. Out flew glass bottles of varying liquids, bunches of dried herbs, white rune stones, a crystal or two and several small pouches.

"Are you going to cast a sp-" he started to ask, before realising that she was looking for her mobile phone. She looked up from her screen, placed the device to her ear and tapped her foot. Alex sheepishly put his hands in his pockets and waited for the line to pick up. The dial stopped as someone answered.

"Hello?"

"Hey, Jennifer? It's Ælla. It's happened. We need to meet. Gather enforcements and meet me at Thurston Manor now. I don't know how much longer we have left to stop him." The voice on the other end said a few things, which Alex could not decipher although Ælla agreed succinctly before hanging up.

"Who's Jennifer?" Alex asked.

"A friend. Or at least, I hope she is." Ælla gathered her belongings and threw the bag back over her shoulder. "Come. We have to go quickly before it's too late for Lars."

And with that, the pair left Shilling and made their way up to the cave that would lead them to Thurston Manor to save Lars.

22. All Good Plans

Alex's heart hammered against his chest as he and Ælla ran back towards the tunnel that would lead them eventually to Thurston Manor. The blood surged through the veins of his body like molten quicksilver and every thought of his endangered friend conjured pangs of sickening guilt and enraged fear.

They pounded through the dank cavern, the same one that they had not long used to escape to the beach after their confrontation with the possessed Mrs Heath. Just a short while ago, they were fleeing Thurston Manor for safety. Now, he and his new companion, Ælla, were charging back to save Lars from his father and the evil influences that were probably trying to corrupt him.

"W- why would he just g-go like that? And d-do you think we should have t-tied up Sh-Shilling?" Alex panted.

Alex was naturally lithe but far from the natural athlete Lars was or Ælla seemed to be, but now in the face of danger and needing to help his friend, he all but flew with the speed his legs were running. Ælla continued to charge, having no problems keeping up.

"Perhaps, but there's no time," she coughed back, "but I've dealt with her once and I can do it again, even if it means cutting her other hand off."

"And-and... what a-about– Lars?" he tried through a series of short breaths that was a dry gasp burning his throat and lungs.

Ælla said nothing and focused on the door ahead, which was well within sight thanks to the glow that traced its outline from the light on the other side, giving the frame an otherworldly aura. Alex knew that stepping back into that kitchen would be like stepping through a portal, one from which there was no coming back. His life was about to change forever. He didn't know how, just that it would.

They both dropped their pace from a sprint to a jog, which eventually petered out to a staggering walk. His muscles burned, his chest ached and his throat was painfully dry. He panted heavily, trying to get his breath back. His pained breathing was laboured to the point where his stomached wretched and any guttural relief was just a bitter taste in his mouth. Ælla placed a sensitive hand upon his back, the gesture being one to help calm him down and also offer silent support for the ordeal that lay ahead.

"We need a plan," she coughed, though nowhere near as traumatised as her companion.

Alex looked to her and then to the door with a pained face. He placed both hands on his hips and bent over to cough. He felt as though he was still going to throw up.

"I know." He eventually admitted. "We don't know what lies behind this door; it could be anything. They'll probably be expecting us, and we don't have Lars here to protect us with his negative-power-thing."

"You're right." She sounded rather surprised at his clear-thinking, expecting him to want to charge through, all gung-ho and that. Ælla looked to the rim at the foot of the door, having noticed the oscillations of the light.

"Barty's our biggest threat right now. We must take her down; either we ambush her with a surprise attack or we find Lars and use him to protect us from her," he stated, almost surprising himself how grown-up, level-headed and authoritative he indeed did sound.

"The latter makes definite sense, but we can't guarantee a positive outcome in either scenario." Ælla sensibly responded, pondering what they should do next. At that very moment, her phone beeped to indicate she had received a text message, which she read immediately. It was Jennifer, "We'll have back up within the hour," she affirmed.

"That won't be enough time. Lord knows how many other extreme-powered witches Jude has at his disposal; teleportation? time travel? superspeed? We can't wait; Lars needs us."

"You know those aren't actual powers, right?" She corrected him. He looked intrigued and confused. With hushed, quick words she explained, "Witches powers are deep-rooted in nature, like, they can bend the natural order but don't completely defy it. Witches aren't gods, so they have limitations to what feats they can perform. Shilling, for example, her power mimics lightning, though I couldn't imagine her going *full Thor* and conjuring an actual storm."

Alex continued to listen, processing what the gypsy warden was telling him before reining the subject back in.

"What I mean is, an hour is a long time, which is a really generous head start if they do go on the run. Not to mention, if he does have a fleet of other witches that are loyal to him..." he stopped and tried not to think about it, "We're in serious trouble and we need to get out of here. We can't wait for your cavalry. Lars needs me – he needs us," Alex stated.

"But we still don't know what they actually want with him." He went to interrupt her, but she quickly carried on by speaking over him. "We don't even know anything about him. This is literally the first time something like this has ever happened.

"It defies everything; boys are not innately magical; they don't have powers; they aren't witches and this shouldn't be happening. The whole thing is unprecedented." She paused, as something struck her, "It means that Jude probably knows as much as everyone else at this point. Lars is obviously valuable; he's the first of his kind, which is something of a blessing since his father probably won't know what to do with him or what Lars even has to do with his own grand design just yet. Thurston will undoubtedly want to keep his asset safe."

Ælla could see that the penny was starting to drop with Alex.

"Alex, I'm itching for some action too, but we have to be cautious. I'm *au fait* with this sort of stuff – and you're just, for lack of a better word, a *muggle* – you have no idea what forces are truly at odds here. You could get yourself hurt, and I don't want the responsibility of having a hand in the death of an heir to Rock 'n' Roll royalty."

He cracked a sly smile. Alex was not aware that this was the first time she had seen him do so. He also did not know that she thought he was angelically beautiful in a brooding, fragile way. Alex did, however, know that Ælla was speaking sense. She had an intoxicating air of authority about her, which Alex could not decide whether or not was due to her intimidating size and strength, or whether this girl genuinely had her shit together. The fact that he had also seen her wield a sword and cut off someone's hand without blinking, meant that she was definitely someone to have on side.

"OK, listen..." She hushed to him as she crept down and rested her ear to the door, which he subconsciously mirrored. "What can you hear?" She ordered.

He strained his senses through the splintered wood, desperately listening for something on the other side of the door. He looked to his feet, then Ælla's sturdy leather riding boots before closing his eyes in an attempt to drown out distractions. The sea could be heard crashing along the shore at the far end of the long cavern, and the moaning of the wind through the ruins at the mouth of the cave was exceptionally loud, considering their distance from them. Above all, he could hear Ælla's panting breath and the drum of his own pounding heart in his chest.

Finally, he heard it; the faint scuff of slowly shuffling feet from the other side of the door. Alex felt the blood rush from his face, leaving a tingly sensation all across his body. Realising the sound of dragging feet, he knew that the moaning wind on the shore was actually a moaning person, or people to be more precise, from the other side of the door in the kitchen. That rasping sound of air laboriously working its way to the chest of the zombies was unmistakable and something Alex was all too familiar with lately.

"There's something on the other side; I think there are zombie-possessed-people-things in the kitchen," he stressed through hushed excitement. "Also, we need a new name for them."

"Enthralled," she piped.

"Huh?" Alex whispered under his breath.

"Enthralled. That's what they are. As in Barty is an Enthrall, she has the power to enthrall and her subjects are enthralled – I think? That word stops making sense when you keep saying it over and over..." she explained.

"Right. Enthralled; got it. Whatever they are, I'm going out on a limb and going to guess that whatever's on the other side of the door is probably going to be hostile, because that's just our luck." Alex confirmed.

Ælla was getting frustrated, not with Alex but with the growing complexities of the situation. Thinking aloud she offered, "Do you think Barty managed to orchestrate them on her way through? Maybe she's no longer with Lars," Ælla strategised. "There are too many variables. Alex, we're in trouble."

"So what do we do?" He demanded with an understanding nod, forcing the situation back on track. "Is Barty nearby?" He quizzed, before quickly moving on to offer answers to his own questions, "I mean, she can't be, or Lars would nullify her power – then again, she can somehow use it with these zomb- *enthralled*."

"To be fair, does it matter? If she's not with Lars, she could be on the other side of the door, in which case, we're doomed anyway and joining the ranks with the rest of the enthralled." She noticed his face drop at the thought and quickly recovered, "But, if she was, we'd probably already be victims, so..."

"You'll need a weapon." She flung her cape aside and pulled around her satchel. "Here!" She gestured a glass vial towards him, quickly changing the subject and putting the focus back on something more productive.

He took it cautiously and held it up to the slice of yellow light that framed the door. It was relatively clear and yellowy-brown like whiskey with flecks of small solid matter. It reacted with what little light gleamed from the cracks around the door.

"What is it?" He asked, still assessing the liquid. She looked at it and thought for a moment before answering.

"On my command, smash it and don't breathe in," she commanded.

Had she waited any longer to respond, he probably would have already opened the vial and taken a huge breath, quite possibly even a glug to ascertain the identity of this mysterious potion. Nonetheless, he refrained and held the bottle tightly with great caution upon receiving her ominous instruction and awaited his orders.

"Can you open the door to get a better view?" She asked, to which he obliged ceremoniously. Alex reached for the door handle to give it a try. It was stiff and would not give way quietly, meaning that the latch would inevitably click and alert them of their presence.

"OK. Follow my lead. And remember, stay away from the contents of that vial once you've used it. Also, I nearly forgot; give me a head's up when you're about to lob it," she ordered decisively.

Before he could even respond to ask what the actual effects of it were, Ælla kicked the door with her mighty foot and unsheathed her sword. In a matter of moments, she flew across the room to the centre. At first, Alex was confused as to why she would jump right into the danger zone. There were bodies all around her and she was immediately surrounded without the enthralled needing to do very much.

The possessed occupants barely reacted to her boisterous entrance before they about-turned on their respective spots to face her in spooky synchronicity. No one looked towards Alex who still stood in the doorway, feeling useless. The nearest assailant launched himself towards Ælla, making a grab for her neck, which she successfully countered having driven an open palm straight into the face of her oncoming attacker.

Just as they suspected, Ms Barty and Lord Thurston had anticipated their re-entry at some point and left guards in the kitchen where the secret cavern door led. The people, or enthralled, were the mind-controlled former staff members of the Thurston estate; the ones that were not already dead or fatally injured. They were bloody and bruised, and each face was glazed and aggressively confused. The entranced masses would lunge with laboured movements towards Ælla in an attempt to overcome and swamp her, just like zombies in pretty much every zombie film you have ever seen.

Before panicking at the outcome, Alex enjoyed a brief moment of clarity where he deduced that Barty and Lars were separated. Being near him would neutralise her and she would not be able to enthrall the people in the kitchen. What the range of her power was, was still unknown, but Alex took pleasure in knowing that she was most likely not with Lars at this point.

This meant Lars was either with his father or alone and being held prisoner elsewhere in the manor house. In hindsight, this was neither good news or bad news for him and Ælla since Barty could attack them and enslave them with her power since Lars was neither with her to nullify her, or with them to shield her enthrall.

In the middle of the kitchen, Ælla was successfully fighting off the waves of mind-controlled servants, who were remarkably normally looking, aside from the glazed look in their eyes. In the absence of Lars, Barty did not have to try and overcome the protective effect of his negation, which meant that the enthralled easily succumbed to her power. This was quite apparent since there were no hideous side effects to these victims, the kind that made them all smelly and readily decomposing.

So this is what people under mind control should look like – Lars and Barty must have a fair distance between them.

Looking at Ælla, who showed little-to-no struggle at fending off the enthralled, Alex tried to decipher her plan. She was fastly becoming more and more enclosed in the encircling attack from the numerous bodies. Alex also observed that she continued to use the pommel of her sword and her fists to keep them at bay, rather than slicing and stabbing her attackers. He considered that these people must have a chance of salvation, otherwise, Ælla would be decapitating them, like Mrs Heath, whose head Alex just noticed was melting into the floor by the cooker where it had landed. He was overcome by a sudden sadness.

She seemed nice.

Aside from the sudden pang of guilt at being distracted by the bubbling head juice of Mrs Heath and watching Ælla the warrior woman, Alex failed to see a creeper sneak up on him from behind.

"Alex, now! Throw the vial!" Ælla bellowed from within the circle of zombified attackers.

But just as he heard her and was about to throw the tiny bottle of brown liquid, he was jumped by the creeping enthrall who had isolated him.

Alex fought back against a young guy who was probably a few years older than himself. His hands were dirty, indicating that he was probably one of Thurston's groundsmen. Unfortunately for Alex, this meant that his hands and upper body were incredibly strong and as he wriggled desperately, trying to release himself from his attacker's clutches, his fists were clumsy but sure, though they had little effect on his attacker.

As he desperately wrestled his own attacker, Alex realised how Ælla's plan was to gather the zombie-guards in one place. But they were rapidly becoming too much for her to handle as their proximity to her became tighter with every desperate breath. Alex caught sight of the desperation on her face as he wrestled this lonely enthrall, suddenly realising the gravity of the claustrophobia she would be feeling. The vial would obviously have some sort of effect on all those that faced exposure from its contents, and she had tried to allow herself enough time to escape before Alex would throw it at them.

It was in a moment of stupidity fuelled with a surge of hope that Alex, gave up his strong position and awkwardly launched his knee into the stomach of the glazed-eyed assailant that was desperately trying to strangle him. His attack caused the young guy to stumble back, allowing Alex a few precious moments and enough space to manoeuvre another, harder kick with his other foot that caused his assailant to fall to the ground completely in Ælla's direction.

He realised that her outlook was not looking positive as she rapidly tried to overcome the swarm of gropers and grabbers. Alex could not see; his vantage point was heavily compromised but he had to throw the vial. It happened within a single moment – "Ælla! Get out of the way!" He hollered, feeling desperately scared for her and releasing the bottle before darting to safety at the other side of the room.

Having lobbed the vial towards Ælla and the enthralled, he held his breath, both as part of her instruction and a reaction to hoping that Ælla would be all right.

In the immediate moment after the small glass bottle left his finger, a powerful figure erupted from the crowding bodies. Ælla leapt out the brawl and landed across the kitchen in the same direction Alex was heading.

The vial smashed behind them and Alex could hear an exceptional hissing noise. He turned to see where the glass had broken, the clear liquid was reacting with the air and forming a dense, yellow smoke. It dissipated and the bodies fell to the floor, one by one.

Ælla muffled through her cloak, which she was using to cover her mouth, "Quick, let's go!" And darted up the stone stairs, bolting the door behind them.

Panting, he asked her "So, what would have happened, had we breathed that in."

She panted too, pondering an easy answer and replied "Hmmm... someone your size? You'd probably face temporary paralysis and blindness for a day or so."

He blinked, unsure whether to believe her or not.

They took a moment to catch their breath and take stock but before they could rest properly and enjoy a brief pause to collect themselves, Ælla's phone went off once again. It was Jennifer.

"She's here and she's outside," Ælla confirmed.

"This doesn't feel right. We should search the house first." Alex observed.

Ælla's facial expression was one of understanding, though she knew better and laid it to him straight. "Two of us aren't going to stand a chance against Barty – hell I'm not even sure Jennifer and her entourage will be enough, but there's safety in numbers. And above all else, you and I both know that we sure aren't safe here."

Alex wanted to argue but knew she was right. "Ælla, Lars is my best friend, shit, he's my only bloody friend." He felt his cheeks redden, "Look, I need to do what I can to help him. This bullshit with witches and gypsies is too much right now and I'm scared for him. I'm scared of Barty and I'm scared of Lord Thurston. Hell, I'm even scared of Lars – but he's going through worse."

"Why are you scared of Lars?" She asked, obviously taken aback.

Alex did not know what to say.

He thought about the way that there's always an element of danger where Lars is concerned, not to mention he is arrogant and generally rather obnoxious. Lars only cares about himself in the grand scheme of things because Lars is the only person he has been truly able to depend on. Alex thought that for all of Lars' flaws, his friend was a very fragile boy underneath it all.

Finally, Alex spoke. "I don't know why I'm scared of Lars. Growing up couldn't have been easy for him, especially in light of all this that's been happening to him. He's damaged and I'm scared of the way he makes me feel. And regardless of whether Lars knew about magic and prophecies and whatever else, these things would have taken its toll somewhere along the line and he might not make the best decisions." Alex offered.

"Hmmm..." was all she could offer and even then it sounded almost like a question.

"That's what worries me. How do you react when the person who has ignored you their whole life, suddenly makes you their very own MVP?" He added. Her silence was enough of a response to suggest getting a move on, leaving the house without searching for Lars.

Alex and Ælla crept through the ruins and rubble, trying not to study the remnants at their feet for fear of finding the organic remains of Shilling's victims. As they moved through the crumbling building, Alex made a point of listening out for Lars' voice or a conversation between Lord Jude and Barty elsewhere in the house. He would inconspicuously poke his head round random doors, hoping to find Lars or his father but the house seemed entirely empty.

Ælla cleaved the way forward with her sword, which had never left her hand, pointing to the exit like the needle of a compass. They clambered over the remains of the once grand, now splintered and cindered door before stepping out into the cool air. They surveyed their surroundings and decided it was safe to cross the courtyard, though Alex grew largely conscious of the crunching shingle underfoot and Ælla looked up to the shattered windows in case they were being watched.

At the far end of the courtyard, Alex spotted the figure of a girl on horseback first, who seemed to be wearing a purple cape that was similar to Ælla's. He was flooded with flashbacks of the purple hoods and their spectacular display as they attacked the strange invisible bears shortly after the train massacre. Memories of being amidst the chaos and fear reminded him of the brief feeling of exhilaration and he was whisked back to fireworks displays on cold November nights mixed with the intoxicating atmosphere of watching a playground fight; neither of which he particularly enjoyed.

"Is that Jennifer?" He asked.

"Yes, and those other riders she's with are the wardens of her clan," she said matter-of-factly.

"Are you different then?" He asked. "Clans, I mean."

"Yes. And she's a dick," Ælla muttered under breath before Jennifer leapt off her silvery horse and approached Ælla with open arms.

"Ælla! It's good to see you looking so well," welcomed Jennifer.

"Jen, thanks for getting here so quickly. Unfortunately, there's not much time for niceties because we're in big trouble." Ælla manoeuvred the situation.

"Yes, of course – couldn't agree more." Her tone now matched that of Ælla's. "Who's this?" She nodded to Alex.

"I'm Alex." He offered blindly.

"He's a friend." Ælla cut him off with a stern voice that rang of authority. "Jennifer, what do we know?"

"As far as the elders are concerned, it seems that everything our people have ever worried about is coming to fruition."

"And what's that?" Interrupted Alex.

She ignored him, instead, speaking directly to Ælla.

"As you know, Ælla, we've had concerns about the Thurstons and the Fold for years and we've stationed spies and moles throughout the family. Well, two of three appear to have been compromised. The first, Professor Lenton, was assigned to watch Lord Lars at the school, and according to our other spy, Mrs Heath, he betrayed us after Jude Thurston made him promises about his new order. Mrs Heath was our second and we lost contact with them both earlier today."

Alex and Ælla looked to each other at the mention of Mrs Heath.

"They're both dead," Ælla confirmed. "The professor was under Barty's enthrall and essentially her man-servant, he was later killed by a witch called Shilling. She's an elemental and currently passed out on the seafront. Mrs Heath, on the other hand, met a worse fate, but she helped us as best she could given the circumstances."

"And the third?" Piped Alex.

"I was the third," spat Jennifer. "I was charged with keeping watch over Lady Lilah and Ms Barty at the school. The previous spy was compromised and I was sent in immediately as the new assistant to the headmistress... It was awful; she was awful."

"What did you do or find out?" Enquired Ælla.

"My job was mainly to observe and report, especially on Barty. However, I unintentionally struck up something of a bond with Lilah. Our contact was small, but I like to think that she considered me a friend, especially after what she was going through with her father. The things that pig made her do..." She trailed off.

What did he make his own daughter do?

"What happened?" Ælla asked, as though having read Alex's mind.

Jen paused, thinking about the words she would use. "She came into her powers and when he discovered what she was capable of, he didn't hesitate to abuse them. Lord Jude made his own daughter bring her long-dead mother, back from the afterlife."

Ælla and Alex were shocked.

"Lilah told me this the night before her death. She went to bed in tears. I had to feign ignorance and that will be the biggest regret of my life. I could've helped... but I wouldn't compromise my mission. The next morning, she came to me with such sadness.

"Silently, she handed me a small wooden box, she said something about not having a lot of time and that blood was thicker than water and that it was for the *Heir,* the Heir of Thurston. This box had to get to Lars and that he must stay away from the Fold because no good can come from the Seven Wonders.

Obviously, I knew more than she realised. Giving me that box could have been a terrible mistake. I should have taken it to the elders, but she was my friend and I knew what was coming. She needed a knife – she said it was for protection. I didn't know she was going to kill herself, but I knew this was goodbye and that I had to grant her last, desperate wish.

"When I found out I was devastated, but I needed to carry out my friend's wishes." She trailed off, her sadness was very sincere.

Alex, moved by the story offered; "So you're the one that gave Lars the box. Did you know what was in it?"

"I didn't. I couldn't open it because it's enchanted or something, but I knew it was important to Lilah." Explained Jennifer. "You see, I needed the headmistress to fire me – taking off after the death of a student would have raised suspicions, both legally and supernaturally. Barty is already suspicious so I needed her to get rid of me. Once I got the sack, I made my way to Kingswould in order to get Lars his inheritance. He wasn't there in person, so I had to leave the box and hope that–" She caught herself before changing the conversation's direction. "Anyway, I had other order orders. And we must focus on the here and now. We're wasting time. We need to get to Lars because he's the key to all this."

23. The Fold and the Seven Wonders

Lars' interest had been piqued back on the beach. Frustratingly, he was fully aware that his father's grand designs were nonsense, but he was passionate and so driven that Lars could not help himself from being sucked in and wanting to know more. Now he sat across the great room and watched as his father spoke with urgent dramatism to his late sister's headmistress. Lars could not make out what they were saying, but it looked heated. Despite looking distracted, Lars knew that trying to run away was impossible because leaving would allow Barty to harm Alex and Ælla.

His father was on the other side of the large room, pacing and talking passionately. Ms Barty sat in her signature pose, cross-legged and feet tucked to the side with her hands folded on her lap. Her eyes monitored Lars in an intense, continual gaze from the other side of the room.

Lars stewed on the guilt that festered in his stomach. From the moment he willingly got up and followed his father and Barty through the cave back to the house, he knew he had committed a terrible wrong. The decision to leave his friends and go with his father had been one that was fuelled by purely selfish motives, and with each passing moment, his thoughts grew darker.

The anxious Lars was snapped back to the present as the couple across the room cackled. Then it hit him like a smack in the face – the realisation that he had obviously overlooked a fatal issue that may well seal the fate of his friends. Lars was nauseated at the prospect of leaving Alex and Ælla and going with his father and Barty, and subsequently leaving them exposed to an attack, magical or otherwise. He remembered Shilling's elemental ability and immediately felt sick.

Lars watched with intense focus as Lord Thurston continued to explain something to Barty. She shifted her gaze to catch Lars' eyes and they were locked in an uncomfortably intimate stare that he had to immediately look away from.

I know her eyes don't work on me, but it's horrible how intense her glare is. And what are they talking about? Whom are we waiting for? She mentioned waiting for a 'guest' back on the beach.

Desperate for an escape or something else aside from Barty, Lars surveyed the poor shape of the house. While he could not see how he was responsible, the current state of Thurston Manor only added to his sense of guilt. The room in which the three of them took refuge was once the manor's grand dining room and Lars barely recognised it, save for the remnants of the chairs and the table. There were scorch marks, smashed windows and red smears that Lars hoped was not blood.

"What happened here?" Lars shouted across the room, "who did this to our home?"

He was met with nothing. They continued to ignore him in favour of their own private discussion.

"Oi!" He called, causing Lord Jude to turn around briefly and then return to his conversation as though nothing had happened.

Ultimately, Lars had no idea what was in store for him and reluctantly admitted to himself that he had fallen right under his father's spell, which in itself was a terrifying notion since Lars was both immune to magic and his father had no innate mystical abilities himself. There was no witchcraft here and Jude's spell had been one that was laced with promises and emotional blackmail, despite having said very little, other than "Come, Lars, we'll talk upstairs."

Lars had to admire how Jude Thurston's power lay in his charisma. He was a majestic and regal creature, who above all, had a way of making things happen. Thinking about the lengths that his father could go to, and what he could actually be capable of doing, terrified Lars now more than ever. Lars had always suspected how morally corrupt his father could be. Now, the veil had been obliterated, leaving Lars to fear for not only his future but also those around him as well.

But still aware of all this, Lars needed to know more. Throughout his whole life, he had been an outsider in his family and until the other day, knew nothing of his true mystical heritage. The dynamic of his family and its weirdness had changed. Lars could not understand the bigger picture, but his recent learnings did give him another viewpoint, one that gave the potential for alternative vistas.

Lars could not quite see from where he was sitting, but he thought he heard one or two pairs of footsteps crunch their way across the gravel in the courtyard outside. The descending sound indicated that the feet were escaping, which gave Lars a pang of hope that Alex and Ælla may well have found safety. He felt a fire of bravery quell the rotten anxiety in his gut.

He looked back across the room and watched the two plan whatever they were planning from across the room.

"Oi! I'm talking to you – what's going on?" Lars bellowed from across the room.

Jude turned, paused, and strolled over to his son with chilling urgency.

"What happened here earlier?" Lars demanded of them, not to be intimidated by either of them.

"There was a commotion with those sodding gypsies." He hissed, cooly.

"I can see that," quipped Lars.

Jude sniggered, "It would seem that our coven had been compromised. We discovered that Professor Lenton was a gypsy spy and that he was supposed to monitor you. However, Barty has her ways and we got him to divulge a few details. There was a gypsy spy amongst us, right here at the manor. He didn't know who the spy was, only that they were a staff member. So, we asked Shilling to help us with our infestation problem. As you can see, she got a bit carried away." Jude divulged. "Word got out though and there was a gypsy attack. Fortunately, Thurston Manor has a few tricks of her own, and the gyspy cavalry was no match for Barty and Shilling."

"That's awful. But why?" Lars asked.

"They thought we had something. Truth is, at the time, we didn't. Now we do." Interjected Barty.

"What do you mean?" Enquired Lars.

"You," the adults chimed in unison. Lars gulped and was sure that everyone heard.

Jude did that patronising snigger-smile. It was a wry, half-smile that demonstrated his pompous arrogance in one swift expression. He offered a change of direction, "Son, do you know what it's like to have people scared of you?"

It caught Lars off guard. At first, he did not know what his father was talking about and remained mute to allow him to continue.

"Unlike you, Lars, I grew up surrounded by magic. You remember my mother, a wonderful lady – and my sisters; you remember them also, don't you." It wasn't a question. "When my father died, I inherited all that was his and as the sole male heir to the Thurston legacy, I received the lands, the money and his title. But I didn't just want what was his, I wanted what was my mother's and my sisters'. I wanted what was my grandmother's, my aunts', and my cousins' – they all had what I did not and could not have."

Of course, it's always about a power trip.

Jude proposed a new question that equally came out of the blue, "It's very lonely, being a Thurston; have you noticed?"

Lars went to speak, but his mouth suddenly felt arid and his words grated on his own throat. He had indeed noticed how lonely it was to carry his father's name. Regardless, he choked the words out.

"You drive your daughter to death before having her resurrect our mother – your wife – you've sacrificed countless lives, in the name of what? The off-chance that you might perform magic tricks someday? What more do you want – how many more lives will it take, Dad?" He pleaded.

"As many as it takes!" Lord Thurston erupted. "Do you think I care about those things? Do you think I care for you? Do you think I cared about your cowardly sister and lying whore of a mother? I see a greater good; the chance to right a lifetime of wrongs. And I will do it, no matter the price. Do you understand?"

Lars' father calmed instantly. His aura bled from enraged red to cool blue. "I will take what is rightfully mine. I will rule the Fold and I will eradicate anyone that stands in my way. And may the Immortals help me, Lars, if you cross me I will destroy you too – mark my words.

"But, it won't come to that, I'm sure. Not if you care about your friends. I know they're outside and you're just the right distance for Ms Barty to violate them with her enthrall."

Blackmail.

Lars felt his heart hammering in his chest. The blood surged through his veins and brought him out in waves of fire that would not stand for this threat. "What do you want from me?"

Lord Thurston sniggered, "I want to wield the Seven Wonders and rule the Fold, of course."

"What's the deal with the Fold and what's so special about it?" Asked a genuinely confused Lars, "And what have the Seven Wonders got to do with me?"

For one thing, Lars knew he had to get his father talking so that if and when he was reunited with his friends, he would have more information to help them. Jude's face changed, indicating that he was about to speak.

Oh great, here comes another monologue; right on cue.

"The Fold are the seven most powerful witching dynasties in the world – the most powerful covens of our people – and hold the key to unlimited power. Traditionally, witches from the Fold have the most sacred, rarest and powerful gifts, so it makes sense that your mother, your sister and now yourself, should have such wonderful gifts; it is our birthright," he explained.

"I still don't get it. Why, Dad?"

Jude contemplated before speaking. "To lead the Fold is to command the most powerful army of witches the world has ever known. To do that, one must wield the Seven Wonders.

It's why they're separated – so that no one coven rules the others. The witch in possession of all the sacred wands will have dominion over all magic. The Seven Wonders are the very essence of the pure, undiluted magic used by the Immortals all those millennia ago to determine our legacies. With the Seven Wonders, I would control the elements, space, time... even death.

"Our destiny is to conquer the Fold, obtain the Seven Wonders and lead an army that would floor the Gypsy clans and eradicate Daemons once and for all. Once I have done this, I will return my dear Evelyn and beautiful Lilah, and we will be a family again. It's all I want."

"And what of Barty?" Lars spoke like she was not there.

"Oh, goodness no, my dear boy. My family is not from the Fold. We are old stock for sure and my gifts are a rarity, but I do not hail from such prestigious ancestry." Lars continued to ignore the headmistress. "And it would seem you have quite the effect on them too."

She had piqued his interest at this point and took the cue to continue, "It seems that the zombification seems to be a side-effect of your nullification when it comes to me trying to compel or enthrall someone. Several times I have tried to influence you and your companions and it has had no effect... at least on you and those physically closest to you.

"It would appear that you and those within your immediate vicinity are shielded from my influence. At first, it came as an obvious surprise! If I may say so myself, I am a tremendously powerful witch and probably the most powerful outside of the Fold; no one has ever been able to withstand my compulsion before. The morning of your *sleepover* was when I discovered that I was unable to compel you to come to me and your father. After countless efforts, I did what was obvious and pushed harder with my powers.

"It's a strange sensation; not being able to do what comes naturally. Not being able to compel was like forgetting to breathe or blink, and having to re-remember something that is usually second nature.

"But nothing I did made the slightest difference. Your ability is like nothing I've ever experienced before. It's neither a shield or barrier, just a vacuous void in which magic does not exist in or around – using my power against you was like screaming and no sound coming from your mouth. Frustrated, I tried even harder, so much so that I nearly passed out. Thankfully your father was there every step of the way to help me. After a splitting headache and relentless nosebleed, I was about to give up, when something tremendous happened, it was the hairline crack of the egg I needed to get around you. I serendipitously could compel those in your not-so-immediate proximity. I admit, it was new and a little overwhelming, but I was able to strip them of humanity and create a pair of drones to carry out my bidding. And once enthralled, it didn't matter how close they got to you, they were under my spell now.

"Of course, you'll know from experience that they were a little heavy-handed and a bit on the primal side, which I am sorry about. I could not control them and my power overwhelmed them, eventually permitting your escape."

"You're a monster," muttered Lars.

Lord Jude stepped in, "We knew where you were and what you were up to – we've been tracking you since Lilah died. Once you escaped, I had my people come in and take care of the mess left behind. It was like they never existed."

Lars was beyond blushing. He was disgusted by these people and their disregard for innocent life.

"And the Seven Wonders?" He asked his father, "They're bones aren't they?" Lars remembered the pen and what Ælla had said. His stomach dropped at the prospect of not knowing where it was.

"It would seem that you are not as ignorant as I anticipated," beamed the Lord. "The Seven Wonders are the sacred relics of the Fold's ancestors. Many thought them lost or just myths and the stuff of bedtime stories one tells children. But..." it was a 'but' that carried much weight. "... there is a prophecy.

"It's said that the Heir of Thurston would wield the Seven Wonders, rule the Fold and bring about a magical balance. Lars, you're incredibly special. You see, everything pointed to your sister – blood magic, runes, even your mother's visions – everything pointed to Lilah being the Heir of Thurston. I believe that the night she died, she somehow transferred her legacy to the next available heir – you, her twin brother – apparently inheriting her borrowed destiny."

Lars pondered on what he was being told. "I don't want it," he muttered.

"Do shut up. The thing with destiny, Lars, is that you don't have a choice. Just like your friends won't have much choice when Barty claps eyes on them."

Lars ' stomach dropped. He thought for a minute, while he was backed into this corner.

"Fine. I'll help you," Lars spat through gritted teeth.

"I had no doubt you wouldn't," sniggered an ever-arrogant Jude. Avar had been preening her feathers and flapped down onto his shoulder before stretching her wings and squawking decisively.

"Now, I believe you have my pen?" Enquired Lord Thurston.

Shit! Alex has the pen – I gave it to him before Barty ambushed us.

The hairs on Lars' neck then stood up for a different reason as he realised something further about the pen and his powers.

Wait – was the night I got my powers the night I cut my finger on the nib of the pen and the ink-sludge penetrated my eyeballs? But my threesome happened before... Have I had these powers all along?

Lars realised that he had something of an upper hand over his father. The pen was instrumental to something, but seemingly not the source or catalyst of his powers. In the moments of desperation at the situation, Lars spared a thought for Lilah and what she was thinking or what her motives had been and he wondered if she even had a hand in any of this at all. Lars was quite certain that his father and Barty were unaware of this.

"Father, I don't have the pen," he confessed.

He knew he had to be vague with his next lot of details, knowing that he would have to give enough information to convince his father that he was telling the truth, all the while keeping the vital stuff back so that he could tell Alex and Ælla and ultimately put a stop to Jude's crazy plan.

Lars was sure they could hear his heart pounding maniacally in his sternum.

"What do you mean, you don't have it! Where is it?" Demanded Lord Thurston.

"What, the pen?" Lars played dumb.

"Yes, the damn pen!" Jude erupted.

"It's in my bag. I left it on the beach," Lars threw. At that moment Avar placed her beak to her master's ear and seemingly whispered to Lord Thurston.

"Liar." Jude hissed, "It's with your friend. No matter, the cavalry will be joining us soon and I'm pretty certain your friends will be joining them."

Lars felt the blood rush from his face immediately. On the one hand, he knew his friends would be safe, thanks to the pen. However, what happens when Jude retrieves it is something entirely different.

24. "I know."

Alex pulled the zip of his hoodie up to his chin. He had retrieved it from the rucksack that had been on his back, which he now placed on the floor as he layered up, remarking how this new garment smelled of Lars and reminding him of the danger he faced. Ælla and Jennifer strategised their next moves with heated discussion, with Ælla wholeheartedly against an ambush, while Jennifer was all for charging in and overwhelming Lord Thurston and Ms Barty.

Alex was beginning to feel a little surplus as he looked around the clan of gypsies and assessed the many men and women on horseback, decked out in their armour and armed with heavier weaponry. Even Ælla with her xiphos and lightweight armour was more prepared than Alex in stark comparison. This hoodie was Alex's way of preparing. It was his armour. That and it was growing colder outside the Thurston estate.

The gypsies discussed the best ways to immobilize Lord Thurston and Ms Barty. No one had yet mentioned Lars. Alex piped in, "It's all well-and-good bombing straight in there, but I've seen what Barty can do – none of us stands a chance if she's not with Lars. And what if he gets hurt?"

"Alex, Lars is a witch. These people... well, they don't look too kindly on his kind." Explained Ælla.

"She is right," barked Jennifer, "our priority is to immobilise the Enthrall and stop Jude. The boy poses no threat; we'll worry about him afterwards."

"But Lars is different! He can help – *his powers* – he can stop Barty!" Shot a desperate Alex.

"What do you mean?" Countered Jennifer, to which Ælla immediately stepped in, knowing that her words carried more weight than Alex's in this situation, diplomatically speaking.

"I think he's the one, Jennifer; the Heir. I wouldn't have believed it, had I not seen him in action, but he stopped an elemental by doing absolutely nothing. Granted, he's indirectly responsible for the rabid enthralls, but I think he could be the key." She stated pragmatically.

"Well, this changes things a bit..." Jennifer considered.

Alex pleaded silently through intense eyes that Jennifer would change tactics and lead a rescue plan. He desperately knew that they never should have left the manor house in the first place and frantically weighed up what he would do if anything happened to his friend while they were out here strategizing. Alex would never forgive himself if anything happened. In that brief moment thinking about Lars, he looked back to the house and spotted a mirage of sweet relief in the window.

"Look, they're up there in that room of the east wing," he boomed. Jennifer, her clanspeople and Ælla simultaneously turned their heads like vigilant meerkats.

"Brazen fuckers," said one of the men, "at least we have no doubt where to find them now."

"I don't like this, Jen." Ælla quipped, her voice steady and confident. You could see that behind her eyes her sharp mind was calculating every possible outcome that could cost them their lives and what their solutions could be. "This feels too easy. It's a trap."

"Ælla, Lars is up there and we don't know what they're doing with him; he could be injured, tortured or they could be planning something worse for him," Alex pleaded.

"That's my point, Alex. We may have numbers, but this is their territory and we have absolutely no idea what their next move is, not to mention Barty – she's a wildcard – who knows where she'll be and what she'll do when we get up there. Just look at the damage just two of them did. I'm sorry, but there's just too much against us." Ælla made good, solid points, but Alex was baying for blood, as was Jennifer.

"Ælla, we must strike. Too many of our people died today and I want blood for their suffering. We must hit them now." Caught up in herself, she continued, "If you still had a clan you would know how it feels."

Ælla felt every word as though each one was a solid punch to her gut.

"What does she mean?" Alex asked.

"It means that Ælla is in exile – she has no clan and has been banished. She's lucky we're even giving her the time of day." Jennifer hissed matter-of-factly.

Alex wasn't sure who felt more awkward, him for his ignorance or the normally proud Ælla. He cast a quick glance in her direction. Her wild eyes burned with a passionate ferocity that had she been a witch, they would have seen to it that Jennifer burst into flames right then and there.

"What happened? Why?" Poked Alex, his face laced with tenderness.

"Not now, Alex. It doesn't matter." She snapped.

Jennifer nudged in, breaking the tension she caused, "We move in. Those in favour, raise your hand." All but Ælla did so.

"This is a mistake." She pleaded.

"Ælla, come on. This plan is the best we've got; these guys are going to take down the enthralled, and Barty, while you and Jen go for Jude. I'll run and save Lars and get us out to safety."

Hearing it aloud did not make her feel any better about this suicide mission. Truthfully, even Alex thought that it did not really make sense and knew that Barty would have them turn on each other before they even entered the room and that there would be nothing any one of them could do about it.

"I'm doing this for you just so you know," she laboured with a tragic smile, "You'll probably end up getting yourself killed otherwise, so someone will need to watch your back up there." He was touched that though they hardly knew each other, she seemed to readily care for him, and the feeling was mutual.

Jennifer called over and ordered everyone to assemble so that they could finalise the plan's remaining details one last time. Alex would have to wait for both Barty and Jude to be preoccupied, then he could get Lars out of the house and as far away as possible. The more he thought about it, the more ludicrous the plan was. It was suicide. There was no way they were going to get past Barty, but they had to try.

The clan gathered their stuff and Alex was about to follow them in when Jennifer called back to him, "Don't forget your backpack." She hollered.

"It's not mine," he responded absentmindedly, "It's Lars'."

"Best bring it," she ordered, "There could be something useful in there." Alex obediently ran back and grabbed the bag, throwing it over his shoulders and joining the clan.

Alex, Ælla and Jennifer and her gypsies crunched up the gravel. Alex turned to Ælla who looked incredibly uneasy about their plan and in the short time he had known her, could tell that this was out of character for her. Alex also considered how shamelessly they were marching up to the house. For the first time since Lars was in danger, Alex was beginning to think that something was wrong.

Why aren't we sneaking up? Lord Thurston and Ms Barty must have seen us from their window.

They slunk back through the house, which they entered through the once grand front door and everyone carefully stepped over the rubble and human remains. The smell of electrocuted flesh hung heavily in the air like burnt meat. Alex first admired the sickly sweet smell, before quickly realising what it was and urgently deciding that he would never crave barbeque in this lifetime or next.

Jennifer led the way by ascending the stairs, followed closely by her small army and Alex and Ælla tailgating behind.

"Alex, I need you to stay away from me when we get up there and I need you to be as far from Barty as possible. If it goes south up there, you could be our only hope of getting the word out. As soon as you see your opportunity, get Lars and go somewhere safer. If he looks like a goner, don't hesitate to leave. Promise me," she pleaded.

He hesitated. She stopped on the stairs and just gazed at him.

"Yes, I promise," he confirmed, and she walked on ahead.

Ælla was not like the other gypsies Alex had met so far. Jennifer and her clan looked like the ninja version of Robin Hood's band of Merry Men, each adorned with embroidered capes of rich purple. The armour they wore was ornate and embellished with gold and silver.

In comparison, Ælla was just as striking, if not more so. Despite the lack of colour and jewellery, she looked more serious, like the other clan was more concerned with the pomp and image that their costume afforded them, which Ælla did not need; she was above it and much cooler.

Alex was reminded of how very unprepared and inadequate he was. If this were a toy box, these guys were all Action Man, and he was very much Ken. Alex could not help but notice and be slightly intimidated by the arsenal that they all carried. There were varying weapons, all rather medieval in style and ornately crafted to be beautifully dangerous. Swords were popular, as were bows and arrows and each gypsy unsheathed his or her weapon and stood poised, ready for battle. Alex clung to the strap of his bag just below his right collarbone, putting his other hand in his pocket where he found Lars' pen that he rolled between his fingers for comfort.

Now at the door, the troop ahead stopped outside. Jennifer nocked an arrow in her bow, while a tall figure poised himself in front of the entrance, ready to bust it down. He wore a cowl that was pulled up over his mouth and his hood shielded his eyes. Due to his height and stature, Alex assumed it was a man, but he didn't want to make assumptions.

The rest of them gathered and listened. Jennifer spoke in a nearly silent tone: "You all know what to do," and with that, she gestured a countdown of three with her fingers.

1... 2... 3... BANG!

The door came crashing down and a puff of smoke magically appeared across the room as Jennifer's artillery launched potion pouches into the room, one of which flew towards Jude and Barty.

The gypsies jeered as they piled into the room brandishing their various weapons. They sounded feral and ferocious and looked even more so, but it was over before it had begun. Alex and Ælla had not even entered the room before the clan went entirely and eerily quiet.

Ælla's gaze was determined and Alex frantically darted his eyes through the smoke for signs of what was happening. Several moments passed and mystical mist cleared, revealing the clan who were now perfectly still with their weapons poised at one another. The clan had fallen already, just as Ælla had predicted.

"We really didn't have a chance," Alex whispered.

"Sssh!" Ælla hushed Alex urgently. "Something's wrong..." she surveyed the room urgently. Alex had no idea what she was thinking or was worried about, but he had already clocked his friend Lars, sat next to his father. Both looked insanely regal. "Where's Jennifer?" Ælla pointed out.

Alex hadn't noticed in the commotion and his primary focus had been Lars' safety. The gypsie clan were frozen at the room's entrance, enthralled and deathly still, like chess pieces on a board.

The room where they stood was massive, like the vaulted interior of an epic cathedral. Barty was at one end while Jude and Lars were at the other. Alex figured that Barty was well out of Lars' reach and why she was able to control the clan as they piled into the room.

But Jennifer was nowhere to be seen.

"Come in, my sweet darlings. I won't harm you, providing you comply." Beckoned Ms Barty.

Alex and Ælla did not need to look at each other or say anything to know that they did not have a choice, and entered the room solemnly. They edged past the enthralled who stood motionless like fleshy statues, making Alex feel exceptionally uneasy at this point and so kept his eyes on Barty, taking what felt like controlled steps towards her direction.

As soon as they were clear of the mentally-captured soldiers, Barty squinted her eyes and released a minuscule smile. In doing so, she unleashed an avalanche of bloodshed behind Alex and Ælla, using her power to set the clan upon one another. Their formerly poised swords involuntarily slit the throats of their kinsmen, bows released swift arrows and those without weapons, used their bare hands to break the necks of nearby gypsies. Within seconds, the clan had been annihilated but for one remaining gypsy, who stood alone, having just killed the last of his brethren. His face, gormless. Barty walked over to him and circled the spot to which he was firmly cemented.

After a full three-sixty, she walked away, leaving the gypsy magically compelled to ram his own dagger up into his jaw, where he choked and gagged before rapidly bleeding out. The sound of him drowning on his own blood caused Alex to look away.

In looking towards another direction, Alex thought he caught a glimmer of something ducking between the shadows that ran parallel to Barty as she walked towards him and Ælla.

"Now, if you would, give me Lars' bag. It has something that belongs to us." Barty suggested, to which Alex looked to his companion, who nodded to indicate that he should do as she asked. Alex slid the bag from his back and into his hand, before holding it out to the headmistress and noticing that same glimmer nearing the headmistress from the shadows.

She took the bag and opened her mouth to say something before the glimmer revealed itself to be a stealthy Jennifer who seemingly appeared from the ether brandishing a wicked knife. Alex saw what happened before Barty knew what was coming. A blood-curdling scream followed as Barty's face was instantly awash with slick crimson. She dropped to her knees and desperately tried to ease her savage injury with her failing fingers. Jennifer stood at the headmistress' side with a blade smothered in the same glistening layer of blood; she had slashed her knife across the woman's face and sliced her eyes in one fell swoop, blinding the headmistress.

"That was for Lilah, and for slapping me across the face, you stupid bitch," spat Jennifer.

Alex and Ælla had no words for what they had just seen.

Meanwhile, Lars and Lord Thurston started walking over. Jennifer picked up the bag from the writhing headmistress and walked towards Alex and Ælla. She bypassed them completely to greet Lord Thurston with the rucksack and gave a passionate kiss on his lips, which he reciprocated.

"What's going on? I can't see. My powers? What's happened to them? I can't use them – I can't use my powers!" Wailed Ms Barty. To see her so scared and desperate gave Alex a sense of pity; a feeling he never expected to emote towards her.

Jennifer and Thurston parted their embrace, "You have done well," the Lord praised his gypsy lover before turning to his distressed friend at his feet before him. He boomed, "I'm sorry it had to be like this Barty," but she was not listening. In fact, she was barely conscious at this point.

"What's going on, Lars – Are you ok?" Alex shot.

"Dad, tell them what's going on." Lars defeatedly demanded.

"Very well," Thurston obliged, "Jennifer was actually a spy sent to watch Barty and Lilah at the academy – in fact – Jennifer, you should tell everyone how you came to be here." He beckoned to his lover.

"Yes, it's true. I was stationed at the school and charged with monitoring Barty and Lilah. Having been there for some time, I learned a thing or two about the prophecy, the Heir of Thurston, and I wanted in. So I approached Lord Thurston, with the promise that I could help him take down the gypsies from the inside and allow him an ascent to power, with fewer distractions. Of course, it turned out that Barty was a bitch and was not watching Lilah as closely as she should have been. Had she done a better job and been more concerned with Lilah's welfare than her reputation and the pride that went with it, then Lady Lilah would be with us today. Barty grew above her station and compromised the prophecy."

"And I just wouldn't accept this," chimed Lord Thurston, "and Jennifer wanted to exact revenge."

"Yes, Lilah was my friend. And what I did to Barty won't even scratch the surface, but I feel a bit better for it."

"And from our misery and despair came love... and a glimmer of hope." Lord Thurston and Jennifer both looked to Lars who sat guiltily in the middle, riddled with what Ælla took for cowardice.

"You traitor!" Ælla shouted to Jennifer, unsheathing her own sword, "You sacrificed the lives of your clanspeople – *for what* – the chance of revenge and the opportunity to be in on this mad man's crazy plan?"

Jennifer about-turned to face her opposition and gave a sickly sarcastic smile. Ælla lunged towards Jennifer in a lightning-quick thrust that would have been lethal for anyone else, but

Jennifer countered the attack with her knife just in time. The two went at each other; Ælla fighting with all the grace and ferocity of a jungle cat.

Jude stepped away from the fighting and began rifling through the bag. "Where's the pen?" He scoffed. But Alex was quick and pulled hard at the bag, which caught Jude off guard. His grip was ironclad, and he was not letting go. With the pull of equal force, Lars' bag ripped open, shedding its contents all over the floor. Odds and ends flew out in a pile at their feet, but the pen was not there. "Where is it!" Lord Jude demanded.

Alex remembered that it was in his pocket.

Jude rifled hysterically among the litter on the floor for the ivory pen, to which Lars voluntarily dropped to his knees and apprehensively helped him look for it too. Without warning, Jude flew to his feet and grabbed his son by the collar with his long powerful arm to pull his face close to his own, before pushing him at arm's length and slapping him across the face with a vicious back-handed slap. At this, Alex launched himself towards Jude, taking him to the ground with a definitive crash. As they tussled, the pen escaped from Alex's pocket and onto the floor.

The ornately carved ivory cylinder rolled across the floor away from them. Jude failed to notice since Alex was busy pummeling his face. Lars spotted the instrument and leapt to his feet and made a dash for the pen. But he was thwarted as a large blur of black and white suddenly darted to the floor. It was Jude's magpie familiar, Avar, who being abnormally large for such a bird, effortlessly retrieved the pen in her beak and bounced back into flight away from a dumbfounded Lars.

Jude used the same backhand to swing at Alex, planting a wallop across his cheek, which startled the boy and caused him to fall backwards, giving Jude the opportunity to get up.

Avar swooped and dropped the ivory pen on the floor, where it rocked back and forth for several seconds at Jude's feet. The hollow rattle of the writing instrument hitting the floor caught Alex's attention. Jude made a slow ceremonial grab for the ivory pen with his long skeletal fingers. He wrapped them around the shaft, clutching it tightly in his mighty fist.

Alex charged towards Lord Thurston, ready to pummel him with his shoulder in a rugby tackle that should have knocked the wind out of him and incapacitated Lars' evil father. But Alex did not see that he was already one step ahead and ready to counter his assault with a violent move of his own.

Lord Thurston brought the pen up to his ear, nib down, before thrusting it towards the chest of an unsuspecting, and nearing Alex. In that short moment, Lars knew that his father was about to do the unthinkable. The gold of the ink and blood-stained nib slid through the air in a golden crescent as it drove down toward Alex's approaching chest.

Lars leapt across the crossfire, diffusing Alex's force and pushing him out of the way at the last minute to put himself in his father's firing line. Alex rolled a small distance and was delirious from what had just happened. He looked up to try and gather his bearings, before clocking a lifeless figure, sprawled out on the floor at the feet of Jude Thurston. Several blank seconds passed before Alex realised what had just happened and what Lars had stupidly done.

He watched numbly as Jude dropped to his knees at the body of his last remaining heir, and only son. Tears streamed from his cold, icy eyes and Alex knew that they were not for hurting his own son but for harming whatever chance he had of fulfilling his pathetic prophecy.

Fire flooded Alex's veins. His eyes stung with blind ferocity. Losing control of his body and erupting into a passionate rage, he flew for Jude and landed a solid fist square on his sharp jaw. He followed immediately with a second tenacious fist that cracked straight across the hideous man's beaky nose. It bled profusely and crumpled like a limp old leaf on a tree.

Alex kicked Jude in the stomach and pushed him away, shouting with such rage that he did not even recognise his own voice. "You fucking bastard. Look at what you've done. Look! You fucking killed him!"

Avar was flapping wildly about Alex's head, scratching and clawing. He felt none of it. Alex moved with fire and speed, laying into his friend's killer.

All the while, Ælla and Jennifer were still fighting. The clang of swords bashing together filled the room with a deafening urgency. Ælla's technique and precision was unrivalled and Jennifer blocked hit after hit. From their position, Jennifer could see the handsome Alex relentlessly beating Jude Thurston with his ferocious fists. She realised that something terribly wrong had happened. She had to help her lover.

In a sneaky move, she quickly kicked Ælla in the shin, though this had little effect. Jennifer took to spiteful tactics in the next instance and scratched Ælla's face and pulled her hair. The icing on the cake was driving the pommel of her sword into Ælla's face, which caused her to stumble backwards. Just as Jennifer was about to take advantage of her ill-gotten upper hand, a pathetic voice called out from across the room; it was Jude, who was not faring too well against a really pissed off Alex.

She deftly approached the juggernaut-like Alex, prised him away and threw him across the room away from Jude. He had seen better days and she knew she had to retreat. She hoisted an arm over her shoulder, supported his weight and left the room, not noticing that Barty's body had disappeared from the spot where she bled out a little while ago.

Ælla quickly came to and hobbled up to Alex. She was bloody and bruised, but all-in-all still looked better than most of the people currently in the room.

"I'll go after them and sort those pigs out. That traitorous bitch is not getting away from me. You must tend to Lars – now!" She fastened her grip on her sword, and threw Alex a mobile phone, shouting "Call an ambulance," over her shoulder as she bounded to the door.

Alex systematically clenched and released his fists. He felt the rage melt away with every breath and in its stead came a dreaded current of blackened despair. Lars was just laying there on the sodden ground; still and unmoving on his side, with his body contorted in an awkward twist.

It's just a fucking pen. How does it do that much damage?

Alex desperately convinced himself that the copious amounts of dark liquid that appeared from under Lars was somehow ink from the pen, despite there being far more than an average instrument would hold, no matter how mystical it might be. Alex stood and watched, not knowing what to do. The phone was in his hand, but he could not bring himself to ring. He knew that it was too late. The pen was solid and had punctured Lars' sternum at an angle that was unable to avoid the heart.

Just as he was about to give up hope and call for help, Lars coughed and awkwardly tried to correct his posture, but he was fading quickly. His life literally bleeding from his chest. For a brief moment, Alex hoped that everything might be ok.

"Alex," he coughed "I couldn't..." he paused for a breath "...I wouldn't let him hurt you."

Alex felt a lump in his throat as his eyes started to burn. The pen was lodged deep in Lars' chest. With every passing second, Alex was growing more and more soaked in the dark liquid of his dying friend.

Lars placed his hand around the protruding handle of the pen awkwardly. "I– I can't do this. I need your help."

"Lars, if I remove this... It's stopping the bleeding." Judging by the amount of blood around them, the pen was not in the business of stopping anything right now.

"It's too late for me. Just promise me that you won't let my father get away with his plan. Don't do it for me – this isn't a mission of vengeance. I don't want that for you. Do it for everyone. My father is a lunatic and the sort of power he seeks should not be entrusted to anyone."

"I will." He paused, awkwardly fumbling the stained handle of the ivory pen. In one swift swipe, he freed the lethal weapon from his friend's chest.

"Lars?" He released his grip and dropped the pen to clutch the cold hand of his dear friend. Alex truly forgot himself in the sorrow and shared a most intimate gesture by planting a tragic and tender kiss across the bloodied lips of his friend. Alex was overwhelmed with sadness, the feeling of shame and cowardice at having waited this long to do what he had always wanted. He could taste the metallic twang of his friend's blood on his lips and the sweet moisture of the mixture of sad tears from himself and his unrequited love.

"Lars, please don't go. I love you."

Lars looked up with his pained brown eyes and answered tenderly "I know." before succumbing to his death.

And that was it. Lord Lars Thurston died by filicide.

Alex whimpered into Lars' chest. His blood was tacky and cool against his skin. He sobbed, feeling more alone now than he had ever done in his whole life. He surveyed his friend's body, desperately hoping that he would miraculously awaken, but it did not happen.

The sounds of steady footsteps approaching nursed his attention back to this realm. It was Ælla, she looked flustered and concerned. She paused, biting her bottom lip before offering sympathy. "The fuckers got away. Sod this house and it's stupid secret pathways..." she stopped, realising what was happening and what she had walked in on. "Oh Alex, I'm so sorry."

Alex looked up from his unrequited lover, blood and tears smothered over the cuts and bruises of his beautiful face. "He knew all this time. He knew how I felt and never said anything..." he mused tragically.

"Come on. This place isn't safe. We have to go." Ælla urged.

Alex obeyed. He grabbed the ivory pen and stashed it back in its box and into the bag at his feet, knowing that he would have to keep his friend's promise and that the pen was the first step.

"What happened?" He croaked.

"The bastards got away," she offered "but let's not worry about that now."

They left the room silently, leaving Lars' lifeless body in his ancestral home, not knowing what the future had in store for them, except that they would at least have each other in the wake of his death.

25. The Heir of Thurston

Several weeks had passed since the confrontation at Thurston Manor where many lost their lives in Lord Jude's quest for, well, Alex still was not sure what Lars' father wanted, just that it had come at a great price and an equally horrible tragedy.

On the day of the fight, Alex and Ælla had managed to escape the house and retreat to the safest place he could think of; a place where no one would ever think to look for them – his family home. After all, it was only the second most miserable place he could think of after anywhere else, and it was somewhere he had no association with Lars. School was out of the question, obviously. For one thing, the headmaster was now dead and Lars would no longer be there. Lars would not be anywhere now.

Now Alex found himself in his father's London townhouse, which had not seen a visitor in years, save for the groundsman and the housekeeper who had maintained the property whilst no one was there since the proprietor spent the majority of his time at his prestigious boarding school. Upon his return, Alex had granted the staff an indefinite paid holiday until further notice.

Alex painfully tried to recall the night that Lars died, right after he had confessed his love to him. He felt sick and angry as he replayed the words. Alex lifted his head from the pillow. It was clammy from fruitless tears and a restless night's sleep. His dreams had been haunted by the jaded memories of Lars foolishly saving his life. From the moment he kissed his friend, everything after that had seemed like a painful blur.

He vaguely remembered Ælla escorting him from the Manor, but how they got to London he had no idea. Flashbacks suggested that there had been the involvement of a hotwired car, but the less Alex remembered about that, the better. When they arrived at his house, the near-catatonic Alex needed to be led in and Ælla had no idea which room had been his, so made do with the first one that seemed occupiable.

She had guided him to bed and sat him down. His face was blank and his eyes motionless. Sympathetically, she pulled off his shoes, which were sodden with blood, as were his trousers and hoodie. Numbly, he obeyed her caring gestures as she stripped him and discarded his bloodied garments. His white skin was mottled with smears and streaks of browning flakes of Lars' old blood.

Ælla left the room briefly to fetch a basin of hot water and a flannel. When she returned, he had not moved from the spot on the bed, and was still staring mindlessly at the ether before him. She dipped the cloth in the steaming water as she caressed and cleaned his skin. Finally, she wiped his face and affectionately swept his damp fringe across his sullen brow.

He thought she was about to hug him or kiss his forehead, but she appeared to remember herself and thought better of it. Alex then rolled onto his side, without a word, and closed his eyes. She pulled the blanket that had been flung across the armchair and draped it across his exhausted body.

And that's all he could recall having fallen asleep and sunk into a bout of depression.

"Rest up, Rockstar." She whispered, before shutting the door and leaving him to his thoughts and designs to rest up. Ælla somehow thought that this would not be the end for Alex and that he would need to be prepared for whatever the future held. Undoubtedly, she would be there to guide him through it, but right now she had one of Lord Thurston's stolen cars to dispose of.

Every day since then was a faceoff with the barrage of varying turmoil and confusion. Alex's days had consisted of waking up feeling heartbroken as it bled into a funk of loneliness by lunchtime. Throughout the afternoon, solace eventually erupted into a fit of rage around dinner, before Alex finally broke down into an exhausted, sopping mess of tears by bedtime. This repeated itself to the point of his own exhaustion.

In the weeks that passed, Ælla came and went. It was obvious that she was nervous around him, probably for fear of doing or saying the wrong thing. She had mentioned occasionally that she was scouting for information and finding reliable contacts to track Jennifer and Jude. But Alex did not care too much. She had also questioned if Jennifer was working alone, or if not, how many other clans had been compromised and were now working with Lord Thurston, but Alex had not paid too much attention. His companion seemed to have everything in hand.

It turned out that the last anyone had seen of Jude was when he fled with his lover, Jennifer, after they betrayed Ms Barty by blinding her and leaving her to die.

On this particular day, Alex was lying on his bed in his old bedroom, idly judging the various posters and trinkets from his youth, all of which served to remind him of a more innocent and naive time. He felt embarrassed and ashamed as he processed the kaleidoscope of different emotions that whirled around his head, just as they had perpetually done for the few weeks that had passed by. Everything seemed bigger than it had then and any remaining folly of youth had been thoroughly plucked, but he was fed up of being fed up.

He washed and showered, got dressed and decided to strip his bed. As he stepped to the frame, his foot scuffed something under the bed. It was Lars' backpack. Ælla must have discarded it all those weeks ago and there it had stayed ever since. Curiosity got the better of him and he decided to see what was in it.

Gently removing the items one by one, he first retrieved an old jumper. It was exquisitely soft and smelled of Lars' boyish scent; a warming musk of tobacco and expensive cologne. He inhaled and remembered all that was Lars. It felt like a stab in the chest. Next, he retrieved the ivory pen; that fatal implement that had robbed his friend's life some weeks ago. Keeping the wand, the first of the Seven Wonders, seemed morbid, but it was safer taking it with them than it was leaving it at the manor to fall into the hands of Jude or anyone else wanting to use it for ill gains.

Alex inspected the pen closer, noting that the browned blood had set and crusted on the intricately ornate carvings and on the gold nib. Alex got a weird sensation as he held the instrument in his hand, as though it seemed to hum in his hands. Upon closer inspection, it looked as though the nib were leaking a congealed black ink that was gooey at the nib. He worked the strange liquid between his fingers before deciding that it was disgustingly stubborn and the texture of melted chewing gum, both sticky and soupy.

Within moments, it had started leaking, first a little, then violent gushes of black gloop that crawled up his arm. He tried to scream but no noise was able to leave his mouth as he was paralysed by the sentient liquid. It whipped across his skin, traced up his shoulder and penetrated his eyes. He dropped to his knees and as such dropped the pen, where it rolled along his hardwood floor behind him.

About to pass out from the searing pain he was experiencing, Alex was immediately brought to his senses by the crash of the front door, as though someone just bust it down and came running through downstairs.

"Ælla? Is that you?" He croaked idly, to which he received no response.

A stampede of footsteps and muffled voices bombarded the area downstairs. Alex stumbled to his feet, feeling both delirium and panic. He knew that the intrusion spelled trouble; his unexpected guests sounded hostile and he needed to save himself. A voice came from down the corridor and it barked, "We must find the wand and..." but Alex did not wait to hear what else they were looking for.

With that, Alex stumbled forwards to close his bedroom door and lock it shut. He then leapt backwards in a desperate attempt to search for the pen that had just assaulted him with mystical sludge. He had no idea what he had to do with it, but he knew that he had to hide it.

Determined footsteps continued towards his door as someone from the other side tried the handle.

Alex clocked the pen, grabbed it and threw it out of the window into the garden below just as the door burst open. Standing in the doorway was a ferocious two-legged creature with a heaving chest as it panted and grunted.

The fur-covered beast stepped into the room as Alex tried to get to his feet in order to better defend himself against an attack. His heart sank as he recognised the monster as one of the same kind that had fought the gypsies after the train incident all those weeks ago. Now out of direct sunlight, the bear-creature had obtained a corporeal form and was terrifyingly feral.

Where is Ælla?

A long hairy leg stomped forward, moving the beast closer. The intruder reached out a massive clawed paw, which Alex assumed was an attack and raised his hands in defence with rapid speed. The act released a bolt of white-hot lightning that zapped it's way across the room right from Alex's palm, just as Shilling had done on the beach.

It hit the beast in the chest and it slumped against the wall. Alex panted in disbelief as he looked at his tingling hand and then to the victim on the floor. At that moment, another beast, similar in size and colour rounded the door frame and attended to its companion.

How did this happen? How do I have powers? What did the pen do to me?

The injured party coughed and revealed to the new arrival, "We have found him. We have found the Heir of Thurston."

To be continued...

Acknowledgements

The Borrowed Destiny and I have come a long way, and I could not have done it without some very special people in life.

To my best friend, Mia– thanks for always reminding me that you're just going to wait for the film adaptation. You were there at the book's inception and I'll forever be grateful for those cold nights when we would bounce ideas over a cuppa, instead of doing our coursework. Those memories stayed with me while writing The Borrowed Destiny, and I cherish them the older we get.

Equally, my dearest Emma Spaghetti, thank you so much for the advice and ideas you gave me. Most of all, thank you for always being there to egg me on and believe in me when I didn't quite believe in myself.

Thank you, St. Sian, of House Cymru, Sister of the Dragon, first of her name and Queen of the Bookshelf. I love you for sharing side-eye when we're discussing the intricacies of important literature and your sister tries to bring up the film version. Mostly, you have my eternal gratitude for taking the time – and having the patience – to read both the first draft and last draft of The Borrowed Destiny. Your feedback is, as always, ineffable. And lastly, thank you for always having the best book recommendations.

Tania, thank you for sending me back to the drawing board. Thank you Hannah R Palmer* for your honest and critical feedback. I look up to as a trailblazer and admire your optimism and hard work. And Roanne O'Neil**, my woman on the inside – thank you for the pep talks, words of wisdom and general advice about all things creative writing.

Much gratitude goes to Laura Byrne for being genuinely excited about my work, asking questions and pointing out my typos. You're a gem and helped get me through some horrible bouts of writer's block, so thank you.

Jessica Everton-Rabbit-Fletcher-D'Laurentis-Wilde, you babe. It was the feedback on your given draft that really helped propel the book. It also made me realise that "this story ain't half bad". Thank you for being both relentless and eager in your approach.

Thank you, Tom, for bouncing ideas with me way back when, and helping to get the story on track.

Danielle, thanks for your advice on the cover and formatting.

Thank you to my family, especially my mum and dad, for just being the best. I'm glad that our family is devoid of drama and that we're nothing like the Thurstons. Also, I hope that after reading this, you don't think I'm a psycho or pervert. Dizzy Bird and Gobshite, I'm mentioning you both by name because I know you'll kick off if I don't.

Liewe Jaco, baie dankie vir jou liefde en ondersteuning gedurende hierdie reis. Sonder jou gekarring sou ek nie gewees het waar ek vandag is nie. Dankie dat jy daar was, altyd gereed met n koppie tee wanneer ek dit die nodigste gehad het. Ek is baie lief vir jou.

Lastly, thank you, Nan. You won't remember the conversations we had while I was writing this at university, but you were and are my biggest cheerleader. To say thank you, I gave you (and Nanny Arthur) the highest accolade and named a character after you.

*If you haven't heard of Hannah Palmer, check her out on Amazon and buy her book, Number 47.
**Also check out Roanne's short stories.

Printed in Great Britain
by Amazon

47875130R00097